FRAGMENTS OF ME

Borgo Press Books by ERIC G. SWEDIN

Anasazi Exile: A Science Fiction Novel
Fragments of Me: A Science Fiction Novel

Other Books by ERIC G. SWEDIN

Computers: The Life Story of a Technology (with David L. Ferro) (2005)
Healing Souls: Psychotherapy in the Latter-Day Saint Community (2003)
The Killing of Greybird: A Novel (2004)
Science Fiction and Computing; Essays on Interlinked Domains (with David L. Ferro) (2011)
Science in the Contemporary World: An Encyclopedia (2005)
Survive the Bomb: The Radioactive Citizen's Guide to Nuclear Survival (2011)
When Angels Wept: A What-If History of the Cuban Missile Crisis (2010)

FRAGMENTS OF ME

A SCIENCE FICTION NOVEL

ERIC G. SWEDIN

THE BORGO PRESS

MMXII

Published by Wildside Press LLC
www.wildsidebooks.com

For Betty

FRAGMENTS OF ME

CHAPTER ONE

The reward of suffering is experience.
—Aeschylus

Let your life be a testament to your beliefs.
—me

"She's from Willow Hills." Mrs. Foster, the ward head nurse, cannot hide her bitterness as she picks at her wedding ring. "Her grandfather was fat with money, so they used to put her up in style."

I absently nod as I browse through the long list of drugs fed to the young woman over the past decade. Perphenazine and thioridazine for schizophrenia, lithium for mania, and fluoxetine and electroconvulsive therapy for depression. No rhyme or reason to the diagnosis or to the drug therapies. The end result is a catatonic patient. Amazing how the frustration of a continuing train of psychiatrists and psychologists comes across in their repeated attacks with ever larger doses of powerful chemicals.

"So why is she here now?" I ask.

"Her grandfather died. The will is being disputed. There is no more money for the time being, and of course, the saints at Willow Hills sent her on her way," Mrs. Foster says. "God, I hate those leeches."

I look up in surprise. Blasphemy from this sixty-year-old woman is most unusual. "Well, bring her to my office, please, Mrs. Foster."

"Yes, Dr. Barash." She turns curtly and marches across the ward. Her given name is Nancy, but I can never address or even think of her other than as Mrs. Foster. She radiates stern authority.

James Barash, M.D. from John Hopkins, residency in psychiatry at Mass General in Boston. These are my current name and my current professional credentials. The profession—healing the tormented mind—is one I have followed for millennia. My nature is uniquely suited to helping humans in need.

My physical appearance is average, not tall, not short. What used to be curly brown hair is receding back from a high forehead now that my body is nearing its fifth decade. I exercise regularly, but not excessively, so I look fit, but not like an athlete. I still have no need for glasses.

My small office is spartan: a desk, a locked file cabinet, and three chairs. A couch dominates one wall, its imitation leather cracked from years of patients. The State of Ohio does not spend a lot of money on its state hospitals. In fact, my own time is donated.

Slumping into my chair, I finish reading the file of Joanna Prall. A damned depressing mess. I close the folder, sigh, and swivel the chair. Sunlight streams in from the window behind the desk, bathing the room in a pleasant glow despite the white streaks on the glass left by the pigeons that nest in the third-story eaves. Through the grime I can see the tall trees that surround the grounds of Jenkins State Hospital. Some of the trees are over six decades old, tall and proud with the dignity that comes with age. I remember when they were planted as fresh saplings. Gary, a patient of mine, had helped. Hopelessly insane, he possessed a magical touch with the soil.

"Joanna, this is Dr. Barash."

Aroused from my reverie, I turn around. Mrs. Foster holds onto the arm of Joanna Prall. Eighteen years old, her blonde hair hangs in strands around her oval face. Her pretty eyes would have been stunning in a movie under soft lighting, but now those eyes are totally vacant. At least one of the diagnoses makes some sense—catatonic.

"Let's sit in the chair, love," Mrs. Foster says, guiding the young woman to the chair in front of my desk. Joanna shuffles her feet, responding to the pressure from the nurse. I got the sense that she would never move unless compelled. She shows no affect or awareness of her environment.

Mrs. Foster smiles at me in her sad way as she leaves the room, closing the door. I smile in response, then return my attention to Joanna. The patients may wear whatever they want, leading to a wild splash of colors and styles in the recreation room. Most people find the disorder unpleasant, but I find it exhilarating, a declaration of individual independence. Joanna wears a white loose-fitting hospital gown.

Joanna does not care about her clothes. Without a doubt, Mrs. Foster or one of the orderlies had bathed and dressed her this morning. Did she even use the toilet without help? Reopening the file, my eyes scan down quickly, and find that she wears a diaper because of her inability to perform this basic function. This is a bad sign. At least she can walk if guided and the record indicates that either a nurse or orderly does this twice a day to keep her muscles toned.

"Hello, Joanna. How are you today?"

No reaction.

Coming around the desk, I kneel next to her chair. She does not turn to look at me. I am struck by her beauty and youth. This young woman had so much raw potential.

I touch her arm, skin to skin, and cast a fragmental of myself into her.

- - - - -

Her mind is a void.

How discouraging. That which made Joanna into a person is no longer there. I explore further, probing for any hint, and find no consciousness beyond simple animal awareness. Moving from being an observer, I take over a small part of her, testing her mind. My thoughts, whether in my host or within a frag-mental, are expressed through the biological mechanism of the brain. I think a few thoughts and find that there is no brain dysfunction.

Unable to help myself, I feel a burst of elation. An unoccu-pied body, ready for me to take if I need it. A rare find, and even rarer, the brain works. Its neurons fire as they should, fueling the mechanisms of thought with no apparent abnormalities.

Inevitable guilt always replaces my elation at moments like this. A woman has died. Maybe her heart still beats, but her mind is extinct. One should not feel joy at such a discovery. True, I need a body as a host to survive, but I am not a parasite.

Setting aside my confused emotions, I consider the cause of her mind's disappearance. Drugs? Certainly the psychiatrists have confused her brain chemistry enough for the mind to lose its mooring and drift away. But what is a mind? Is it an ethe-real entity, a spirit or a soul, superimposed over the biology of the brain? One might think that my ability to fragment gives me an answer to these timeless questions. Ironically, it is not so. I know that the mind is more than the sum of neurons, but whether normal human minds can exist outside of the brain, I do not know. I only know my own nature. I need a body to exist, even though I can flow from body to body.

Since there is no mind to detect my interference and thus be terrified, I manipulate her memories. Her procedural memories seem intact. She still knows how to walk, how to sit, how to feed herself. Her general memory also seems intact. She knows where New York is and how a car works. Now for the most important and intimate form of memory, episodic.

I visualize a white pill in our mind and the memories come forth, activated by this trigger. She is five years old and staring down at her purple vitamin that is shaped like a dinosaur. Like most memories, the edges of the stage of her mind are fuzzy. The pill and her feelings are the core of the memory.

Every morning her Mom made her take one. "It is good for

you." But she hates the bitter taste. When her mother's back is turned, she grabs the pill and goes to the bathroom to flush it down with her pee. She feels triumphant and guilty. She hates feeling guilty.

Another image comes. This time a paper cup full of pills and capsules of many colors. Total despair rebounds back and forth in her mind. A white-sleeved arm offers her a glass of water. Laboriously, she begins to take the pills one by one, following each with a sip of water. The doctors say that it will make her feel better but she has no hope of that. She has gone beyond depression or paranoia. Both of those emotional complexes require energy to sustain. She had no energy to offer.

I draw back from her brain chemistry, allowing the memory to fade. Still, I can taste the utter lack of the will to live. Rarely is a person so beaten down as this.

But while I have found her despair, the answer to her missing mind proves elusive. It will take days of sifting her memories to find the answer. I am curious and willing to devote the time. One must always continue to learn. Of course, in the end, I might find that her memories do not hold enough clues to arrive at an answer.

Diving back into her mind, I prepare to focus on her hand and the memories that it triggers....

- - - - -

While my fragmental trolls through Joanna's mind, I sit in my chair, gazing out the window at the trees and remembering Gary. A different time, seventy years ago, a different host. I was not James Barash then, but a nurse. Locked within me are all the memories of all the people that I have been and everything that I have experienced. Normally, I avoid those memories and live in the present. My life as a healer has involved so much misery and included so much failure that I try to learn from my mistakes and put them behind. But some memories are pleasant, and this is one of them.

Gary had the misfortune to grow up in a family that savaged its members. A sensitive child, he weathered these buffetings with considerable courage. After escaping, he fell in love. He put his trust in a woman and when he was betrayed he retreated into insanity. By the time that I examined him, all hope was gone. Never again would he be able to view people with anything less than total distrust and paranoia. A man gifted with extraordinary empathy was lost.

One day I took Gary on a walk through the grounds, which were mostly dirt and weeds since the hospital had just been built. We were located far enough away from the city to put the insane out of sight and concern. A thin, wiry man, Gary stopped and bent over a wild violet that was struggling to survive among the wild grasses. I reached out and touched him to find out what he was feeling. He was already pulling the grass up and casting it aside to give the violet the necessary space to flourish. My unique nature was not required to understand the situation.

Over the next couple of months, Gary transferred the empathy he had once had for his fellow humans to an empathy with the fruit of the earth. I arranged for him to tend a garden. So boundless was his energy that he rapidly outgrew the garden and soon was landscaping the entire grounds. From dawn to dusk he moved soil, planted seeds, pulled weeds, and cut grass. The director of the hospital was quite thrilled to have such a talent who would not strain our state allocation of funds.

Gary even began to communicate with others, yet only when he needed something for the grounds. He also found satisfaction when the staff and patients walked among his flower beds and across his grass. When Anthony had a tantrum and destroyed one of the flower beds, Gary handled himself with grace. To him, Anthony was a natural force, like rain or snow, to be suffered through and the resulting damage repaired.

The memory calms and comforts me. Gary was a success. Looking at my wristwatch, I find that it is time to go. It is Thursday and I have an appointment in the city. I turn around to look at Joanna, hoping to see a spark of life in her eyes, hoping that my fragmental had found the key to unlock her vitality. As usual, I am disappointed. She still stares at the floor vacantly.

Most therapy takes considerable time, many days or even years, yet I always yearn for the quick fix. Such speed would allow me to help even more people. I am just one, with so much misery to fight.

I touch Joanna and the fragmental passes through our skin, rejoining me. Instantly I know all that it has learned. I feel a sense of dismay and exhilaration. My current body is still strong, only forty-three, but it is always wise to have an alternative waiting in case of an accident.

Fragmentals is a word that I use to refer to the other parts of me, though perhaps that is not the right word. They are more like copies. Each fragmental contains all that makes me unique, memories and personality. Like a flock of birds, I split apart and come back together. The joining is sweet, like long-lost siblings reuniting. With the fragmental reabsorbed, we are one again and the memories of the fragmental are integrated into the whole.

On my way out to my car I talk briefly to Mrs. Foster. "There is some hope." I despise the need for deception. There is no hope for Joanna Prall, but someday she might come alive when I animate her, so I need to lay the groundwork for such a dramatic turnaround.

CHAPTER TWO

Over the centuries I knew the Slavs, peasants who toiled in the fields under the heel of their latest conqueror. Whether Hun, Mongol, or Teutonic Knight, they persevered as a people, even if many individuals perished. As with so many peasant folk, unschooled in written lore, they thrived on the spoken story. Their singing and dancing touched me whenever I passed through their homelands. I had visited the Czech, the Pole, and the Jew in the Pale and their urban ghettos. Finally they found an escape from stagnation and misery.

When the Eastern Europeans emigrated to America in the late nineteenth century, they crowded into the industrial centers of the north. It had been a century since I had last visited the New World, and my wanderlust urged me to follow this massive emigration. The Europeans had clustered together with others of the same language and religion and recreated the old ways of life in their ethnic neighborhoods. The singing and dancing continued. Every day they trudged, men, women, and children, to service the smoking behemoths and textile mills. And like their Europe neighborhoods, the sharp points of church spires soon defined their American skyline.

After a while my restlessness had abated and I found myself in Cleveland, which had been booming from the invention of automobiles. For a time I used my talents among these ambitious dispossessed peoples, calming fears and healing their heartaches. I took hope from the promise of their new situation.

I was away when Cleveland begin to rust. In 1969, the

Cuyahoga river caught fire when an oil slick engulfed two bridges. During the seventies, the city went bankrupt and acquired a derisive reputation. When I returned, I found that the children of the immigrants had become Americans. The city had become bland; the only ethnics left were those two groups that always survive, the children of Israel and the children of Africa. Now the city was like so many northern industrial cities. The heart of the city was a forest of metal and concrete, where commerce thrived. Sprawling away from this were long streets of ramshackle lumber houses where the Africans lived, having migrated from their slave roots in the South to find work. White suburbs surrounded the city like a necklace of prosperity.

There is a human desire to be at the boundary of different spaces: the seashore, the foothills, or a park. Why else do we have so many suburbs as sanctuaries draped around the necks of so many American cities? Normally I like to live on the verge between city and country, where different types of people mix, but Cleveland did not offer that.

Cleveland did have certain attractions. Nostalgia mostly. Part of the sentiment came from the hospital.

Jenkins State Hospital is south of the city, set among the hills that ring Cleveland and its daughter suburbs. Dairy cows, their udders waiting to be sucked dry by a milking machine, dot the green fields around the hospital. The freeway is not far and soon I am in the city. I turn east to cross to the suburb of Euclid. The setting sun casts long shadows before my moving car. The routine of driving and flicker of deep shadow and light from the passing buildings lulls me into a dreamy contentment.

The city is undergoing its daily conversion from work to play. The nightclubs will soon be seeing the early crowd and in the many working-class homes that line the freeway, people are eating dinner and watching television. Of course, there are undoubtedly many domestic arguments also going on. Humanity is truly a paradoxical species, capable of switching from love to anger in the space of a heartbeat, without the intervention of conscious thought.

The neighborhood where I maintain an office is familiar and comfortable. After parking, I linger to scrutinize a line of trees planted when the medical office building was built twenty years earlier. I remember those trees as saplings and find a great deal of satisfaction in seeing them grow. Most of my life has been spent wandering, interspersed with periods where I try to settle down. Now is such a period, and I am content, or rather, am as content as I can possibly be.

These remembrances are comfortable, unlike so much of my past. I am not one to revel in my memories. It is true that I have an eidetic memory, in that I remember everything that I have experienced in vivid detail. But I do not lose myself in sentiment. I have seen and felt too much. By focusing on the present and what good I can do here and now, I avoid the pain of my failures.

My receptionist has already gone home for the day. A final patient, Senator Handlin, waits for me in my office. In town for a couple of days to visit constituents, he called and asked to visit. This is not uncommon. He had first come to me after the death of his wife. They had enjoyed a relationship that few couples ever experience, then a hidden cancer cut their joy short when she died at the age of thirty-nine. While I have been married before, the experiences were dissatisfying.

I had guided him through the mourning process, and soon came to function as a surrogate for his departed wife, serving as the repository of his fears and joys. Eighteen-hour workdays did not leave him the time to achieve such peace of mind on his own.

Normally I do not waste my precious time on someone not in desperate distress, but he did much good for the people of this country. In my own nonpolitical way, I wanted to help. Every year I am able to count on him defending federal funding for mental health care.

"Hi, Bill," I say as I drop my briefcase on my desk. The senator remains in his chair, reading from a folder. Even here, where he is supposed to put aside his responsibilities and service only his own inner needs, he has brought work. As always, he is in the overstuffed chair. Many of my patients prefer this chair over the other three that I keep available. The softness of it has a tendency to enfold them, like a womb or a hug. Against one wall is a couch, for those patients who cannot conceive of their care as being anything other than Freudian.

I walk over to shake Bill's hand. He looks up, his reading glasses perched on the tip of his nose. A handsome man, whose rugged features appeal to the electorate, the senator cracks a grin as our hands meet.

My fragmental collides with another of its own kind and reels back inside me, crazed with terror. The senator's eyes widen in astonishment and surely my own face must also betray the same emotion. I am unique, I am the only one of my kind, or so I have thought. Yet another just like me is already inside the senator. And the innermost essence of this one is malevolent, a dark lump of lust and cruelty.

These conclusions are arrived at later, since I do not then have the time to process my sensations into thoughts. Only a fraction of a millisecond elapses during the meeting of our fragmentals. The grip of the senator's hand tightens on my hand, holding me. The other one inside the senator rips at me, trying to tear my defenses aside as if with taloned claws. A miasma of hate and hunger filters into my mind, suffocating my thoughts. I have never fought a battle in the nether world of the mind. But I sense that neither has it, and so as it rakes at me, I push away.

The fear takes control. My other hand sweeps across my desk, desperately fumbling for something, anything. I brush against a bronze statue, about fifteen centimeters tall. One of my grateful patients sculpted the dramatic imagery of me, wearing a lab coat, leaning over to lift a fallen patient to her feet.

I grasp the statue and swing. The heavy base collides with the side of the senator's face, spraying blood across the room. He collapses. I drop the statue next to him, run to the door, grope for the door handle, find it, twist, and burst free.

Someone is in the hallway. I crash into a tangle of arms and legs, sending whoever it is sprawling. My normal reaction is to stop in concern, appalled at my thoughtlessness. But the fear holds sway. I dash beyond, unaware of whether the person was man or woman, adult or child.

Now in the parking lot. My car? Where's my car? There. I run over to it and tremble as I pat down my pockets. The thought that I might have left the keys in the office begins to form, but is stalled when I reach my jacket pocket.

I pause a moment to try to calm my racing mind. It is no good. Total concentration is required to just put the key in the door. Then I am in the car, its engine roaring to life as I push too firmly on the gas pedal. Lurching out of the parking lot, I bump over the curb as I take the corner too sharply.

CHAPTER THREE

Eight blocks later, the red warning of a stoplight penetrates my haze of fear. Ingrained habit forces my foot from the accelerator to the brake. As I numbly wait for the light to change, I become aware that my clothes are saturated with sweat. The shirt and pants stick to my skin in a most uncomfortable manner. My vision begins to narrow as darkness kaleidoscopes in. My body is going into shock.

The light changes and I drift through the intersection. Like a distant foghorn, braying horns signal the annoyance of the traffic behind me. I pull over to the side of the road, push the gear column into park and collapse across the front seat. The blackness rushes in.

I am out for only a few minutes. A tapping on my window pulls me back.

Using the steering wheel for support, I tug myself upwards and unroll the window.

A woman's anxious voice. "You alright?"

I nod and breathe, "Yes."

"I don't know." The voice is a nasal drawl. "Do you want me to call an ambulance, or the paramedics?"

Instinctively I know that is a bad idea. It is so rare for me to feel fear that I hardly even recognize the paranoia that it brought with it. I look at the Good Samaritan. An older black woman, skin stretched across her gaunt face, her concerned eyes exaggerated by her eyeglasses.

"I'm okay, really," I say, growing more confident as the lie forms. "I have a medical condition and this happens every once in a while. It's passing. I'll be all right...thank you for your concern."

She smiles in a matronly manner, waving as she walks away. "You be careful, young man."

Laughter tickles up within me. This body is in its forties, yet to her I am a young man. If only she knew the many countless years that separate us. I bite my lip to stop from tittering aloud.

She returns to her own car, where an elderly man waits behind the steering wheel. They exchange a few words and pull back into traffic. I look around and recognize where I am. A large cemetery is only a block away. Putting the car into drive, I go there.

Tombstones and miniature mausoleums fill the ground between trees and brush. I find a secluded spot and switch the engine off. When I open the car door, the cool evening air sweeps across my body, chilling me. I walk briskly about for a moment, relishing the isolation. If I stop to actually listen, I can hear the rumble of cars on a nearby road, but for a city, this is being alone.

I slump onto a marble bench in front of one of the larger mausoleums. Moss grows on the base of the bench legs. The long shadow cast by the mausoleum covers me.

Now I allow myself to recall the office by forcing my mind to replay the memory. Never have I met such evil, so repulsive and so filled with hatred. And I have experienced the worst that history and humanity has offered. Even Attila the Hun, as he terrified the crumbling Roman Empire, still possessed some redeeming qualities, though I cannot remember just what they were. This person contains only darkness. Yet this is not just a person, a human, but another of my own kind. How truly extraordinary.

Replaying the memory in my mind, I realize with a sinking feeling that Bill Handlin, the man I have called friend, is dead. His body still walks, his memories still exist, but his mind, his essence, is another's. He is now occupied—possessed—by the enemy.

But where did this other one come from? I do not know. That is because I do not know my own origin. I have always existed, or I assume that I always have. Had I at one time emerged from the womb of a woman and cried at the chill and abandonment that the newborn feels? In modern times, adopted children often seek out their natural parents in order to find their roots. Knowing their origin gives them a foundation to build a life upon. That urge has never come to me. While this may seem curious, I do not like to think about where I have come from. Whenever I follow that path, I so often experience the same emptiness as when I think of what there was before there was God. God has to have a beginning, because everything has a beginning. But if there was a beginning, what was there before the beginning? How can the human mind conceive of total emptiness, no matter and no time? How can one absorb and comprehend absolute nothingness with no beginning?

Does my ignorance about my origins gnaw at me? It does not, and that is because I deny any curiosity and avoid the very thought of it. Are we all not entitled to a bit of denial? The price of searching always seemed too high.

But the equation is changed. There is no longer just one, but two. And if there is two, might there not be three, or even more? Am I one of many? I have always been the many, the sole many.

The question of origins may be interesting, but I have more pressing problems. My very existence is at risk. Was the enemy able to absorb any of my memories during our contact? Certainly I absorbed none of his. That was because of my instinctive drawing back in repulsion. Carefully scrutinizing my memory, I realize that he had pushed eagerly forward and only my resistance had kept him on the outer edge. Perhaps he had absorbed some of my memories, and maybe he knows where I live or where my fragmentals are currently located.

While capable of fragmenting some ten or eleven times, I have just one fragmental away from myself right now. It is with a small boy in Shaker Heights. I need to retrieve it, then flee.

The life I have known as James Barash, M.D. is over. I need a new life and that means a new body. There are two possibilities: a man who languishes in the criminal insane asylum outside Canton, or Joanna Prall. Both of them are void. She is the healthier specimen by far.

It suddenly occurs to me that maybe the enemy is not exactly like me. It took over Bill, but maybe it cannot fragment. Maybe it is a single entity, bound to a single body. An interesting thought to be pursued when I have the leisure to mull it over. Now I must run. Every instinct urges me to escape.

Night has wrapped the city in its shroud by the time that I pull up to the curb in front of a large, red-brick mansion in Shaker Heights. I have always thought that context and contrast are absolutely essential. Before me is the wealthy home that houses the Horgan family. James Horgan works for Society Bank as an executive Vice President and as befitting such a position, his family lives in this private neighborhood.

These gently rolling hills had been homes to animals and the Native Americans for millennia. I almost called them Indians, but why continue Columbus's mistake? Then the Shakers came, fervent in their belief in God, communal ownership, and strict celibacy. They called themselves the United Society of Believers, but everyone else called them Shakers. When I first came to America in 1775, I met some of the Shakers back in eastern New York in the small town of Watervliet. A woman, Ann Lee, led the church. She was called Mother Ann by the faithful. At their meetings, they trembled and chanted songs that contained no words. Intrigued, I cast a fragmental into one of them and was overwhelmed by the intense emotions coursing through the crowd. This type of communal fervor is the closest that I have found normal humans coming to the wholeness that resides within myself. They felt a oneness with each other and with God. I have found such energy in others: the dervishes of North Africa, the flagellants of fourteenth-century Germany, the ancient Dionysian rites of northern Greece, the rites of modern Haiti.

The Shakers took in orphans and converts and new colonies were sent out. One group of Shakers came to Ohio. They repressed their sexual energies by channeling those forces into other avenues. As a prayer to God, and with skilled hands, they made beautiful furniture. Their orderly communities were filled with love and hard work. While not sharing their theology, since I have no God-knowledge, I respected them. They constantly strived for the good of the whole and not the individual. That I can always appreciate, regardless of the place or time.

When I left America in 1788 to return to France, I left a thriving community. Unfortunately, it could not last. A religious community cannot survive when celibacy restrains procreation. Each generation needed to be replenished by the fickle seeds of orphans and converts. They gradually died out, though a few still exist here and there.

Speculators bought the land, and two brothers turned the communal soil of Shaker Heights into a planned community of curving streets, lakes, and designated locations for houses, apartments, schools, and commerce. The brothers never married and left no children, but they left a legacy—an exclusive neighborhood of fifty-year-old homes with great full-grown elms and oaks lining quiet streets.

These thoughts of context and contrast dominate me as I stand in front of the house. The only lights on the empty street come from the windows of the other mansions. While I often lapse into retrospective, at this moment the exercise is pure escapism. I do not want to do what I feel driven to do.

As I stride up the curving walk toward the front door, I see the flickering of a large-screen television through a window. Tim Horgan sits on a cushion, entranced by the cartoons on the screen. The boy looks so calm, not betraying the rage and schizophrenia that had dominated most of his six years. Visual and auditory hallucinations haunt him when I am not there to calm the misfiring electrochemistry of his brain. A curious word: hallucination. A convenient word to use to deny the reality of another's perceptions. For Tim, the snakes and spiders are vividly real.

It is always odd to look at a person that one of my fragmentals currently inhabits. After retrieving the fragmental, our memories merge and reconfigure so that my memory of a scene then comes from two points of view. It is like having multiple cameras on the set of life.

Tim's mother, Jennifer Horgan, opens the door to my knock and smiles. Long, straight brown hair drapes down to the small of her back, and her eyes are alive with intelligence and warmth. "Dr. Barash, what a surprise."

"I apologize, ah, for coming by, ah, unannounced and at such a late hour." The lie grows smoother as I talk, and my guilt rises its warning wrath. Just as pain warns the body that something is going wrong, guilt warns our psyche. I brutally squash it. "But I wanted to see Tim for a moment, if I may."

"Of course, please come in," she gushes. "You can come by anytime you like, you have done so much for Tim."

My smile feels awkward at her praise, which she surely must see and interpret as embarrassment. But I am more than embarrassed, my deep shame borders on humiliation.

Tim is happy to see me, and bounces up off the cushion to hug me. I take back my fragmental then. In that brief moment that we merge, I feel his distress at my fragmental's leaving. He has not been consciously aware of its existence, but he has felt its calming effect. It...I...have kept the demons at bay and now I am abandoning him.

The young boy wanders back to his cushion in bewilderment. Making excuses about time, I manage to leave only a few minutes later. Finally outside and escaping. How can I leave that boy so defenseless? I cringe at the question and push the answer away. But...but...maybe I should go back.

A car passes by, driving slowly, its headlights briefly tracking across the lawn and illuminating me. I freeze, ready to dive for cover. The fear tugs at my muscles with tension. The urge to urinate pushes against my bladder, peaks, and declines.

The car moves on, a dark shape in the night.

I cannot go back and return my fragmental to Tim. If the enemy finds him, it will cut him down to get to me. He is safer with me out of his life. Safe from death, but not safe from the demons.

Walking quickly, I reach my car and jerk open the door with sluggish fingers. My body feels like it weighs two or three times what it should. A piercing scream from behind causes me to spin around. It is Tim. The demons are back.

My tires squeal as I flee.

CHAPTER FOUR

Jerry Cowen, the security guard at the hospital, approaches my car with puzzlement writ all over his features. He has not buzzed me through as usual, but left the gate closed, forcing me to stop. I roll down the car window. "Hi, Jerry, what's going on?"

"Dr. Barash, the police called," he says, placing his hand on the window sill. The fingernails at the end of the stubby fingers are ragged from being gnawed upon. "They were looking for you."

I touch his hand and cast forth a fragmental, quickly assimilating a knowledge of his surface thoughts and basic personality.

- - - - -

Jerry found his job so boring. Watch the cars come in, write down the license numbers. Watch the cars leave, write down the license numbers. He recognized almost every car or their driver and so he hardly ever stopped anyone. Every once in a while he would stop Ann Reese. He always put on his sunglasses so that she would not see him staring so hard at her. Her blonde curls surrounded her oval face and trailed down over the hills formed by her breasts. She was always so nice to him and just looking at her gave him a woody. Looking was sufficient, actual contact was too frustrating. His ex had proved that.

His only friend was the radio on the shelf behind him. An older model, with a broken cassette deck, but it picked up the all-sports AM station and that was all that mattered. In the fall it was the Browns; in the spring and summer, the Indians; and in the winter and spring, the Cavaliers. He never went to the games, but he could quote every statistic. His wife divorced him for that and took the kids back to Canton. The only good reason to go and see them was to go to the Football Hall of Fame.

Tonight was a bit more exciting. Normally he ignored the hourly news updates on the radio, but the name of Dr. Barash had caught his attention. Someone had been found dead in the shrink's office. That surprised him. The doctor, always so quiet, yet friendly, did not seem like the type to wind up dead. But you never know.

Only minutes later the phone rang. It was Dr. Hollis's line, the hospital director, but he was not there. Jerry considered not answering the phone, but remembered how angry the doctor had gotten last time. Hollis was a prick. He did not have an answering machine because he thought that he was too important for such a contraption. He expected his secretary to answer the phone and take a message, and if she was not there, then the guard was supposed to do it.

Taking a deep breath, Jerry picked up the phone and pushed the line button. "Dr. Hollis's office."

"To whom am I speaking?" The voice was quiet and authoritative.

"This is the night guard."

"May I speak to Dr. Hollis?"

"Nah. He's in New York or something."

"This is Detective Morris of the Cleveland Police. We are looking for Dr. Barash. Have you seen him?"

Jerry straightened his stance and brushed his hand across his hip. Damn, he wished that Hollis would approve guns for the guards.

"No, ain't he dead?"

"Why would you say that?"

"The radio said they found a dead man in his office."

"That was someone else. When did you last see Dr. Barash?"

"One moment," Jerry said. "Let me look at my log."

For once all his faithful scribbling was useful. He had Dr. Barash's license number memorized and found the last entry. "He left at three minutes after eight, sir."

"If he returns, will you please call me."

"Yeah, sure."

"How long are you on duty?"

"Till six in the morning."

"You will pass this message on to the next guard."

"Yes, you can count on it."

The detective left his number and hung up.

Only minutes later, much to his excitement, he recognized the green two-door Taurus that Dr. Barash owned.

- - - - -

To prevent Jerry from making that phone call, I decide to leave my fragmental with him. Jerry returns to the guardhouse and presses the button to open the gate and thus allow me to drive up the gravel driveway and park before the four-story hospital. Getting out of the car, I look at my watch. Five minutes to eleven. Only a few windows are illuminated. The tall trees whisper as the wind soughs through them.

This place is a good place and I hate to say goodbye. The gravel crunches under my shoes as I stride over to the front door. It is locked, but I have a key. Inside is quiet. Joanna Prall will be on the third floor, in a room of her own. I take the stairs and find the orderly sitting with his feet propped on his desk, a romance paperback in one hand and a cup of coffee in the other.

He looks up in surprise as I approach.

"Dr. Barash, what you doing here?"

He acts genuinely surprised but I have to be sure, so I touch his shoulder. The fragmental enters and immediately returns. The orderly is ignorant of my fugitive status.

"Nothing too important, Pete." I have met him once before, some six months ago when they hired him and introduced him to the staff. A college pre-med from Case Western. "I came to get Joanna Prall."

"Huh?"

"Didn't Dr. Hollis tell you? I am taking her to my private clinic for further evaluation."

"At this time of night?"

"Strange, I know. But this is the first break that I have had all night. I get too busy sometimes. She won't mind the time."

"She's completely catatonic. How's she's supposed to mind?"

I smile indulgently. "Find a release form for me to sign while I get her, okay?"

He nods and I pass through the door into the hall beyond. It has occurred to me that the police might very well be on their way here. This idea does not disturb me so much as the possibility that a fragmental of the enemy might be in one of those uniforms. Speed is of the essence and I do not have any time to chat.

Joanna's room is 316. I open the door and find her lying on her back in the bed with a sheet drawn up over her. I remember that she is the type to curl when asleep, but even that instinct is gone.

My fragmental animates her and she stands. Together we search her room and find her clothes in the chest of drawers. The hospital staff prefers jogging sweats for their catatonic patients because they are so much easier to get on than tighter-fitting clothes. Joanna peels off her diaper and we look for underwear. There is none. No panties, no bra. She pulls on the sweat pants, a dark tee shirt, some socks, and slip-on shoes. There is a picture of her family on a shelf. I look at it briefly; a blonde girl sitting in front of her father. She looks about twelve years old at the time.

We leave, Joanna acting catatonic as I slowly guide her down the hall. The orderly is talking on the phone and looks up as we walk in.

"Dr. Barash, I couldn't find any release forms and so I called Mrs. Foster." He holds the phone out towards me. "She wants to talk to you."

A momentary flash of anger surfaces. I quickly put it away. I only permit anger when my moral sense is aroused. Frustration is more difficult to cast aside and I struggle to not grind my teeth. I smile at the confused young man and take the phone.

"Yes, Mrs. Foster."

"What are you doing, Dr. Barash?" Her voice does not sound the least bit sleepy. A television drones on in the background. "Pete says that you are taking Joanna Prall out of the hospital."

"Yes."

"At this time of night?"

"Yes." My mind races to find a lie that will convince this good woman to relent.

"And why are you on the news?" she says. Her voice sounds puzzled.

I look at my watch. A few minutes after eleven. I am on the nightly news. Though curious to know what they are saying, I realize that the trap is closing in. Mrs. Foster runs her floor like a queen. I may be a psychiatrist, but her patients always come first. She will never let me leave.

Placing the phone in its cradle, I touch Pete.

"Pete, she said that it was okay for me to leave," I say. "Will you please help me take Joanna to the car?"

The fragmental inside Pete soothes his suspicions and he nods with a smile of confidence. We walk to the stairs and behind us the telephone rings twice before it is picked up. I know that Jerry the guard, acting as switchboard, has answered it. That will stall her for a while.

We stop on the second-floor landing. There are so many people I want say goodbye to and will miss, but I cannot leave without seeing Mary and Jane one more time.

"Pete, please take Joanna to my car," I say. "I will be along in a moment."

The second-floor orderly is asleep. A skinny woman with nicotine stains on her left forefinger and thumb. I touch her and leave a fragmental to keep her asleep. A rising full moon is shining directly through the window at the end of the hall and I walk down a lane of milky light. The last door on the right is slightly ajar. I push it open.

One double bed with two sleeping forms. On the right is an empty wheelchair. Even without the wheelchair, I could tell that Jane is on the right side. Her stiff body occasionally twitches. Fifty-seven years old, Jane is Parkinsonian, with compulsive tics and a rigid left side. She is confined to a wheelchair. Her voice is so slurred that only Mary can understand her.

Mary sleeps on the left, snoring slightly. Sixty years old and severely mentally retarded, Mary provides the body to propel Jane about, while Jane provides the mind. Together in a symbiotic relationship, they form a whole. I love these two women for their innate goodness and for the way that they strive to overcome their handicaps to create a coherent sense of self. In this case, the self is a merging of two. I have seen how their example positively motivates other patients to strive. It is in striving that we find our humanity. It is in striving that I find my own humanity, though at times I must confront the fact that in so many ways I am not a normal human; I am multiple, not single.

I long to touch them, and visit one last time. I know that I will find their night thoughts: simple dreams. Jane is running through a meadow, her legs strong, her body a source of pleasure and freedom. Mary is there running alongside her. The bright sun makes the world seem clean. Mary also dreams, but she has never known a meadow, only the hospital. They sit in the common room, playing checkers with any challenger, moving the pieces at the behest of Jane. And winning every game. This dream is also the reality of their lives. Fortunately, there are patients who doggedly return again and again, driven by the hope that they might actually win a single game against the formidable duo. I have lost every game that I have ventured to play with them. These familiar dreams, or variations of the same themes, will be all I will find. And while I find comfort in them, I decide not to touch them. Time is pressing, and why prolong the misery of departure? Taking one last look, I leave the sleeping counterparts.

After retrieving my fragmental from the sleeping orderly, I hurry downstairs and find that Pete has already put Joanna in the front seat of my car, and now waits patiently. "You can go back to your station," I say as I touch him.

He blinks as my fragmental leaves him, and sways a bit before looking at me with puzzlement. He mumbles some parting words and wanders back into the building.

Jerry meets us at the gate as we are leaving. I touch the guard, and my fragmental returns, reintegrating into a greater whole. While waiting for me to retrieve Joanna, my fragmental had been mulling over the implications of the police calling Jerry and the phone call with Mrs. Foster. He had told her that he, as the guard, was already in contact with the police and that Dr. Barash was wanted for questioning for something. He would take care of it. That ought to satisfy her for a few hours.

The dead man in my office must be Bill. No doubt the police thought me responsible for the death of a United States senator, yet my blow was not strong enough to have halted the biological processes that gave the body life. Though its host was injured, the enemy must truly fear me to so casually abandon such a plum. But, of course, it could so easily take over another politician, and maybe already had. After all, I can fragment, so why cannot it do the same? It probably has a fragmental in one of the police officers, or maybe even in a half a dozen officers, goading them into a frenzied search for me.

CHAPTER FIVE

Trees fly past the moving car, momentarily exposed by the headlights, like the columns of an endless Greek temple. Joanna sits beside me. Why had I taken her? It seemed like a good idea, a way to rid myself of the body known as Dr. Barash and start anew. Several times before in my life the authorities have sought me, forcing me to elude them by switching. They had not sought *me*, since no one had ever known about me, but rather they sought my host. Now I am known by the enemy, and a switch now will not achieve anything. The enemy knows my nature and will deduce that a woman missing from the hospital where I worked is possibly a new host body for my core. Even so, two bodies is a much better idea than just one.

I have gone from complete control over my life to no control.

Joanna reaches over to touch my shoulder. My fragmental in her and my core in Barash are then in direct contact, self to self. While this is my natural mode of communication with myself, we decide that Joanna should talk and exercise her vocal cords.

The sound of a voice that had been mute for so long startles me. "We should discard this car."

"I agree, though it would be nice to get to the cabin first."

"That's two hours away."

In the distance ahead of us the bright red of brake lights flash. I remove my foot from the accelerator and we coast towards a roadblock. Two police cars block the road with flashing lights. Flares have been placed farther forward to guide the traffic into a single lane. A line of cars and a truck and its trailer wait. I slow to take my place at the tail of this awkward snake.

Joanna is the safer host for the moment.

I turn to her and move my core self into her body. Now only a fragmental remains in James Barash.

Exiting the car, I walk toward the police. It has been forty years since I have taken complete control over a female. So different than a male body. The lower center of gravity, the sensitive skin, and the breasts getting in the way of moving my arms. The ability to walk is not part of the self, but a training of the nerves and muscles. I move awkwardly as I struggle to master a body that has had very little exercise for far too long.

"What you looking for?" I ask a police officer who is directing his flashlight into the trunk of a car. My voice rasps in my throat, demanding a drink of water.

He spins around in surprise, reaching towards his holster.

I smile and suck in air, expanding my chest. His eyes naturally focus on my smile and then on the movement below. I do not need a fragmental inside his mind to see the effect of the smile of a pretty, young woman and the resulting surge of hormones.

"Oh, I'm sorry," I say, gently touching his arm.

He is part of a massive manhunt. Four counties have been mobilized, calling in all their personnel and setting up numerous roadblocks. Seared into his mind is a faxed image of James Barash. He knows nothing of Joanna Prall.

"That's okay," he says. "Will you please return to your vehicle."

I nod, smiling again as I walk away.

The line is moving slowly, so it will be a few minutes before it's my turn. I walk up to the side of the car and James rolls down his window. I retrieve the remaining fragmental and he slumps to the side of the car door, his brain paralyzed and his autonomic functions slowly failing.

Trying to dash into the woods, I stumble and scrape my hands on the pavement as I break my fall. The body is just not used to such activities. Shrubs grow only a few feet from the road and I crawl past them before rising back up to my feet. The forest provides excellent cover.

The police officer knew of a small diner only a mile down the road, beyond the roadblock. Hopefully the discovery of my other body will be such a shock that I will have time to gain other transportation. It is probably too much to hope that the officer will forget a young blonde woman.

My steps disturb the carpet of dead leaves, causing smells of decomposition and renewal to float past my nostrils. I pause to inhale deeply, gratified by the intensity of life around me. Knowing the void that some people move in, so self-absorbed that they do not notice other people or their surroundings except as they apply to themselves, I have long ago learned to relish every moment. I kneel down and rub a handful of leaves between my fingers and palm. The leaves crumble in a shower of decay while the stems resist destruction.

I bring the leaves to my tongue, tasting them. I swallow and my throat spasms with the gag reflex. Closing my eyes, I return to the smell...so musty...so intoxicating. A person can so easily lose themselves in their senses.

A whiff of cigarette smoke tickles my nostrils, pulling me back to rationality. Dimly I remember that the other police officer had been smoking. I am not too far away, certainly not out of danger. Grasping at the threads of fear, I use them to find the strength to haul myself to my feet and stagger through the woods.

Blinking my eyes furiously to push away the sensory overload, my groping hands find a large oak, and I work my way around, tripping over roots, but not quite falling. A path. Probably used by deer. I rush along it, fleeing the enchantment of smell and taste.

Branches whip against my face, waking me even more. I trip and smash my chin against a small rock on the ground. A stab of pain explodes back through my skull, down my spine, to the ends of my body. My testicles contract, or so it feels like, since I do not have testicles anymore.

I jerk up from the ground, bringing up my hand to my face. It is wet with blood, but the enchantment is gone. It has been so long since I have transferred my core self to another host. I have tended to forget the hazards of being in a new body. While people see much the same, our senses of smell and taste diverge in subtle and wonderful ways from individual to individual. Until I get used to the change, it is so easy to surrender to its allure and wallow in its wonder, like a pleasant LSD trip.

There is time enough for that later; now there is only time for survival.

Marybell's Diner is a combination café, gas station, and convenience store. Several of the letters on the neon sign are burned out or flicker on and off at irregular intervals. A dozen or so pickup trucks and cars are parked haphazardly about in the manner that one sometimes finds outside of the city, where drivers are not used to parking lines and order.

My sneakers crunch across gravel after I leave the cover of the woods. The sound seems far too loud, as if it will alert the police officers down the road. Which car to steal? A couple of years ago I examined a man at the hospital who had a habit of taking cars that he did not own. From him I learned how to hot-wire many models.

Two men come out of the diner and I freeze. In their early twenties, they are dressed in dirty work clothes. Construction workers perhaps. They are laughing and walking away from me.

I make up my mind and hurry after them.

"Excuse me," I call.

They stop and turn. One is red-haired and clean-shaven, with an abundance of freckles covering his face and bare arms. The other is bigger and a dark bushy beard covers his face. One of his bottom teeth is missing.

"Could you give me a ride?"

"No problem, honey," the redhead says.

Needing more than a ride, I reach out to touch them both.

- - - - -

I am a fragmental, a complete duplicate of my core self. I have my own memories and think my own thoughts. When I reintegrate with my core, our memories resynchronize and we know all that has happened to each other. My core remains behind in Joanna.

The redhead is named Greg. His thoughts about Joanna are unimportant. The sight of a vulnerable pretty woman so often resonates with the most basic desires to procreate. Taking absolute control of his body, I push his self deep down into his brain. He is vaguely aware of my presence, experiencing me as a irritating headache pounding at his temples. Greg has just finished two beers with a dinner of chicken-fried steak. The beer is a good idea, so I reach back to touch Joanna and the other man. A rapid conference and Willard, the other man, goes to the store to buy a case of beer.

The truck has a large toolbox in the bed up against the cab. Greg keeps various odds and ends in there and a quick examination reveals that there is room for the woman to hide in there. I do not want my core exposed if we are stopped by another roadblock.

Five minutes later, I am behind the wheel heading south. Greg was born in Copley twenty-two years ago and still lives with his widowed mother. He is a good man who supports his mother and younger sister in spite of a weakness for drunken parties. Trolling his memories for possible escape routes reveals a pond on a large farm that a friend's father owns. He and his friends often fish there while drinking. A road through that farm passes near the freeway that circles past Akron.

A quick touch and the fragmental in Willard agrees with my plan. We find the entrance to the farm road a bit later, and Willard climbs out to open the gate. It is unlocked, since there is not anything of great value beyond. Moments later we are bumping down the farm road past fields of corn and soybeans. The scale of modern agriculture never ceases to amaze me. Hundreds of acres farmed by a handful of men, not like the life that I knew for so many centuries when nine out of every ten people served the needs of the land.

Willard touches me and I slow to a stop. We open the toolbox and help Joanna out. The bumpy road has already bruised her forehead. A pang of guilt at my own thoughtlessness. To some it might seem curious, to feel guilty of what one has done to oneself.

Joanna sits with us as we creep along the road with the lights turned off. We approach a copse of trees that surrounds the pond of Greg's memory. Coming around it, we see the lights of passing cars on the freeway. A rig pulling three trailers rumbles past. Leaving the road, we jolt across rows of half-grown corn.

At the end of the corn, we stop. A small forest obscures the freeway. The trees are placed by the chaotic logic of nature, not the linear logic of man who thinks in straight rows. Willard takes some wire cutters from the toolbox and clips a path for us while I help Joanna back into hiding. Her body is so exhausted that we are concerned that she might collapse.

After waiting for a moment, there is no oncoming traffic. We crawl up onto the freeway and then race south, having successfully circumvented any possible police roadblocks around Akron.

The radio is tuned to a country-western station. Personally, I normally listen to a classical station, but now was not the time for relaxation and contemplation. I scan for an all-news source and find WNES on the AM band. The various reports cover sports, the economy, the infidelity of an Akron councilwoman, and then comes the top story.

After a brief introduction, a recording of a police spokesperson is played. "At six forty-five p. m. today, Senator William Handlin was found dead at the Euclid office of Dr. James Barash, a psychiatrist. He was bludgeoned to death and Dr. Barash is being sought for questioning." The recording ended and the announcer continued, "Senator Handlin was the junior Senator from Ohio, serving his second term after winning re-election two years ago."

We leave the radio on as the dim ghosts of the night flicker by.

Later comes an update. "Further information is becoming available about the mysterious Dr. Barash, who is being sought in the death of Senator Handlin. An anonymous source within the Federal Bureau of Investigation has informed UPI Radio that a search of the doctor's home found child pornography. He said, quote, 'boxes full of videos and still photos.' Another source reports that there were also negatives, which would mean that Dr. Barash produced this material himself."

A search of my home? Child pornography? How had the other one got hold of such vile filth in so short a time? After a while, I begin to think about the radio broadcast, what was said and what was not. It had been unusually well informed, as if the police were freely releasing information to the press. They did not even bother to use the word *alleged* when referring to me. None of this was normal. The enemy must be manipulating the release in order to increase the frenzy of the search for me.

CHAPTER SIX

I am now fully integrated, with no fragmentals. Greg and Willard lie sleeping in the cab of the truck, empty beer cans piled at their feet. My body trudges away from the road, the darkness of unconsciousness gnawing at the edges of my vision. My head feels like the anvil of a blacksmith and he is busy at work. The pain throbs so intensely that I find my gait is in sync with its cresting and ebbing. The cabin is only a quarter of a mile away through the woods.

Dawn is three hours away. When the two men awake from their drunken stupor I expect a blackout to obscure the past several hours. They might remember a blonde woman, but hopefully confusion and embarrassment will stifle their questions.

A dog starts to bark nearby and I freeze. There are other cabins up here, weekend getaways for the more exclusive sort. I last visited two years ago. Sinking to my knees and pressing my fingers against my temples, I will my tired brain to function and draw out the memories of that visit.

It was spring then. Green leaves everywhere. Bright flowers among the underbrush. The gravel road twists and turns, going from cabin to cabin. Each owner has five acres. There was a pond, three or so acres. A houseboat on it. That should be off to my right. The gravel road to my left.

Another dog joins the first in frenzied barking. Are they agitated over me? Sometimes dogs just like to bark. Standing, I move to the left. One hundred yards. Two hundred. The crunch of gravel under my feet.

I am so tempted to stay on the road and just follow it to my cabin. But the chances of being seen are too great. Across and into the trees on the far side, up a slight rise and then the glow of a lamp through the trees. The Saunders lived there. They keep that lamp on year-round, even when not here, a habit born of suburbia. My cabin is the next one.

A whiff of skunk jerks my head up. Faint, yet pungent. So that is what the dogs are complaining about. I turn about a bit, sniffing. Running into that frightened critter would be a complete disaster. I do not have any way of cleaning myself if it marks me. It is to the left, deeper in the woods, where I had wanted to go.

I move back to the road and travel on its edge, pushing branches aside. Past the Saunders'. There is the cabin. A key is hidden in the bole of a tree around back.

Once inside, I pull out a sleeping bag and unroll it. The dust from the wood floor causes me to sneeze. The night is too warm to get inside, so I rummage around in a closet for a blanket. Lying on the sleeping bag, I pull the blanket over me and immediately fall into a deep sleep.

It is past noon when I wake. I would have slept longer, but my muscles and shins are aching too much. Besides, my bladder demands attention.

The toilet in the bathroom has antifreeze in it. Of course the water is turned off. Awkwardly, I squat and pee into a bucket. This is the first time in years that this body has voided under its own control and not into a diaper. Heavy ammonia proclaims my dehydrated state. The cupboards in the kitchen contain a lot of canned goods. This cabin is insurance against the unforeseen, owned under a different name, with money hidden in three different places. There is some fruit juice, which I open and drink straight from the can.

Pulling a cover from the couch, I sit down to eat a meal of canned ravioli. The last food that Joanna had eaten was dinner from the hospital cafeteria. The motions are deliberate: spoon in can, up to mouth, back to can. Depression is a strange and bitter quandary.

The stress of running and of having my life torn apart, the fear of death, tends to weigh down the self. Brain chemistry diverts my thoughts down forlorn paths where hope is a dim light and self-recrimination waiting for an opportunity to pounce. My fear rules me and that is humiliating. I abandoned a boy in need, deceived a young orderly, and left two young men drunk. Will that boy cower in fear for the rest of life? Will Pete be fired for letting Barash take Joanna? Medical schools hated any indication of scandal, making him a pre-med that will never become a doctor. Would Greg and Willard be fired for being late to work today? Blackouts can be so terrifying, such a loss of self-control that self-confidence suffers a fatal blow.

The can of ravioli is empty. Lurching into motion, I walk to the kitchen table. My muscles moan with every move. Setting down the can, I pull up my shirt. In the truck toolbox I had lain on my right side. Now my ribs and hip are black with bruises. What I really need is a hot bath, lasting at least a couple of hours. There is a bathtub, but do I dare turn on the water?

What is the risk? The valve to turn on the water is inside to protect it from the winter cold. If a meter reader comes by, he would see that the house was occupied. I do not want anybody to know that. But how often does a meter reader come? Every couple of months? Twice a year?

My imagination readily supplies the sense of heat and wet enclosure and the decision is made. The water valve is under the kitchen sink and twists easily. Then the tub. It spits air for a few moments, then brown water, then pure water. I wash the dust from the tub and turn on the hot water. Water comes, but not hot water. Of course, the water heater. That requires natural gas. To turn that on requires going outside to the meter.

"Damn it all to hell," I say through clenched teeth.

Returning to the living room, I pick up the blanket and lie down on the couch. I lie on my left side, my body aching so badly that tears trickle across my nose and off the side of my cheek. Fortunately the oblivion of deep sleep comes quickly.

There are deeper shadows when I awake. The sun is going down. This time I flush away the antifreeze and use the toilet. I hope that it's not too loud. A can of beef stroganoff and another can of juice serve as dinner.

On the shelf is a radio covered with dust. A quick search of the refrigerator locates enough batteries to get the radio going. No power to keep them cool, but they work anyway. I find WNES, put an earphone in my left ear, and patiently wait for news.

"The FBI alleged at a press conference this evening that Dr. James Barash apparently has committed even more murders. Dr. Barash worked at Jenkins State Hospital and today the bodies of a nurse, an orderly, and three patients were found. According to the FBI, each had been beaten to death.

"The nurse, Rita Foster of Cleveland, had earlier been in contact with the police about Dr. Barash. When she failed to report for work today, police were sent to her home and found her dead—"

Sick with sadness and guilt, I turn off the radio. I don't even want to know which three patients are dead. The orderly is most certainly Pete. I had only met him once before last night and now he is now dead. Beaten. They had seen their attacker, felt his rage, felt their own terror. Obviously the enemy has a scorched earth policy, killing everyone I leave behind. Would he find the boy, Tim Horgan? The possibility leaves me terrified.

It is dark now. To even think about the enemy brings ever increasing surges of despondency and grief. Briefly I rally, self-righteous indignation rising: I did not kill them! It did! But they are dead because of their contact with me, even if my hands are not bloody; to rationalize otherwise is too humiliating. I refuse to be morally handicapped by denying the situation.

While acknowledging my responsibility, I take care to not let my guilt overwhelm me. There is serious thinking to be done. Why is the enemy killing everyone? That makes no sense, regardless of how I look at it. Another thought strikes. Wait, why were they still searching for James Barash? Surely they had found his body where I left it in the car. Most curious, and most ominous. How was the enemy manipulating the authorities to continue the chase for me? What purpose did it serve to look for James Barash when that body is so easy to find? Are they searching for Joanna, a missing patient? This will take some time to mull over.

Sneaking out the cabin door, I carefully scan the surrounding woods. It is clear. A quick twist turns the gas on.

An hour later I lie in the tub, drawing comfort from the water. All night, I doze fitfully, waking only when the water loses its warmth and I have to replenish the supply.

My brain chemistry summons dreams to rationalize my neurons into harmony. Nightmarish images flash back and forth, finding some material in Joanna's memories. A new baby brother whom everyone fawns over. A well-loved doll lost. Her father in uncontrollable fury. Sniffing an industrial inhalant that her friend brought over.

New material is found in my own memories, images of time past and places distant. A young boy breaks through the ice. His sobbing cry for help is lost as the air rushes from his shocked lungs. As he flounders, the chill leaks through his thick coat.

I gasp awake, tears running down my face. The water is too cold for a summer morning just before dawn. Crawling from the tub, I pull a towel from a musty drawer. After drying myself, still shivering, I ransack the bedroom for some clothes that might fit me. A pair of sweat pants and an oversized tee shirt. Two layers of socks and a pullover sweater complete my attire.

Enough light is coming in the windows now so that I can move about the kitchen. I quickly boil some water to make tea and oatmeal. My eating is not so awkward as yesterday, though my right side is very stiff.

After rinsing the dishes, I return to the living room. A skylight casts a yellow square on the floor. Pulling over a rocking chair, I settle down and lean back. The sun is refreshing, cleansing, as if

I am absorbing vitamins by osmosis. I rock back and forth ever so slightly. No thoughts interrupt my worship.

Finally the warmth becomes too uncomfortable and I shrug out of the sweater. Ah, much nicer. Calm thoughts come.

Introspection is not a skill that a person easily acquires. It requires a degree of unflinching moral courage that so many lack. Looking into the self and acknowledging the cruel impulses, the selfish motivations, or something even worse, is incredibly difficult. Even I struggle with this skill.

Now is the time to assert my rationality and regain dominance over chemistry. I am more than chemicals. While I think with Joanna's brain, my core self is beyond her. My thoughts are expressed through her neurons, but do not originate there. What to do about my situation? I am safe for the moment but the enemy will surely track me with every effort for as long as it takes to kill me. Why? Does it hate me because I am like it? Two of a kind with no other peers.

Does it think that I am a threat to it? An intriguing possibility. Certainly, in the past, I have come across evil people and judged them and slain them. My nature makes such a moral choice easy to implement. This is a new situation. Can I even kill the enemy? Possibly. Knowing its dark nature, my immediate inclination is to destroy it. But what if it kills me instead? It has been centuries since I have almost died, and then it was due to my own lack of caution more than anything else. Unlike true humans, I have rarely been forced to confront my mortal nature.

How evil is this creature? In our one touch I found such spite and hatred. And fear. Was its reaction merely fueled by fear? Maybe it might behave better if that emotion was not dominant. Certainly my own fear has sometimes made me act without forethought, like taking Joanna. I should have retrieved her in a way that disguised my involvement. The enemy is slaying everyone in its path, not a simple kill like I might do, but savage. Does it enjoy the terror of its victims? I think it does. How repellent.

While I was not in contact with it long enough to be sure,

perhaps a diagnosis of fear is not quite accurate. Perhaps the dominant emotion was hate. Yes, hate. An all-consuming hatred. Why?

I excel at analyzing people, from afar and from within, but thinking about the enemy's dark nature is so uncomfortable. Wiping my brow with my sleeve, I find that I am soaked in sweat. It is not hot under the sun, just the reaction of my new body to stress. Perhaps there is a better approach. The enemy is like me. I thought I was alone, but I am not. Reason suggests that our origins may be similar. Is there an answer in my own past?

My true memories are encoded in a way that I do not understand. It certainly is not physical. The memories are so complete in every detail that no brain could actually hold them all. They contain much joy and much misery. I have always avoided remembering too much—the details overwhelm me and I cannot see the shape of the beach because the grains of sand are too overwhelming. But I cannot continue to avoid my memories. I must regress backwards as far as I can go.

Closing my eyes, I begin to dredge up the specters of the past. My life and my memories are as fragmented as my nature. Lengthy journeys, short episodes, long relationships, and quick encounters, all come together in a narrative that reflects what I am.

CHAPTER SEVEN

The present is fast-time; the past is slow-time. My memories slowly unreel before me. The slower pace allows me to more fully understand them than when I lived them.

Certain highlights provide guideposts on my journey when I think of this turbulent century. The awe I felt when Neil Armstrong stepped onto the moon, the joy at the end of World War II, the exhaustion at the end of the Great War, and a fascination with new technology. The first time that I saw a long line of black Model T automobiles in a progressing state of assembly in Henry Ford's massive plant in Detroit, it astonished me with the scale of the effort. The first time flying in an airplane exhilarated me in a way that cannot be conveyed to people who have grown up knowing that machines can make people fly. The explosion of population was bewildering and somewhat intimidating. One feels smaller when one is a part of six billion, instead of part of only one billion. People everywhere, loving, living, hurting.

People have always soiled their home, but the demands of billions began to tear at the ecological foundation and so the Cassandras of science raised their wail of doom. The images from Hiroshima and Nagasaki terrified me to a more profound degree than I had ever experienced. I had seen too much, had known the inner drives of too many people, to believe that such a weapon could be kept caged. Here we are, more than a half a century later and the atom has not again been used in anger. More than anyone else, I am astonished. Perhaps people are maturing.

The more important part of my memories is the people who have touched my life; or I touched theirs, hopefully for the better. Jenny in Toronto thirty years ago, who finally broke from her compulsion to marry men like her abusive father. Daniel in Austin, only a decade ago, whose first words to me were, "I'd shake your hand, but it's full of worms right now." The new miracle drugs managed to calm his paranoid schizophrenia.

There are little traumas within the lives of individuals and bigger traumas that scare nations. During the time that Europe consumed the lives of its young men, we called it the Great War. Only later did we realize that we had to rename it the First World War.

The time was the late spring of 1918. War had raged across Europe for the last three and half years, toppling dynasties, and consuming the lives of men with voracious abandon. Germany faced famine at home, and the Allies took new heart at the sight of doughboys coming from America and marching into battle with the enthusiasm of the naive. With the capitulation of Russia only months earlier, the war had entered the end game.

Amid such misery I did what I could to help. My current host was Baron Gustav von Hof, the sole survivor of an old, obscure Junkers family from Prussia. Gustav had served as my host for twenty-two years. I took him when he was only fifteen.

When I met Gustav my previous host was dying. The cancerous tumor visibly bloated my girth. Desperate, I was seeking a new host and it so happened that I visited a military finishing school as part of my work as a Catholic priest. The Germans called such schools gymnasiums, which only confuses non-German readers. I was there to receive the confessions of those young men who were Catholic. The gymnasium was a model of order, the students sitting quietly and alertly at their desks in sharp uniforms. The linear rows of desks reminded me of soldiers on the parade ground.

The instructor summoned each Catholic boy forward in turn and ordered him to march out to the chapel to give his confession. There were only six of them, since we were deep in Protestant territory north of Berlin. Each boy submitted to the ritual and dutifully recited in detail each sin of the last week. Among the petty fights and lustful thoughts toward girls, three of them had been involved in liaisons with other boys at the school. This activity was growing in popularity among German military youth across the nation. I forgave each of them their trespasses, though only God can forgive, assigned each of them some penances, and bid them to go and sin no more.

I returned to my own parsonage and ministered to the needy there, but a preoccupation with the growing lump under my belt interfered with my concentration. Finding a new host in a manner that did not violate my own moral code was always so difficult. One of the confessing boys had talked about a liaison with another boy, a Lutheran, named Gustav. Apparently Gustav liked to hurt his playmates and few sought him out any more.

After a few inquiries, I identified the boy in question. His father was Baron von Hof, a high administrator in the Prussian government. Responsible for some aspect of agriculture. He lived on an estate outside of town and every weekend his only child visited. Standing on the street corner across from the grey stone wall that surrounded the gymnasium, I watched as the youth came out. A strapping lad, with blond hair and the high cheekbones of the Nordic people. He wore his uniform with careless ease, its lines crisp and straight. I crossed the street, dodging a horse-drawn wagon and approached him. He glanced my way and turned away. The collar and frock of a priest did not interest him.

As we passed, I contrived to discreetly touch his arm.

The next day I waited for him, reading a book as I loitered. It was by a Frenchman named Jules Verne, who told such wonderfully outlandish stories. A carriage drew up and the young man alighted. He walked directly toward me, which startled me. He touched me and I knew the story.

A petty bureaucrat by day, Baron von Hof was a twisted man

at home. And he twisted his son. Even though only sixteen, Gustov had been totally corrupted. I could describe their crimes of corruption and brutality, but to what purpose? After centuries of experience, I can see when a person is redeemable. Gustov was not and so my fragmental destroyed him. I now had a fresh, young body.

Gustov and I returned to my quarters at the church. Three canons and two priests lived there. My own small room contained a bed, writing desk and straight-backed chair, and a bookcase full of leather-bound volumes. Gustov sat on my bed and patiently waited. Sitting at the desk, I wrote my will. It was simple enough, granting what little money I had to the parish poor and giving away my books and other treasures to particular friends. I turned to look out my window and contemplate my impending demise.

Frau Stettin was kneeling at her daughter's headstone in the small graveyard. During my first year here, some thirty-three years ago, the girl of only seven had died. Every day the good frau came to place fresh flowers from her greenhouse on the grave and spend an hour with her only child. Herr Stettin handled his grief differently and never came to the church. He was a prosperous tanner now, unlike the poverty of the past that had prevented them from taking the girl to a hospital in Berlin. I often comforted the Frau during her weekly confessions. Some might see her prolonged grief as an illness, but I knew better. She had twisted and turned until she found a mode of life that she could live. The daily visit gave her reason to continue. A lesser woman would have just lain down and waited for the reaper to harvest her.

Beyond the stone wall of the graveyard was a playground. A contribution of Herr Ruderman, owner of three dairies. After a sermon on why it is easier to pass a camel through the eye of a needle than for a rich man to go to heaven, he had come to me in contrition. He asked how he could make amends and I suggested the playground for the local children. He gave in the proper spirit of caring and loving, not begrudgingly. If there is a judgment day, I am sure that this will be a mark in his favor.

There, side by side, death and life. Frau Stettin was alone while the playground was full of laughing children. Death is always lonely. While I was not about to die in an absolute sense, in another way I was dying. It was hard to give up the life that I had created for myself here and the people that I loved so dearly. My books and my other knickknacks, while only made of paper or leather or wood, were invested with emotional meaning. I would leave them also.

My physiology reacted to my emotions and tears streamed down my face. After a while, I wiped them away and smiled at the antics of the children. Children know such raw joy, unrefined by the weight of years. Taking my will, I went to find Father Braun. He was in his room. A younger man, he deferred to me as the senior priest. Normally I waited for a visit from the bishop to say confession.

He opened the door to my knock and I entered. After a few pleasantries, I got to the core of the issue. "Father, I am dying. I have only a short time left, perhaps only hours."

"Are you sure?" The young priest was alarmed. "Shouldn't we summon a doctor?"

"No, no, of course not. I am at peace with my fate. I am here to ask you to hear my confession and administer last rites."

"Isn't that premature?"

"No, absolutely not."

He heard my confession, which was not much, mostly regrets that I could not do more for those that came to me. I am a healer and being a priest or minister was the best mode to deliver my comfort. Then he performed the final sacrament. While I am not Roman Catholic in the usual sense, I honor the beliefs of the community. Last rites provide closure.

Pressing my will into his trembling hands, I asked him to run to the store and buy me some sweets. He gladly complied. This was his first experience with the final sacrament and I could see that it had unnerved him.

He was a good boy, one who had the potential and drive to

care for my parish when I was gone. Returning to my room, I lay down on the bed and passed my core self to Gustov.

As Gustov, I slipped out of the church and returned to my home. There would be no gymnasium for me today, and besides, a military gymnasium was not for me. Society and culture was changing ever more rapidly around me. There was a new profession called psychiatry. The medical men were encroaching on the territory that only priests had heretofore occupied. Medical school was the place for me.

That night I pushed the self of the Baron from his body, slaying that which made him a person. With my fragmental in complete control on his son, the new Baron, I tried to heal some of the decades of horrible damage that the petty Junker had caused.

With my new body, I decided to head to the front. There were surely many there who were crippled in mind and needed my help.

CHAPTER EIGHT

A French schoolhouse on the outskirts of Lille served as a hospital. Most of the children of the city had fled with their parents in 1914, so their classrooms now housed about four hundred patients. Most of the men were recovering from gas attacks or the damage caused by bullets and shrapnel. Shell-shock casualties occupied a single room on the second floor.

The windows faced south and bathed the room in a warm glow during the morning that by afternoon made the room a humid sauna. The sweet-sick smell of gangrene drifted in from the first floor. Of the nine patients in the upper room, a man named Hans Kruppen lay in the third bed on the left. A large Frenchwoman, Mrs. Joulet, quickly and efficiently changed his clothes and bedding, cleaning away the feces and urine-soaked sheets. As she rolled him back and forth in the process, he lay limp, neither resisting nor assisting her efforts. The good woman worked in the hospital and earned just enough money to support her six children. Her husband had left with the reserves only days before war erupted. Fate decreed that her children be stricken with fever when the Germans swept through, preventing her from fleeing. Letters funneled through Switzerland kept her in contact with him, but the letters stopped coming after the opening battles around Verdun. It took her six months to find out that he had died during an artillery barrage.

Some might think that she should not be here tending the wounds of the countrymen of those who had slain her husband, but she was better than that. She worked as a nurse to save lives. Most of the other nurses were German, and none of them would take care of the shell-shock victims. After all, they were slackers, unhurt, and should return to the front. Their disdain was not justified. These men were just exhausted after too many months on the line. After some rest, most would willingly return to their units and bravely continue to endure the horror.

Finishing with Hans, she moved to the next patient. I had already examined the other patients. Most of them would recover their mental health and even some self-respect. Those that would not I had helped the best I could. Hans was new.

Sitting down next to him, I touched him, placing a fragmental inside. Since I wanted more than just his surface thoughts, a complete mining of his soul, I sat and waited. It was pleasant to enjoy the grace of the sunlight.

"Your children are well, Mrs. Joulet?" I asked in French. She spoke enough German to get by, but her native language was much more comfortable.

"Yes, Dr. von Gustov, though I do worry about Lucien."

"Your oldest? Seems like a fine young man."

"He is almost sixteen. I know he longs to be a soldier."

"This war has claimed enough children. He should wait."

She smiled, though a distant sadness filled her eyes. "I know," she whispered.

Then she was gone to tend to others.

My fragmental entered Hans and lurked unaware in the back of his mind, learning his story.

- - - - -

Hans Kruppen was not the sort to dwell on his memories, a lot like myself. And like me, the moment and the future always tugged at his attention. Yet, during those moments of melancholy brought on by too much dark beer, two memories often dominated his thoughts. The first comes from when he was five years old and always begins with his spinster Aunt Ruth softly shaking his shoulder and whispering his name. He struggles up and blinks at the summer sunlight that filters past the blinds in his darkened room. Without a complaint, his bare feet shuffle across the fine wooden floor.

Down the hall and into his mother's room. His father sits next to his mother's bed, his hand holding hers. As usual, he is dressed in a business suit, with long coat and tie. Hans's other aunt rocks in a chair in the corner and quietly blows her nose into a handkerchief. His mother's pale face is slack. The white frilly covers barely rise underneath her shallow breaths. There were no other children in the room; his own birth had drained what vitality Golda Kruppen ever possessed.

He is guided over to the side of the bed and Aunt Ruth stands behind him with her hands resting on his shoulders. His mother's eyes are closed. She had not been the center of his childhood; no doubt she wished that she had been. Sanitariums and doctors claimed too much of her time, but she always gave him gifts, toys and books and candies, and little hugs.

Only minutes later, she ceased to breathe.

His father took his hand and led him from the room, leaving his aunts to care for what remained. They went to the drawing room. The morning sunlight bathed the room, giving it a gay life and warmth that seemed so inappropriate for a memory of death and loss. A cold stove squatted in the corner next to an empty coal box.

He sat on his father's lap, enclosed by burly arms. He distinctly remembered the odor of his father's freshly laundered suit, the crisp tie and stiff collar. His father cried and Hans cried. Then David Kruppen began to mumble in a strange language, a litany of mourning and hope. Hans remembered the word Yahweh, but did not know what it meant. Years later he found out that it meant God. His father had prayed! A man who shunned religion and found strength in atheism had prayed.

That was the only time that he could remember his father hugging him or crying. From then on the hugs came from Frau Johnson, his nanny, or Aunt Ruth.

The next memory was of June 5, 1909, the proudest day in

his father's life. Hans was thirteen years old, awkward with puberty. Wanda from down the street had already treated him to his first kiss. She was Lutheran and they saw each other only at night when she crawled out her bedroom window and he slipped past Frau Johnson's bedroom out the back door. It was so exciting, like being spies at a rendezvous. As a Jew he knew that his kind was not always tolerated by the neighbors and that her mother would beat her if she knew. Though Wanda was a fond, bittersweet memory, that memory rarely demanded his attention. In May, his father had completed the construction of a newer, larger factory. He had moved beyond making dyes to processing chlorine for industrial use.

The factory had been designed by an important architect who gloried in the forms and lines of steel girders and glass. Two long chemical plants with a smaller office building in the front. A rail line came up to the rear, bringing salt from the mines and taking away the highly toxic chlorine gas. The workers, some three hundred in all, stood in four long lines, like troops on parade, their clothes freshly laundered. David Kruppen stood in front, his own suit immaculate. Hans waited beside him.

Four officers of the German army drove up in one of those new automobiles. The points of their helmets made the tall men look like steeples. Even at his young age, Hans knew that the true heart of Germany was the army. Its conservative class of officers supported the Kaiser and brought dignity and glory to the nation. Even if the nation had not been at war since 1871, that great war had seen the humiliation of the weak French and the unification of Germany under the royal house of Prussia. Hans was well aware of all of this because their home was filled with books on the exploits of the Prussian and German armies. He also knew that Jews could not be officers.

The officers toured the factory, making compliments about the shiny machinery, and asking detailed questions about the potential of the business. Germany was the world leader in the chemical and dying industries and his father now had customers in sixteen countries. Hans remembered the pride on his father's face and Hans shared in that pride. If the army accepted them, then anyone would accept them. They were not truly Jewish anymore. They were Germans.

These two memories so often surfaced during drunken binges while a student at the University of Berlin. He was studying to be a lawyer, but yearned to be an archeologist. Famous men were finding such fascinating artifacts amid ancient cities that had been lost for millennia, exotic faraway places like Troy, Assyria, Babylon, and Minos. His father expected him to inherit the factory and continue to run it. At the end of his second year of study, he returned home for the summer and argued once with his father about the subject. There was no resolution and for the next two months, he made a point to avoid the strong-willed man. While he could not face up to Herr Kruppen, he did not relinquish his defiance, either.

Tension filled the household for the rest of the summer, and outside the machinations of states began to tumble like dominoes. Armies mobilized and in the heat of August the continent rushed into war. Enthusiastic crowds of patriotic citizens surged through the streets of Frankfurt, singing *Was blasen die Trompeten?* and *Deutschland, Deutschland über Alles.* Hans was there with them, a stein of beer in his hand. The ecstatic sense of unity, an mystical union with his fellow citizens, filled him with a sense of purpose he had never experienced before. He enlisted in the army.

A couple of weeks later he was summoned to the local barracks to begin training. A recent change of policy now allowed Jews to become officers and, because of his education, he was selected to command a company. By the spring of 1915, he was a fresh lieutenant in a newly formed division. A train took them into Belgium and they marched the rest of the way into France. He strode alongside his company, proud of their smart uniforms, clean weapons, and fierce patriotism.

The sight of hundreds of marching troops strung along the road provoked a sense of invincible power. Such discipline, precision, potential to wield death. How could France stand against them much longer? They had whipped the effeminate Gauls in 1870, and though the Western Front was now stagnant, their superior morale and national character would surely crack the back of the Allies.

That night they bedded down with warm meals prepared by the cooking wagons. It was almost like a country outing, camping with his schoolmates. The enlisted men slept in large tents and he found quarters in an abandoned chateau with the rest of the officers. Before bedding down, he walked about his company's bivouac to ensure that his soldiers were happy. Their jokes and general demeanor were familiar to him. They were just like the stalwart souls who worked at his father's factory.

The next day they came to a village that was little more than ruins, their first symbol that war had passed this way. The sign outside the village was half-gone, and ended with "alans." Bullet holes pocked the plaster walls of burned-out houses and stores. Craters marked the surrounding fields. There were no civilians to encumber a picture of desolation worthy of a great painting. Such a painting would have been even more dramatic if the church tower still stood as a solitary counterpoint for the scene. Alas, the tower was a pile of rubble. Glory had been found here, Hans thought to himself, feeling somewhat envious.

Beyond the village they passed a crude cemetery. Wooden crosses in neat rows marked each hero. Healthy green grasses had already started to cover the overturned soil. Two taller crosses presided over larger mounds, which Hans realized were mass graves.

That night they stayed in an abandoned village. Its homes were still intact and at least dry. In the distance thunder boomed, which according to a liaison officer was really the sound of German and British artillery. It rained that night. Hans had always liked the rain, its fresh scent and aura of cleanliness, but already he realized that rain was bad for men at war.

They slogged through the mud the following morning, coming ever closer to the angry roaring. The 195th was supposed to replace a worn division on the front line. Two long lines of hollow-eyed troops had passed by, heading to the rear on the way to much-deserved rest. Hans led his company in a rousing cheer for them. At noon, they stopped to divide into individual units and receive detailed written orders and maps.

As he was standing near two of his sergeants, examining the complex contours of the map he had just received, an errant shell crashed nearby. He flew through the air, aware of only silence and surprise. Crumpling to the ground, he felt a cold blanket of darkness collapse over him.

When he regained consciousness, two days had passed and he found himself lying in a hospital bed. His entire body was sore, inside and out. Bandages tightly bound his chest and he could at least hear some faint sounds. The doctor explained that both his eardrums had been ruptured and would take quite some time to heal. A piece of shrapnel had cut through his chest, missing his heart by half a centimeter. Lucky to be alive, he would be able to fight again.

He was evacuated back to Germany and his father came to visit him, proud of his only son. Hans accepted the congratulations with a smile but knew that his wound was not a noble cut, but an accident of fate. Even so, he found it chilling how close death had come to severing life from him.

CHAPTER NINE

I come awake abruptly. Confusion scraps at my thoughts. Where am I? Who am I? My hands fumble across my body, seeking answers, finding a tee shirt, no bra, soft flesh, thin arms. Up to my face stumble the fingers, revealing delicate features and long hair. I am Joanna Prall.

My eyelids are so heavy that I don't bother to open them. All I want to do is sleep, return to my memories. There I will find answers, of that I am certain.

For some reason my journey back through my memories persists on lingering with Hans Kruppen, recalling the smallest details. Why, I cannot really say. I usually try to stay away from wars, too much danger there, and so often there is so little that I can do for soldiers. They die so soon. Perhaps I am attracted to my memories of Hans because I felt that I might truly succeed with helping. With him, I could honor all that is good, to use my unique nature to do good.

I think that maybe I haven't always tried to do good.

That thought pops open my eyes with a bit of shock. What about my enemy, who is obviously not good in any way? The problem with hiding is that not only can't anyone see you, but you can't see anyone else. Completely isolated, my knowledge of the world outside grows more outdated by the minute. What has my enemy been up to? Are people under its control, or at the very least, its influence, closing in on me. I need to find some access to the web and google some facts.

There is a small town only two miles away, an easy walk

along a trail through the woods. A plan forms. Walk into town, but don't follow the trail, in case I stumble across another hiker, but make my way through the woods, using the trail as a guide so that I won't get lost. The thought of using that much energy makes me feel ill. Joanna's body is still weak from years of inactivity. I am concerned that my face is everywhere, on television, on the web, and in newspapers, like a wanted man in an old western movie. Anyone could recognize me.

There would also be cameras in town, for traffic, stores, and automated teller machines that might see me. There would be people that might see me. I could find someone and contrive to put a fragmental in them and send them to the small public library, a small red brick building that used to be a post office, where they could do my research for me. My hunger for information, to feel connected, tugs at my fears of the enemy, threatening to bring them to full bloom. I want to know what is going on!

Calming myself, I realize that going into town would be too risky and too exhausting. Better to find answers in my memories and trust that my hiding place will remain secure.

Best to find out if I am as good a person as I think (no, as I hope) that I am.

CHAPTER TEN

By early summer of 1916, Hans had regained his strength.
A troop train took him to a bivouac near Lille. A Hauptmann
from the division staff of the 195th found him and announced
that he would be placed in command of a company near the
town of Montdidier. The next day Hans left with the Hauptmann, driving in an open staff car along pleasant French roads.
Farmers who had not fled the war worked their fields behind
plow horses. The Hauptmann pointed out two specks in the sky,
swooping around each other. The war had left the ground and
taken to the realm of the birds.

They left the car over a kilometer behind the front and
descended into a trench. The boards that had been laid across
the muddy bottom squished under their boots as they walked.
Wooden posts, some with bark still on them, and interwoven
branches formed the walls of the trenches. Sentries asked for
the day's password, then saluted at the correct word, as they
worked their way through the three parallel trench systems and
connecting trenches.

The 2nd company, one hundred and thirty-three men,
manned a stretch of the trench some four hundred meters long.
The previous commander had been promoted to command a
battalion in another regiment and taken his orderly with him, so
a new man was assigned to Hans.

That night the Tommies welcomed Hans with a bombardment. Not much, a shell every couple of minutes, but it was
enough to keep him wide-eyed in his cot. He knew that the stout

layers of logs and dirt above the bunker protected him from anything less than a direct hit from a seventy-five, but that did not keep him from shivering for most of the night. His orderly slept on the other side of the room and a hanging blanket separated them, hiding his terror.

For the next three nights, the shells pounded them. Six men were wounded and were replaced by only one, who returned from the hospital, having recovered from a broken leg. His soldiers began to look listless from exhaustion. Division headquarters predicted that it was a feint to cover an attack some five miles down the line near the Somme river. The next morning the bombardment did not stop. The telephone lines to the rear were cut and Hans began to get nervous.

At about ten o'clock, it began to rain. The pickets squinted out into No Man's Land while everyone else huddled in the bunkers. A half hour later, the shelling stopped. Hans emerged, astonished at the silence. He removed the cotton from his ears and tried to listen, but could only hear the familiar ringing. He joined a soldier who was on his tiptoes to see over the parapet. They could only see the grey of rain. The Tommy trenches were some six hundred yards away. A running man could cross that in less than three minutes, but considering the shell holes, debris, and wire, it always took considerably longer.

The whine of an incoming shell. It hits with a sick crumble. Only a small explosion. His companion's eyes go wide. Hans's nostrils are tickled by a scent that he hasn't smelt for over a year, since strolling through his father's factory. Chlorine.

"Gas!" the soldier shrieks, fumbling for his mask. Fear speeds the cry down the line.

Hans moves more deliberately, aware that as the officer, he has to set an example. His orderly has already put his own mask on. Hans orders the bunkers emptied and the men to prepare for imminent attack. He sends two runners back to the rear trenches to alert them to his suspicions and ask for artillery support. Damn the phones. A full-scale attack will certainly overwhelm the 2nd company, since the front-line trenches are usually overrun in a big push. It is the second and third line that holds. His only consolation is to make the Tommies pay.

A new pitch to the ringing in his ears. He concentrates and realizes that it is a whistle, shrilling the signal to attack. Out of the rain come vague forms, inverted saucer hats on their heads. The wide-eyed goggles and hoses coming from their mouths make them look like something from the imagination of that other Tommy, H. G. Wells. The men of the 2nd company are veterans and their two machine guns open up on either side of Hans. The forms tumble. The rattle of rifle fire joins the noise.

Hans runs down the trench line, checking on his troops. He trips over someone lying in the mud. Ready to scream out his anger at the shirker, he rolls the man over. His left eye is a mess. Grey stuff oozes from a hole behind the left ear and into Hans's outstretched fingers. The scream struggles to emerge but the internal image of an officer, restrained and strong, manages to suffocate it. His first dead man. A man whose life he was responsible for.

"Grenades," his orderly shouts.

The young officer becomes aware of a new sound, sharp cracks. That must be the grenades. It is from further down the line; the Tommies must have got to the trench there. Drawing his revolver, Hans runs down the trench, tapping the shoulder of every second man and shouting for them to follow. Half a dozen men later he comes around a corner and finds grey and brown coats struggling with each other. With a shout to bolster his courage, he joins the fray, putting two bullets into the back of one brown coat and another two into a second. Some instinct causes him to look up. A Tommy is on the parapet of the trench, a grenade in one hand, rifle in the other. Their eyes meet and, much to his own astonishment, Hans shoots the Tommy without hesitation. The man falls back and the grenade explodes.

Hans jumps up out of the trench, fascinated to see his own handiwork. The Tommy is still alive, but his left arm is gone, and he is shrieking. In pity, Hans pulls the trigger once again. The pistol is empty. He pulls again and again. Still no bullets.

His orderly steps into view and plunges his bayonet into the stomach of the man. Hans notes that his orderly gives the rifle a half turn before tugging it out, just like they had been taught in training. Entry was easy, but spasming muscles and bone often conspired to keep the blade in the body so that a twist was necessary to get the bayonet back out.

Then the battle is over. The Tommies retreat back into the mist. Hans is completely astonished to still be alive. The heavens seem to agree and the rain stops. The moans of the wounded and cries for medical help are now heard. An hour later, Hans is still preparing for another wave of attacks. There are seven dead and some twenty wounded. A quick count has revealed thirty-nine dead Tommies. Two of them are found still alive, but wounded; taken prisoner, they are sent to the rear with his own wounded. One of the runners returns. There will be no artillery support and division intelligence believes this was a feint. On the Somme, entire armies are engaged.

Only a few shells mar the peace of the rest of the day. Hans wants to talk to someone or get drunk. But he is an officer and does not have a peer to talk with. And of course, drinking on the line is a capital offense. That night his exhausted sleep is haunted by the Tommy without an arm, shrieking his sanity away.

The following months become a blur, like a reel of film set wrong in the projector. The memory even had that black and white quality, no color. He earns the Iron Cross, Second Class, in a battle that he can barely recall. That battle was like so many of the others, and he did as he always did, but this time a superior officer was there to watch him. The decoration only confirms what Hans knows, that he is an effective officer. He writes regularly to his father and through return letters basks in his father's praise. His father keeps him abreast of the German victories on the Eastern Front. Russia is collapsing. That is where the war is being won, not here in France.

The war, which seemed that it would never end, is changing. While the Fatherland may be winning, it does not feel that way in the trenches. The world for Hans has become a few square miles of dirt. Lice are everywhere, biting constantly, leaving little red itches behind. Sometimes the men groom each other, picking lice from a comrade's hair and crushing them with a thumbnail. Rats appear to thrive in the mud and more than once, Hans awakes with a start as the filthy beasts run across his blanket. What if they touched his nose or mouth? A completely revolting thought. He learns to sleep with an arm flung over his face.

Always, the shelling. Once a shell collapses the side of a trench and the lower half of a decaying corpse spills out, left over from some previous battle. The rest of him cannot be found. There are no clothes, not even boots, to show if he was friend or enemy or just a civilian. The shells made Hans feel so damned helpless. A man should be able to affect what happens to him, have some control, but the shells fall at random, picking whom the shades of war choose.

March 3, 1917. Markus Buchhiem, a picket, is found asleep at his post. A bottle of cheap wine is with him. No raiding parties had come across that night and so no harm was done, but Hans knew that he could not let these two crimes go unpunished. Discipline was already going to hell. Repairs to the trenches and barbed wire were getting shoddy. Many of the soldiers only shaved when they thought he was going to visit their section of the line. And most telling, a dozen men in the last week had contracted trench foot. Soldiers who cannot keep their feet dry are not ready to fight. Soon the regiment would notice that in the medical reports and know something was amiss. His men were in the grip of a malaise and it was his duty as their commander to correct it. He had even heard rumors of unofficial truces between other units and the enemy where they refrained from firing at each other, or if they did, they did not try to kill. One wild rumor described nightly card games.

The swift court-martial is held in a cramped bunker under the pale glow of a single oil lamp. Every corporal and sergeant is present as Hans announces the verdict prescribed by regulations. He borrows the firing squad from another company, but personally steps forward to direct the proceedings himself. On March 5, 1917, Markus Buchhiem, nineteen years old, a veteran of sixteen months of war, is executed for dereliction of duty. His body is not buried with honors or even with other soldiers and his family is informed of the disgrace that they must now bear.

Another year. The war grinds on. The rations get sparser and worse. There is talk of a failed harvest and famine at home. Before the dead are sent back for burial, their boots are stripped. Boots are hard to come by.

March comes, cold and wet. Markus Buchhiem comes to Hans in his dreams. The apparition does not condemn or condone, but merely stands there, hands bound, eyes covered, waiting for the bullets. Hans wants to remove the blindfold, look into the youth's eyes, but cannot; he must follow the script of the dream, of life, and order the firing squad into action. Such a waste, a useless waste.

He does not go to sleep the next night, but lies in his cot watching Markus Buchhiem in the darkness above. An hour before dawn, shells begin to fall. Hans welcomes them. Mechanically, he eats his breakfast. Muscles in his neck and back ache from the lack of sleep. At midday airplanes strafe the trench line. The shelling continues, grinding up the earth and blowing holes in the strands of barbed wire and minefields. The Tommies are softening them up. It is either a feint or an attack will soon come.

Two days until the anniversary. Again Hans does not even try to sleep. He prowls the trenches, crouching at every incoming scream, checking his pickets and the six machine gun pillboxes, making sure that his company is alert and ready. Sleep is not an option. A headache pounds at his temples and his joints ache. He will not allow the sacrifice of Markus Buchhiem to have been in vain. The 2nd company will survive.

This attack will be different than the rest, he feels it in his gut, which has been tuned like a violin by too much experience. Already six men have died, another fifteen wounded. At the last staff meeting, the liaison from the General Staff mentioned that seven out of every ten casualties came from artillery. His orderly fills his canteen with strong dandelion tea. Coffee is simply unobtainable; damn the Tommy blockade.

With dawn comes rain. The shelling stops and now the familiar piercing of whistles being blown. The first wave appears and the pillboxes cut them down. The sun is hidden by such dark clouds that the day is like twilight. The deluge provides good cover for the second wave, who manage to overrun two forward pillboxes. Hans collects a few dozen soldiers to counterattack. They are soaked and shivering. There will certainly be a lot of reports of trench foot after this. At least the rain will provide cover for his troops, just as it has for the Tommies.

The mud sticks to his coat as Hans scrambles over the parapet. They are halfway to the first pillbox, moving as quickly as can be expected when the rain slows to a drizzle. He can see the pillbox now, its concrete washed clean. The Tommies have set up a few machine guns of their own and open fire.

Hans dives to the ground and scoots into a crater, where he tumbles into the water pool at the bottom. It is only a foot or so deep, but thoroughly soaks him to his underwear. His orderly splashes in behind him. The staccato of the machine guns trails off and Hans dares to peek out. Grey forms litter the ground. He counts twenty-one before the drizzle turns back into a downpour.

Never has he lost so many of his men at one time. His stomach, full of tea, rebels, and he retches. How could so many be dead? He had let them down, let Markus Buchhiem down. He whispers to his orderly to call for a retreat. Only two soldiers creep past their shell hole. Hans follows, slithering through in the mud with his loyal orderly trailing him. A fragment of barbed wire snags his cheek, drawing a deep streak of blood. He welcomes the pain, a form of penance.

Back in the safety of the trenches. Now the 2nd company has only enough soldiers left to cling to their own defense positions. The rain continues and streams of water flow along the bottoms of the trenches. According to his watch, it is now night. A strange silence settles over the battlefield. He can hear scraps of English when the wind is just right. The Tommies are that close. Then comes cries of terror and shouts for help—in English and German. The wounded have crawled into shell holes for protection and the rain is inexorably filling up the holes like bathtubs. Hans imagines the horror of slowly rising water and wounds so severe that the men cannot move. He cannot afford to lose any more troops and so he listens, his face slack, eyes wide. Finally the piteous cries cease. Hans continues to stare into the dark rain.

March 5, 1918 arrives but Hans does not notice. Only wisps remain in his memory...sitting outside his bunker...diarrhea filling his pants...his orderly slapping his face...urine seeping down his legs...the hospital...a kind nurse who reminds him of his Aunt Ruth, who always treated his mother with such tenderness.

CHAPTER ELEVEN

In a small garden near the hospital stood an old elm tree, some thirty meters tall. I enjoyed its company, and often sat on a stone bench underneath it. What to do about Hans? This awful war had claimed so many casualties, and not just the dead and maimed. My medical colleagues thought that the large number of psychiatric casualties were caused by the introduction of mass armies. More troops were at war than any time ever before in history. The soldiers of the twentieth century were not hardened veterans, but inferior conscripts. And this war was a factory war, with each side pouring out mind-boggling amounts of artillery and shells.

Some physicians thought that shell shock came from physical damage to the brain, while others thought that it might be a temporary nervous disorder. One doctor at a nearby hospital studiously applied electroshock to shell-shocked patients, arguing that it would clear the nervous system. Unfortunately he was quite successful. The temporary amnesia helped clear their mind of the horror and destroy symptoms of paralysis that so often affected their right arms. You cannot fire a rifle if your right arm will not move. Hypnosis was also quite in vogue as a treatment. The reality was that we did not know how to help our patients; even I, with my special access, had difficulty helping these shattered soldiers.

Other doctors thought that the number of patients was due to weak character. That implied that there were soldiers of strong character who could endure the continual rain of explosives that did more than chew up land and flesh. But I knew that war had always battered the psyche, crippling many, even in the wars before gunpowder. Most people are just not equipped for war, and that was something to be proud of, not dismayed. On the whole, people have an innate resistance to killing and overcoming that reluctance always leaves scars.

Hans clearly suffered from nostalgia. He yearned to be home, away from the killing and the dying and the mud and the misery. Such a desire was not surprising. Almost every man and officer on the line shared that sentiment. And for most of them, home would be a welcome place. Hans would only be welcome there if he was a hero.

Much worse was the horror. It created a blanket of oppression smothering his spirit. He needed to be able to step back and find some distance, some perspective. But right now his memories would not suffer that favor. When a man punishes himself, perhaps it is deserved. Markus Buchhiem would always be there. In no way could he ever find absolution for that execution, but maybe some accommodation could be reached.

- - - - -

"Don't drink that!" Hans roared.

Private Holt looked up him at with sullen eyes and deliberately poured the brown water from his cup. For a moment, Hans thought he might have to draw his revolver to defend himself, but then the defiance melted from Holt's eyes and he slumped to the ground. The water came from a puddle left over from the rain two days past.

Hans walked on, keeping the corner of his eye on Holt. A direct hit had destroyed their water barrels and new water had not yet been sent forward. In a bitter irony, he yearned for fresh rain. Holt was the sixth man that he had shouted at. Who knew what germs and toxins were in the puddles? They would have to wait and suffer.

His memory lurched, skipping from one image to another,

fascinated by the horror. Four horses in harness, pulling a gun. Incoming shells lacerating them with shrapnel. They scream, twisting about in agony, bright drops of blood splattering each other. A handler, tears in his eyes, brings a rifle to his shoulder and picks each of them off in turn. One can see the terror in their eyes as their mates are stilled and slump, dragging them down with dead weight.

A tabby cat, gaunt and grimy-looking, chewing on the leg of a corpse that is protruding out from under a pile of village rubble. One of his soldiers shoots at the cat and misses. One last tug for a final mouthful and the animal disappears.

Bloated corpses left in the sun for too long. Flies clinging to them, growing fat and greasy.

The rippling of Markus Buchhiem's chest as bullets tore craters into his torso.

- - - - -

Hans was still caught in the nightmare. He continually replayed in his mind the horrors of his memories. If this went on much longer, the web would become a permanent prison. He would spend the rest of his life in an asylum, stripped of the will necessary to even yearn for hope.

Every day a courier brought mail to each of the patients. The letters were placed in a bag under their beds and one often saw a soldier reading the scraps of paper as if they contained the salvation of scripture, which they most certainly did. The bag under Hans's bed contained six letters. Withdrawing my fragmental from Hans, I waited for Mrs. Joulet to leave before I broke a cardinal rule and pilfered them.

Outside in the park, I read each of them in turn. Two were from Ruth Kruppen and filled with the longing of a mother for a son. The rest were from his father. The last had arrived only today. Handwritten, only a single page. His father was coming on a train.

Three days later I was at the train station, almost skittish with anticipation. In the half-hour that I waited, two supply trains passed, bringing flour requisitioned from the Ukraine to feed the German Army.

The third supply train had a single passenger car just before the caboose, from which a well-dressed man of about fifty was the only one to disembark. The haughty bearing that he projected has to be cultivated; we are not born with it. I introduced myself and presented him with the gift of a fragmental. It was only a short walk into town and to the hospital.

- - - - -

David Kruppen was now a Count, a title awarded by the Kaiser himself, all records of his Jewishness having been stricken, a reward for the chlorine gas that his factories pumped out with such awful efficiency. He was still the tall, lean man that his son remembered, though the dark hair had a liberal dose of gray in it. He thought the gray made him more distinguished looking, appropriate for a man in his position. Across from the train station was the headquarters of the town occupation authority. A guard stood in front of it, his rifle resting against the stone wall. Anger flashed in the Count's mind at the slothfulness of this soldier, even though he was obviously middle-aged, with a substantial paunch, a third-rate reservist. The younger men were at the front.

When his son joined the Army in 1914, he had been so proud and so envious. He had even tried to join himself, but the local regimental commander persuaded him that he could contribute to the war more effectively by personally running his factory. That was still true, but he so often regretted the decision. He had missed the chance for glory. When word came of the awarding of the Iron Cross to Hans, he had thrown an extravagant banquet for the local garrison officers.

He still yearned for the scent of gunpowder, but gradually the war had turned ugly. The first indication of this struck him quite suddenly when he found himself unable to buy quality cigarettes at anything less than shocking prices on the black market. The British blockade was strangling Germany so slowly that it was sometimes easy to ignore in years past, but not anymore. Inflation and the gaunt appearances of the children continually reminded even the most dense.

He now owned three factories, feeding chlorine gas to the army. Fortunately he had not been disrupted by strikes like so many of his fellow industrialists. But he was tired of giving presents to his weary workers each time one of their sons was reported dead. It was not the gifts that bothered him, but rather the continual need to confront the reality of his workers' lives as the town was stripped of joy at the loss of its young men.

Increasingly his thoughts had been drawn away from the business and back into himself. He thought a lot about Golda, remembering summer picnics and soft nights before she became ill. He thought about their son and so longed to see him. When the letter arrived saying that his son was in a hospital, he talked to his army contacts and secured permission to visit.

And here he was. He wondered if it had been gas or a bullet. Hopefully, it was something serious enough to take Hans from the war, but not cripple him permanently. He was not sure if he could handle another invalid in his life, to every day be reminded of health that once was. Must look on the positive side. A hero would be good for the business.

The Herr Doctor von Hoff escorting him was evasive about his inquiries. A queer sort of man, not solemn enough for a man in his position.

The town seemed deserted, which was odd considering that it was a bright, invigorating spring morning. Warm, but not the heat of summer yet. At least there was one man who was taking advantage of the day. He perched on a wooden bench outside the hospital, wearing the uniform and insignia of a master sergeant of the army of Saxony. His pant legs hung empty, as did his right sleeve. The right eye was gone, replaced by a white scar. His left arm was casually flung across the back of the bench. A man at rest, his eyes closed.

As Count Kruppen passed, the man spoke, his scratchy voice quivering with the effort. "Excuse me, sir."

The Count stopped. The smell of urine and sweat clung around the soldier.

"Could you light my pipe?" The words seemed labored, even forced, by a great effort. "The breeze keeps snuffing out my match."

"Yes." Taking the soldier's matches, he scratched one to life and shielded it with his cupped hand.

The pungent odor of Turkish tobacco trickled from the sergeant's mouth. A Pour le Mérite hung around the man's neck. He was not a general or important industrialist, so he had earned it through valor. The highest medal possible. The Count had always wanted one of his own, yet did not feel envious of this man, for the soldier deserved the honor. He sought a small share of his glory by sitting down next to the man.

"How were you wounded?" the Count asked.

"Grenade...maybe two of them."

A reticent man, intensely aware of social protocol, the Count could not bring himself to ask the question that burned in his mind. My fragmental wormed forward and pushed the words out of his mouth. "How did you get the Pour le Mérite?"

The Count was somewhat surprised at this strong impulse, so out of step with his own character. But the words were out and he was eager to hear the answer.

"Verdun...I had cracked up before that...sent to hospital...a bit of rest and I was back with my company...led a rush on a Frenchie pillbox...machine gun got most of my men and I took a round into one leg...I crawled the rest of the way and pushed a charge through the gun slit...dragged my sergeant back to aid station...I didn't want to go back after that, but did...cracked up again in '17...heat and bugs was too much...now here."

The master sergeant fell silent, his chest slumping and his eyes closing as if intensely exhausted.

"You are a credit to the Fatherland and a true hero," the Count said, his voice choking with emotion. He tucked his business card into the right pocket of the Sergeant's tunic. "If you ever need anything after the war, do not hesitate to contact me. It is the least I can do."

"Thank you," the Sergeant whispered.

Further words seemed inappropriate, so the Count simply stood up and walked away, feelings of pride and sadness smothering his soul.

- - - - -

Master Sergeant Wilhelm Zeitler sucked on his pipe with contentment, enjoying the aroma and the pleasant buzz that came from not having smoked for so long. My fragmental struggled to maintain control of his nervous system. Gradually the battle was lost and the hand holding the pipe increased its shaking. The palsy won and the pipe slipped from fingers that could no longer grasp it. The pipe bounced on the cobblestones, spilling the smoldering tobacco. The only thing that kept him from toppling over was the belt looped through the wooden slats of the bench behind him.

I had been forced to insert words into the man's mouth in order to serve my own purposes. Master Sergeant Zeitler had never cracked up. He was one of those few people who are natural warriors and thrive in the chaos and danger of war. Before the war, he had been a troublemaker, drinking all the time and getting into fights. When he stayed sober, he was a hard worker; but it was in the war that he found his purpose and felt completely alive. It was only fitting that he should die in battle, but that was not to be. His body was slowly wasting away as his nerves and brain continued to fracture. He was not aware of much anymore. Six months to the end, no more.

- - - - -

Hans lay on his cot, his chest sunken, hands clutching the sheet, eyes wide open, seeing visions of the past. Small, clear bubbles decorated the string of spittle that trickled out of the corner of his mouth.

The Count was shocked. Where was the ruddy glow of life that his son had always had in those cheeks? What had happened? What wound? Was it nerves, like the Sergeant outside? The older man stepped quickly from the door and knelt next to his son. He reached out to touch him, but paused in midair, unsure of what to do.

He glanced around the room, seeing the other patients. Some were sleeping, one gazed out the window, and a few more were reading. They did not seem hurt.

"What is this room?" The sharp tone cut through the air and demanded an answer.

"Shell shock, sir," answered one of the men before returning to his book.

The Count felt like someone had just slapped his face. His rabbi father had struck him many times when he neglected his studies of the Torah and Mishnah. Then his stomach roiled, wanting to vomit, and he fought for control.

Oh, dear God, the humiliation. How could his only child be here? He flashed back to a time a couple of years ago when he had caught the flu. His bowels felt weak.

He thought of the Iron Cross, Second Class, which Hans had sent home, in a frame on the mantel in his study, where he could see it. Anger washed over him, calming the stomach and bowels. Was the medal even deserved?

Now was the chance for my fragmental. Having found the closet that held the memories of Golda, I opened the portal and pushed them forward. The memories most associated with anger slipped onto the stage of his mind. She was so weak, always sick. Other women had babies with no problems. His own mother had birthed eight, all strong, except Lev, who caught the measles and succumbed. Golda was always going from one doctor to another, in and out of sanitariums, creating bills almost as fast as he could earn the money.

More memories of Golda. Sitting in her father's parlor when

he was courting her, laughing at a quiet joke. There were other girls who attracted his attention, but none with whom he felt at ease. With her, he was always relaxed, spontaneously bringing out his noblest behavior. She listened and made soothing suggestions. He had loved her so much. And then a proud winter day when she presented him with a son.

His son! A disgrace, collapsing under the pressure of battle. Would be that he could have gone instead, instead of working in the factory, to find the glory and bring home the medal. None of this cowardliness.

But there was Sergeant Zeitler. He was a genuine hero and he had cracked up twice. Maybe it was natural. What did he know of true war? He read avidly, but it was all intellectual, not blood, mud, and horror.

The anger began to abate, exhausted and confused. My fragmental opened up that place where Count David Kruppen kept his love. He had sometimes been so angry with Golda and her weakness, but he had been consumed with their love. Could he not love her child in the same way? Hans was weak and maybe that was okay, maybe it should be okay.

As the years passed, he had so rarely talked to his son or played with him; he just did not know how to. It did not feel natural to pick up a ball or tickle the boy. So he watched his sister play with the child, and was happy when the boy was smiles and laughter, and sad when the boy cried.

All of these turbulent emotions crested and tears began to trickle down his nose, the first since Golda had died. He crumbled to his knees and took his son's hands into his own, oblivious to the other soldiers who were watching.

"Son, please speak to me," he whispered between sobs. He paused then spoke in a louder, declarative voice. "I am proud of you. I love you. I need you. Do not go away like your mother did."

- - - - -

Hans wallowed in the war, mixing up the memories of his life. He stood in front of Markus Buchhiem, pointing his pistol. Three quick tugs on the trigger and brain splattered everywhere, like the first dead soldier he had seen.

The scene repeated; this time four bullets. His troops applauded, like an appreciative audience at the opera. Bravo, good performance, do it again. And again, bullets ripping skull.

My fragmental struggled to get past this litany of images. There was more to life than the last three and half years. Remember Wanda, who had quick lips. Aunt Ruth, who always gave love. The street in front of their house, with familiar cobblestones, where he used to play a game, jumping from stone to stone. If you slipped, you fell into the lake of acid that surrounded those islands of safety.

Then came the sound of crying, so much like something he had heard before. He knew that memory. A warm, sunny room and his father, crying and praying at the death of his mother. He still found it difficult to feel anything about her loss, but he always felt sorry for his father. How to tell his father that? How would he feel if he had a wife and she wasted away? This imagined feeling was a good sadness, a natural mourning, not like the self-pity and misery of before.

He became aware that his hands were being held by unfamiliar hands. It was not the nurse or that doctor.

He opened his eyes to find the hospital room. The war clamored for attention but he saw his father first and heard his words.

"Da!" Hans sobbed, breaking free of the silence that had confined him for six weeks.

- - - - -

I was so pleased with myself after I left the two men to be alone. A young man brought back, an old man finding his buried love for his son, a family reunited in affection. Walking through the hospital ward, my attention was drawn to a young soldier coughing up blood. I assumed he was a gas casualty and was about to pass on. He coughed again and let out a moan that chilled me. He needed comfort and so I sat with him and soothed him with a fragmental. His name was Otto and he called Nuremburg home.

Gas was not his enemy. He had been on the front lines when he fell ill from influenza. Later that night he died. His body was too wasted from malnourishment and exhaustion to fight back. He was the first victim that I met of the great pandemic of 1918 and 1919. At least twenty-seven million died, most of them in India and Africa. It hit the young particularly hard. For some, it was as if the Black Death had returned, but I knew better. The Death killed so many more and came back for repeat performances, whereas the influenza burned itself out after a year and never returned.

CHAPTER TWELVE

It is mid-afternoon when I emerge from my memories. The intensity of the sun has made my skin sticky; my clothes cling to me. Wiping my gummy eyes, I stumble to the kitchen and take a long drink of water. My thoughts play lightly across the memories fresh in my mind as I eat another can of food.

Sifting through my past is an arduous, time-consuming path. So many people, so many stories, so much that I found meaning in. Some I skim over, like a flat rock dipping into the waters of memories, but some I cannot; they compel a full examination. My memory of a man that I met during the Great War is like that, a soul so lost that he almost broke loose from the moorings of meaning. Often I feel the same way. His set of problems were not unique in any way, even mundane. But there are some people that I feel drawn to understand and to help, as opposed to others who are as much in need, but I do not always help. Hans touched my soul and I was compelled to help him with all the powers I could command.

After we parted company, I continued to take an interest in him. In the thirties, I hired a detective to find out what Hans was up to. He was running the family firm and staying afloat despite the severe economic depression that hit Germany earlier and harder than the rest of the world. A new Chancellor, Adolf Hitler, was promising better days to come.

After the war Hitler ignited was extinguished, I hired another detective to check up on many of my former patients. Hans had married a Catholic and hid his Jewish roots from the Holocaust.

He left a widow and three children when he was executed by the Gestapo for his part in the 1944 plot to assassinate Hitler and end the war. His first two sons had already been offered to appease the insatiable appetite of war.

What a horrible waste, yet so noble. That's the problem with hate and war, they strip our personalities of all pretense, exposing the most noble and the most base in those that survive.

Why am I so drawn to my memories of Hans? I think it is because I feel a kinship. If I were a true human, and not the sum of my fragmentals, I think that I would be very much like Hans: filled with love of life, but so sensitive to the horrors of life that I might very well break.

But Hans is dead, the way of all other people. I return to the labor of retrieving the past.

Six or seven days pass. I lose count. Eat, sleep, and remember.

Going backwards through history is like visiting different alien cultures. The one common theme is the fundamental need in all people to feel connected to other people. People come together in families, villages, cities. In community we find our purpose. Often our purpose is found in God. Religious faith is an expression of community, not individualism. People like to think they are individuals, but I am the only true individual.

In my memories, a couple of centuries pass.

CHAPTER THIRTEEN

The winter of 1764-65 was spent in solitude at a small monastery in Kerga dedicated to St. Peter. A palisade of logs, as high as a tall man, surrounded the rough buildings of the monastery. The monks thrived on their work, a picture of mental health, and required nothing from me except a strong back. These pioneers were cutting down the forest and pushing the boundaries of Mother Russia and her Holy Orthodox church farther into the wilderness.

Normally I tried to head south when winter approaches. Not out of some phobia of the cold, but because I did not want my work of healing curtailed by the enforced seclusion of winter. An early blizzard caught me and many others unawares. With spring came the rains, and when the first fresh sprig of grass pushed its way up through the slush, I prepared to leave.

"Are you sure that you won't stay with us longer?" Abbot Utechin was a thin, wiry man with an oddly strong, soothing voice. We were dressed the same, a brown habit with a hood made of wool, tattered pants and well-worn boots of leather. We shared a vow of poverty. Another monk walked past us, slapping at the flanks of cattle with a stick to drive them out of the gate and down to the pasture near the river where there was some brown grass left over from last year.

"My heart and prayers remain with you," I replied, smiling at my own humor. A fragmental of mine rested in his mind, quietly observing.

The abbot smiled in return. "God be with you."

He was a healthy man of God, in no need of succor, but he served as a safe place for a fragmental to wait. If my core died through some mishap, I wanted a fragmental available to carry on. My fragmentals knew when my core self perished, as it had twice before. How they knew this, by what mechanism, I do not know. It is the classic problem of action over distance, where something causes action in something else even though there is no intervening medium to transmit the influence. Isaac Newton struggled with this when he elucidated the law of gravity; he finally surrendered to the beauty of the equations, though he could not explain how the sun could compel the planets to orbit about it. Gravity remained a spooky irritant in the craw of science until Einstein modified the beauty with new equations.

The sad part of the scenario was that if my core died, then the fragmental in Abbot Utechin would be forced to take his body in the name of survival. Certainly an unjustified kill, but one necessary for me to survive. I pushed the implications away from contemplation, queasy at the consequences. In more honest moments, I am forced to admit that I will kill anyone to survive; I have proven it before. The only consequence of my fragmental becoming the core is the loss of all the memories accumulated in the old core since its last contact with the fragmental.

All winter long, while sitting at the supper table during the long nights, the conversation centered around the wondrous happenings in Krist. It was said that a young woman, only thirteen years old, was receiving visions from Our Blessed Mother. Krist was only ten miles away, so I decided to see for myself.

The path was no more than a track winding though the barren forest. Snow still covered most of the ground and the naked trees looked forlorn without their leaves. Several carts had already passed this way, leaving deep ruts and turning the track into sticky mud. I walked along the edge of the track where clumps of brown grass grew, taking care to jump over the deeper slush. Even so, my boots were soon damp.

The way led downhill into the river valley. After five miles, the elevation dropped enough that buds decorated the trees and the snow was completely gone. The ground was still mushy and I slipped, sprawling forward into a puddle. The front of my coarse habit was soaked. Fortunately, the leggings were dry. I pulled off the habit and wrung it out as I shivered. This body was healthy and a winter of good food had given me a bit of fat.

Putting the habit back on, I began to trot, hoping to warm up. The sun was already beginning to dip back towards the horizon. Damn the short days of the far north. My teeth started chattering uncontrollably.

A movement out of the corner of my eye halted me. There, again, a shadow moving among the trees. And another, and then four more. A pack of wolves. Despite myself, I could not stop shaking and chattering. I pulled back the hood of the habit to get a better view. The long winter had caused bones to jut from the grey backs of these scruffy hunters.

I skipped across the ruts of the road to a large tree, placing my back to it. The lead wolf was already rushing me, silent and quick. At his shoulder, he was half my height; certainly he weighed just as much. I put up my arms as he leaped for my throat. As he collided with me, I pushed a fragmental into him.

The wolf tumbled away and rolled on the ground as if stricken with a deadly palsy. His legs twitched; his tail went rigid and straight, and froth streamed from his mouth. A low mournful whining escaped from his throat when he could draw in enough breath.

The rest of the pack stopped its circling to watch their leader. Four adults, with a half-grown pup in the background. One of them, a bitch, drew closer, approaching at an angle. She stopped to sniff the air and I was certain she could smell the fear in my sweat. My teeth still hammered against each other. I hoped she would not take that as a sign of vulnerability.

The lead wolf went rigid for a moment, as if frozen by the chill air, then its chest sunk as all the air in its lungs flowed out. Its legs sank to the ground. I glanced at the pack and found that they were all tense, pacing with anxiety.

Switching to approach from a different angle, the bitch

moved closer. Some ten feet away, she stopped, then began to circle. I was focused so much on her that I did not immediately notice that the fallen wolf had began to breathe again—short, shallow pants under closed eyes. Each exhalation came out as a whine, brief and high pitched.

After only a few moments of this, the bitch began to snarl at the fallen male. She knew that it was more than hurt; it was alien. I wondered if they were mates, though I must confess that I knew little about wolves. Perhaps the young wolf was their offspring.

Having successfully blunted the first attack, my fear calmed, though I remained tense and alert. If more came, I would use more of my fragmentals.

The bitch backed away, still growling, the hair on her shoulders raised in what seemed like revulsion. Once back far enough, the other wolves came to her, clustering around in confusion. She howled, and they joined in with her, gradually bringing their individual voices into harmony. Even the half-grown one joined in.

Returning my attention to the former leader, I watched with fascination. In the past I had put fragmentals into different animals, always with awful results. Unfortunately, those incidents were so long ago that it would take hours to retrieve memories from that far back. Some things have to be relearned over and over.

Leaving my tree, I approached the wolf and crouched. The others broke off their howling and watched, but made no move toward me. I reached out and gripped the wolf on the leg. His fur was sodden with sweat.

Like a wounded animal skittering away from the light, the fragmental fled from my touch. The mind of the wolf was a maelstrom of chaos, the aftermath of battle. The vigor of the wolf's life was slowly fading away and my fragmental intended to stay. We did not communicate with each other, for my fragmental forbade that contact. My fragmental was insane, yet still—amid all that disintegration—retained enough sense to self-preserve. Not preserve itself, but to preserve me, the core. It did not want me infected with its lunacy.

I backed away. The rest of the pack still watched me, and so I returned their scrutiny. Oddly enough, I felt a slight sense of loss, as if a finger had been cut away. Five minutes later, the wolf lay still. What an awful way to die.

I touched the wolf again and found nothing there. It might as well be a stone or a tree, neither of which had the neural pathways needed to be a nest for intelligence. The wolf was gone and so was my fragmental. The Scriptures explain what happens to the souls of people—the final destinations in heaven, hell, and purgatory. Where do my fragmentals go?

The sun was even farther down on the horizon and my wet clothes were not getting any drier. I walked away, looking back with every other step. The pack followed for a while before dropping back and disappearing.

My body continued to shiver in an attempt to keep the flesh warm. The chattering of my teeth grew worse. I broke into a jog, then a run. It felt good to let my body heat up with exertion and soon I was not shivering. But I was keenly aware of my limits. This was the last week of Lent and I was eating only at night, fasting during the day. It cleansed the mind and the body, but left me without energy.

My run petered away into a walk. I refused to stop and rest. My bag contained a small loaf of bread, hard from the cold, which I gnawed on as I walked.

As the shock of the experience with the wolves began to wear off, rational thought reasserted itself. I left the trail and found a small clearing sheltered by a large boulder. Breaking dry twigs off of some trees, I went to the south side of the boulder. A north wind was already rising. Using flint and steel from my bag, I soon had a merry bonfire roaring. Some years ago I touched and healed a woodsman in Germany and learned from him the skills of forest survival.

A couple of hours later, my clothes and cloak were dry and I felt well roasted. The sun had set, so I hunkered down and went to sleep. Not only was my body tired, I also felt a deeper weariness. The fragmental I had lost would soon rejuvenate within me, keeping my total ability to split constant. My feelings at the death of a fragmental are always confused. I did not mourn, but rather regretted that the memories of that fragmental's experiences since we last joined were now irretrievably lost.

When I arrived at my destination the next morning, the first man I met was the parish priest, a small, wiry man with an impish smile and an eagerness to please. We shook hands and I slipped a fragmental inside him. The miracle at Krist is not one story, but many smaller stories. So I wandered about the village, scattering my fragmentals about to learn these stories.

CHAPTER FOURTEEN

Because Krist was only a couple of decades old, most of the villagers came from farther up the river, from villages no more than fifty miles away. Alexsey Chkalov, the priest, was different. He came from the far south, where trees grew only along the streams and the rich loam of the grasslands yielded fodder for cattle and horses and bountiful gardens. Like his father and his father before him, his fate should have been to be a peasant, scraping at the earth. But rampaging Cossacks left his father and half the village as part of the dust. His mother, distraught with grief, sent him to live with a distant cousin who served as a priest. His new guardian was an old man who moved slowly about his parish. He lived in a hovel like his charges, but he owned two books: a Bible and a volume of liturgy.

For the first time in his life, Alexsey touched a book and found awe in the experience. His guardian tried to teach him to read the block letters inside but Alexsey could never understand. He learned to write his name and memorized the liturgy and a few stories from the Bible. After ordination, he headed north to find a village that needed a priest who could not read.

On the way he passed through Moscow. So many people, so much filth, so much wealth. He hoped to see the Archbishop, but the busy man had no time for an unimportant priest. He did see his Holiness pass on a rutted street in a carriage drawn by six fine white horses, like a great lord. The dried flecks of mud on the white paint did not detract from the power, both heavenly and earthly. The Archbishop was heading to the Kremlin for an audience with the new Czarina, the German princess Catherine.

Leaving Moscow, he went from village to village, seeking one that did not already have a priest. Three months later, he heard that the priest of Krist had died, so he went to the provincial capital to seek that position from the local bishop. A dispensation was granted, and Chkalov left for his new home, still dazzled by the gold rings, fine clothes, and large home of the bishop. Such wealth, awarded by God to his anointed.

He first met the girl Sonja when she came to tell him of her latest dream. She was short, even for seven years, with thick, wild blonde hair. A livid birthmark covered the right half of her face. Chkalov had already heard of her. The villagers thought that she was touched by God and they indulged her prattle. This was not right. She was a child, not a man of God. Only the scriptures gave the words of God, not some child. He had been looking forward to putting her in her place.

She came to him in his log cabin, which doubled as the church. When the weather allowed him, he said mass outdoors rather than have the villagers crowd into a room that was no longer than three men lying down.

"Father, I have dreamed a dream and saw Our Lord in all his glory."

Complex ideas for one so young, Chkalov thought. He wondered what the previous priest, who had died only a year ago, had told her.

"And what did Our Lord say?" Chkalov asked.

"Our Lord says that you are a good man, but vain. What does vain mean?"

Chkalov gaped at her...how?...who had put those words into her mouth?

He sputtered his confusion. "Where?...what?...why do you say that?"

"It is true. Our Lord spoke it."

The priest grasped for something to say. "And what does Our Lord look like?"

"You cannot see His face. The light of His glory is too strong.

Blinding like the sun."

"Where is Our Lord when you see Him?"

"In heaven," she said simply, seeming to get bored by the questions.

"What does heaven look like?"

"It is like a meadow in the forest, with great trees surrounding it, going all the way up into the sky. He has baby animals and angels all around Him."

"No gold?"

"Gold is for man, not God."

She spoke with such sincerity and certainty that he saw why the villagers held her in such awe. Some of them said that she was a sprite, akin to the spirits of the woods and water. Such pagan nonsense. Perhaps he had stumbled onto a saint in the flesh, like St. Olga. Of course, Olga was originally a princess, not a peasant.

- - - - -

When the labor pains began, Mariia Gladkov sent one of her sons to fetch the baba, while she headed for the bathhouse. She was not like other women, who grunted through hours of labor; after six births, she had learned that her babies came quickly.

An hour later, the child slipped from her womb and after the baba cut its cord, she laid it in the mother's arms. Mariia looked down at her new daughter, who quivered beneath the blanket. White mucus and streaks of blood still covered the tiny features. Finally, after six sons, a girl; someone to help cook and sew in the house and help her father and brothers in the fields; someone to look after her in her old age. Then the exhausted mother slept.

The next morning, she again took the girl into her arms. This time the girl was asleep, snug and comfortable in a blanket that bound her so tightly that she could not move. The birthmark was quite apparent now. Mariia choked on a sob. What man would want such an ugly woman?

As she felt the child suck at her breast, Mariia remembered a story she had heard when just a girl. In another village a girl was born with her face covered with a birthmark. On that hapless girl, the mark covered all her face, except for around her left eye. If she had been missing and arm or a leg they would have let her die, but she was a healthy bawler and her mother fought to keep her alive. The children teased her and she left the village when she was only fourteen to go to St. Petersburg, where she sold her body at the waterfront. The sailors did not seem to care what she looked like.

Was that to be the fate of her daughter? The loss of three of her six sons to various coughs and fevers had hardened Mariia somewhat. She accepted that God allowed life to be cruel, but she could not accept the idea of her daughter lying with strangers for a few pieces of metal.

She prayed to the Virgin to show pity on her new child. Let the other children be kind and let her find some happiness. Perhaps a nunnery when she was older, where she would be useful and not have to worry about attracting the attention of a man.

On the eighth day, Mariia emerged from the bathhouse, now purified from the stain of childbirth. She took the child to her husband, Marek. She saw his eyes flinch at the sight, but he leaned forward nevertheless and laid a kiss of acceptance on his daughter's forehead. Mariia came closest to crying then, so relieved and grateful to her man. She took the child to the priest and had her baptized. She named the child Sonja, daughter of wisdom.

Every night from that day on, Mariia took the time to offer a prayer to the Virgin for Sonja's sake.

Before the first year passed, the girl was speaking in full sentences. The other women marveled at this. She was a quick learner, always asking questions and using her nimble hands to emulate whatever she was watching. People always found a ready smile on her face and a kindness that enchanted them. Such goodness from another adult would be embarrassing, an affront to the inadequacies of all, but acceptable in a child. Only her mother noticed when she threw silent little tantrums, eyes shut, teeth clenched, and hands tightened into fists.

She also never lied, even when other children went through those times when they tested the limits of reality and parental tolerance.

One summer evening, when the girl was five, Mariia and Sonja were cutting potatoes for a stew.

"Why does Our Lord wear a dress?" Sonja asked.

"What?" What a strange idea, Mariia thought.

"Every time that I see him, He is wearing a long dress, not pants, and He has bare feet. Doesn't He have shoes?"

"When do you see Our Lord?"

"All the time."

"Where do you see the Lord?"

"Behind my eyes."

Further conversation revealed that her daughter saw almost continuous visions, and the girl did not realize that she was unique in this. She thought everyone saw Our Lord, why else did they worship Him?

Soon Sonja was telling the neighbors what the Lord looked like and what he was saying. That Misha's son, Sasha, would recover from a fever. That Our Lord loved us all, except when we sinned, which He hated.

The villagers were mystified at these statements, then accepting. After all, the girl was known to have never lied, and had not the village enjoyed good harvests ever since her birth. Few died of sickness or from accidents. Perhaps God protected them because He protected her. Through it all, Mariia watched her child with intent interest. In so many ways, Sonja was like a carefree, innocent child, and in other ways she seemed like the oldest, wisest, kindest person anyone had ever known.

In the autumn when she was twelve, Sonja asked her father for some planed wood. He had to borrow the tool from the monks at Kerga, but had it done before the snow drifts cut them off from the rest of Russia. Sonja kept the wood in a sack with other secret materials and during the long winter nights she worked on the project. She only did this when she was alone and soon the main topic of gossip turned to speculation about what she might be making. Her parents and brothers honored her request to not peek.

When spring came, she showed the creation to her mother—an icon drawn in brilliant colors and unlike any icon that Mariia had ever seen. Childish and natural-looking, Jesus Christ stood in a meadow, with trees and flowers all around. He wore a full-length robe of grey and His face was a splash of white and gold. A small child knelt at His feet, her hands clasped in prayer. The child's face was partially covered with a birthmark.

For the first time in her life, Mariia genuinely feared for her daughter's life. She did not know who was supposed to paint holy icons, but she was sure that it was not small children. What would the soldiers do? A Russian army patrol only came by every few years, but they maintained the purity of the faith in the name of the Czar.

"I am taking it to the priest," Sonja announced as she left their cabin.

- - - - -

Even Chkalov had joined in the speculation about what Sonja's secret was. He thought that it was a doll, probably a gift for someone. Why else hide it?

Sonja came into his church, bowed before the altar as she always did, and went to his room.

"I have brought something for the church," she said, handing him the piece of wood, no longer or wider than his forearm.

Chkalov stared at it for a long time, uncertain how to react. It was an icon, but unlike any icon that he had ever seen, and certainly he had seen many more than any of the villagers. Despite its oddness, breaking the formal conventions of icon painting, he liked it. Natural curves replaced straight lines and rigid forms. The colors were a bit off, having been made from berries and whatever she could find. The church did not have an icon, a luxury they could not afford. He had no idea if creating this art broke a rule or not. Perhaps he should go ask the bishop, but the head of the diocese was some sixty miles away, not a journey to be contemplated lightly.

"It will perform miracles in return for worship," she explained. "Our Lord wills it."

Miracles. That would bring pilgrims. They would bring money to buy food and lodging. There was potential here. Maybe the bishop could wait. Besides, to reject the icon would surely provoke a serious crisis among his flock, with most people favoring her. Chkalov genuinely loved the villagers, but recognized who was more popular.

As soon as he put the icon above the altar, the villagers streamed into the church, kneeling and worshiping. Just as the essence of God is found in every part of the universe, they believed that He lived in that icon. Offerings piled in front of the altar. Never had so many visited the church, even when Chkalov had first arrived and people were curious to see the new priest.

The first healing happened two days later, when the old woman Matryona hobbled into the church and prayed. Moments later she declared that her knees felt much better. Casting her cane away, she left the church proclaiming praises for the icon and Sonja.

After that, more healings occurred and word began to spread. Some monks from Kerga came and worshiped. Peasants from other villages came.

Four months later, in the pleasant warmth of August, the noble who owned the village of Krist traveled the forty miles upriver from his manor and paid homage to the new icon. He pressed a sack of coins into Chkalov's hands. Such a wonder needed its own church.

Chkalov went to the monastery at Kerga and sought out a monk with a reputation as a master carpenter. They returned and the carpenter put the villagers to work. They labored so hard that summer that the fields were neglected and Chkalov had to buy food. Imagine that, buying food for peasants. By the first snowfall, the church was finished, with a real floor and a single onion-shaped dome over the entrance. Inside, the icon was hung behind the altar. The number of villagers doubled as more peasants came to live near the new building.

With coins in their pockets, the peasants could now pay for weddings and baptisms, and some of the money returned to Chkalov. He thought about hiring the carpenter to return the next summer and build him a house befitting a priest. Visions of possibilities competed for his attention. If he was lucky enough, maybe he could even buy a bishopric of his own. Even better, maybe the icon and the girl would become so popular and pilgrims so numerous that they would make him the bishop of such an important site. He would have to be cunning to prevent the current bishop from stealing Krist away from him.

All winter the visions danced in his mind, entertaining him during the frigid nights.

CHAPTER FIFTEEN

All because of one girl, the village of Krist flourished with prosperity; or rather, Our Lord's favor on that girl. The church symbolized that favor. The church was a solid piece of craftsmanship, a form of praise to God. There were no stray axe marks, as one found on the peasant cabins. The walls were made of uniform logs, with mud caulking. The doors, window sills, and shutters were made of carefully planed wood, though there was no glass in the windows yet. A cross topped the intricately constructed onion dome.

Most of the villagers were of a uniform mind about the girl: grateful and in awe of the miracles and healings. For ten years, ever since her birth, the fields had yielded plentiful harvests, the longest run that anyone had ever heard of. Even the wolves stayed in the forest; at least they kept away from the villagers and their children, if not me.

The only exception was the crabby, old bachelor Koyla, who hated Sonja's mother for spurning him in their youth, and transferred that feeling to each of her children. He was certain that Sonja was a witch. This was not a popular view and he learned to keep his accusation to himself. Pushing the point could easily lead to the accusation that he was a witch himself. After all, everyone knew that most witches were men. Koyla had spent some time in the monastery, but never took any vows because the monks could not tolerate his presence and sent him on his way. He did learn to write a bit, much better than anyone else in the village.

I went into the church and approached the altar. The nave was half full of pilgrims, murmuring in prayer. Carefully set candles bracketed the icon, illuminating Our Lord. My perception of the icon, formed from the memories of others, changed as I viewed it with my own eyes. The different color combinations resonated with me, making a different emotional impact. The young girl in the corner of the icon drew my attention. How could she not fascinate me?

I crossed myself and bowed before the icon before moving back into the shadows to make way for others. My gaze swept across the church. Young and old, rich and poor, knelt with bowed heads. Everyone needed what the icon offered.

Life on the northern taiga was harsh. The meadows were too soggy for farming and trees covered almost all the rest of the land. To make a field required felling the trees and farming around the stumps. Eventually the stumps rotted enough to allow a horse team to pull them up. The harsh winters demanded secure housing and a store of food to tide the villagers over. Such a life puts a premium on hope, and the icon brought hope, a gift as precious as grain or salt.

With Easter so near, even more pilgrims were appearing. Besides the icon, the travelers sought out the girl. She avoided most of them, though the richer ones often forced their way into her presence. Certainly I should seek her out and learn more, but I was afraid.

A vague apprehension, difficult to describe, inhibited me. What I might find? Or not find? Certainly I feared God. Would He be offended at my intrusion into her? Would He strike me down? A serious possibility.

Maybe I would find that she was a fraud. How? She was only a girl. A mere girl does not create such elaborate fantasies, especially beginning at the age of five. If she is no fraud then she is a possible source of answers to so many questions.

Did I fear the answers? The problem with answers is that they compel action. During my centuries of life I have decided to accept certain attitudes and created a system of morals to guide my behavior. For instance, I assumed that we really do have control over our destinies. Calvin and the Anabaptists were wrong and God did not predetermine our fates. But if God did not know what will happen to each of us, then how could He be all-knowing, omniscient, aware of all that had happened, is happening, and will happen? Such a question is well suited to philosophers.

Other questions have more immediate meaning to my life. The Bible prohibited murder, but I have at times deliberately taken lives. What if I found out that I was wrong? Maybe these acts were not justified. Maybe I do not have the judgment necessary to both condemn and execute another. Certainly, if I was a human, a single mind, I do not believe that a person could make such a judgment. But I am not human, or at least not a normal human. I can truly know the innermost thoughts of a person and find their condemnation within those thoughts.

These deliberations only succeeded in frustrating me, so I went to find the girl. She was sitting on a bench in front of her parents' cabin. A crowd stood around her, staying a respectful distance away. One by one they detached themselves and moved forward to kneel on the dirt before her, even the nobles in fine dress, and ask her a question or for a healing. Composed and courteous, she touched them and gave an answer.

After a few minutes in the crowd I realized that most of her answers were not particularly satisfying. At least not to me. A young noble lady explained that after four years she had yet to conceive and asked if she would ever bear a child. Clearly this was an issue of importance beyond the personal urge to leave one's progeny behind. Noble lineage and lands and money were probably at stake. Sonja told her that "Our Lord rewards those that follow His commandments and give aid to His church."

A old man, his limbs twisted from some past famine, asked her when he was going to die. Her reply, "Only Our Lord knows and you should not fear going to join Him."

Another man, dressed in the rough garb of a peasant, carried a child forward in his arms. "My son cannot walk," he mumbled in a voice so low that I barely heard the words.

She drew back the hood covering the child's face and tenderly touched his face. He was half her age with wide, innocent eyes. She blinked twice, then looked at the father. "In Heaven we are reunited with all that go before us." When the father turned away, his shoulders were even more hunched, bearing his child and the answer away.

My turn came and I approached and knelt. "I am Pëtr Alekseyev, a monk. I have no question or ailment."

"You are easy to answer. Go in peace with Our Lord." When she touched me, a fragmental slipped into the fourteen-year-old girl.

- - - - -

She is so exhausted that even her teeth ache.

All day the people come, bringing their pain or their vanity. The vanity annoys her. Rich people who already have more than her village can ever hope for, asking who their daughter should marry for the best advantage, or how to best manage their estate and serfs. Despite her annoyance, she strives to love them, for Jesus Christ loves the rich as much as any other.

The pain is worse. The Lord is a harsh taskmaster, causing misery among those who deserve only joy. When the man with the crippled son came to her, she knew that the boy would die by next winter, wasting away from the strange disease inside. She could only offer the hope of heaven.

More come to her, laying their burdens on her, and when the sun reaches its zenith, she raises her hand. "I must rest. I will return later."

The crowd does not murmur in complaint. They move aside for her as she goes to the door. A few hands reach out to touch her as if she were a holy icon. Once in the privacy of her home, her mother kisses her, gives her some bread and piece of dried meat, and lets her out of the back door. Sonja does not spend her time in the house, but in the forest. Within moments she is among the trees, taking refuge away from everyone else.

She has been up since dawn. The night's sleep did not give her a complete refresh, but only enough relief so that she can push on. As she follows familiar paths, munching on the bread and meat, the tension flows from her body. Unlike other people, she does not fear the forest and the wolves and the darkness within. Many of the villagers have noticed this and say that she is most certainly guarded by angels.

Her mind is filled with prayer, seeking answers and divine companionship. The answers come bubbling up from her hidden mind, the part of each human that is a cauldron of contradiction and confusion. Nowadays we call it the unconscious, but at that time only I knew enough about the ways of the mind to understand that it existed.

It is hard to delve into the hidden mind. When my fragmental pushes down inside, it is buffeted by passions and horrors. The raw emotions live here, pushing up feelings of futility, hate, and love. Her fears live there, clamoring for her attention. Different selves live down there, bound within complex matrixes of emotion and intellect. To summon up those selves now and examine them more closely would interfere with her current perceptions. My fragmental did not want to contaminate the experience for myself, so I choose to bide my time.

A flower drew her attention. Yesterday when she had passed by there, the ground had been drenched from the melting snow. There are still patches of snow under the trees, where the sun cannot reach. Now a scattering of yellow petals hugs the ground. Another miracle from the Lord.

She reaches one of her more favorite places. The forest is filled with wood spirits, but here lives the most powerful wood spirit. A large oak, white with age, sprawls next to a stream. The wandering stream had tried to topple the magnificent tree; in an angry response, the tree had forced the stream away. The spirits do not speak to her, not like the Lord, but she feels them and their worship of the Lord. All bow before the Christ.

She hugs the tree; the spirit is so solid. A bird chirps above her. She breaks the embrace and cranes her neck back. A newly finished nest of twigs lies at the meeting of a branch and the trunk. The bird chirps again, singing a song to attract a mate.

Suddenly it flies from the nest, all blue with a touch of black on its tail. Another bird of the same type appears and settles on a branch of the old oak. It chirps at the first one, which circles about, replying with its own words.

Despite the beauty of the flower and the bird, Sonja still feels worn out. No child should have so much thrust upon her. To sustain the hope of others is an awful burden. She looks to the sky and a feeling of pure love streams from her hidden mind, flooding every cranny of her being and calming her agitation.

It is an extraordinary feeling and my fragmental feels it too. I absorb her reaction, though it does not calm me for more than a moment. The existence of the feeling is too exciting. Is this feeling a blessing from God or from some recess of her flesh? If I killed and possessed her, would I still get these holy thoughts and feelings? Would I then be a messenger of God? I am horrified that the idea even occurs to me. May it always horrify me. Besides, certainly God must speak to her soul, not her flesh.

She sits and leans against the oak. Closing her eyes, she basks in the afterglow of the love. Such experiences sustain her when the demands of the crowd clamor so loudly. She wonders if Jesus Christ Himself ever felt so weary that He wanted His mission to just end. Did Jesus hope that another would come to replace Him? Another Son of God?

There is no answer to this question and she knows that her own mission will only end when she dies. An ordinary life is not to be her lot. She cannot even conceive of marrying or having children; that is for other girls.

As I contemplate her thought patterns, I realize that they are like poetry, not mathematics. Most peasants, lacking the opportunity for education or even sustained contemplation, ride the waves of their hidden mind, rarely imposing discipline upon their thoughts. Scholars, educated and adhering to logic, follow one thought to another, striving to keep the impulses of the hidden mind away from the topic that preoccupies them. They find glory in the structure that they impose on their minds.

Sonja is different. She is neither that raw cauldron of feelings, nor the analytical student. Her thoughts center around love and the other positive emotions. She thinks logically when required, but mostly she is just creative. All of us have creative flashes, inspiration that reorders how we look at a problem or life, but her entire existence is filled with neverending creativity. Her abiding fear and joy are the Lord and His purposes. The liturgy of the mass sings directly to her.

Time passes, random thoughts of little consequence cross her mind. An impulse to play with other children seeps up from her hidden mind, which she must reject. She is not like other children.

When she returned from the forest, she passed through her cabin, giving her mother a brief hug, then returned to her bench. The supplicants crowded closer. The afternoon sun almost seemed too warm for people used to the sharpness of winter. My core is the third to approach her. I touch her, instantly retrieving all that my fragmental within her had learned. I decide to leave the fragmental within her for the time being.

CHAPTER SIXTEEN

Though only a girl, near to being a woman, Sonja was compassion personified. Rarely have I met someone who loves so unconditionally. She cared only about others, her village, and God, not herself. Meaning in her life was found without, not within. How is such a love possible? Does God sprinkle the world with His gifts? Am I and my fragmentals a gift, here to give comfort and lead those that I can to sanity? Does Sonja possess any more gifts?

Sonja prompted more questions than answers within me. In her I sought miracles, but so far I had heard only stories of great healings, and had not witnessed one myself. But I had seen changes within people: hearts mellowed, pains healed, grief softened. These are miracles in their own way.

Does her icon really heal through supernatural intervention or just activate the mind's own mysterious healing powers? Some philosophers, especially those French ones, argue that God is bound by natural law. He does not interfere in the clockwork universe that He has created. It is a lonely thought to think that God is not there to help and comfort us. But there is much misery in this world, and if God allows such misery, then perhaps He is a cruel God, and that is a cold thought.

The next day was Easter and visitors packed into the village. Even the most wretched hovel had people sleeping shoulder to shoulder across the dirt floors. Father Chkalov performed mass soon after dawn and kept going though the day as the crowds took turns kneeling in the church and receiving communion.

Even with everyone standing, the church could barely hold more than a hundred souls.

At midday, Sonja entered the church and stood toward the rear of the crowd. It was my fortune to have two fragmentals there inside other people so that I might observe her. The crowd thrilled to have her visit during their mass, even though the Eucharist had already been blessed.

Sonja joined the queue for communion, finding herself in the middle. Those in front of her wanted to pass her forward, but she refused. She waited her turn. The priest looked haggard from his tasks as the line slowly filed pass him, each kneeling to take a wafer and a sip from the cup. After Sonja drank, she left the line to step up to the altar. She stood there, staring at her icon. The service stopped and everyone waited expectantly.

She turned to them, her face passive and worn. "The words of the mass are wrong," she declared.

"What?" Chkalov exclaimed.

"You speak the words of the Greeks, not the words of Mother Russia. This is wrong. You will change and so will all other priests throughout our Holy Land."

The crowd was stunned. She was an Old Believer! I had not noticed this before because I had been so entranced by her that my fragmental did not delve deep enough within her. The Russians had learned their Christianity from Greeks and over the years, the liturgy had wandered from the Greek Orthodox wording. Over a century ago, the Patriarch Nikon had changed the wording back to conform to the Greeks. Peasant and learned alike knew that words have power and thought that this was wrong. The Old Believers clung to the archaic rituals and by denying the authority of the Russian Orthodox Church, they threatened the head of our faith, the Czar. The north country was a stronghold of Old Believer beliefs.

While I felt a cold dread, the crowd did not. There were murmurings of support. Someone called out for the priest to do the mass over again with the old words.

"I do not know the words," Chkalov muttered.

"Do you not have them in a book?" another asked.

"Those books are gone," he replied, a note of alarm in his voice.

"We know where one is," an older woman called out. "We will bring it, but it will take a week." An older man who stood next to her gripped her hand and vigorously nodded his agreement.

I longed to enter that woman and learn her story, but only my fragmentals were watching, not my core. My core was still unaware of these happenings and only the core can release a fragmental.

"What am I to do until then?" Chkalov blurted out. I felt sorry for him. He was no theologian and certainly he felt alarmed at the new direction that Sonja was leading them.

"You may use the Greek words," Sonja said. "The Lord listens to our hearts. But He yearns for the worship of the Russian people. Let the Greek worship Him in their way, and let our people worship in our own way."

Communion was forgotten as the crowd streamed from the church to tell their fellow pilgrims of the new day.

The old woman and old man disappeared down the road before I could intercept them. In a week, they would return with the book.

Within the next hour Chkalov held another mass. Only a few attended. He tried again and no one came.

Three days later a company of soldiers arrived, led by an officer on a horse. His uniform was quite smart, and his regal bearing showed that he had been raised as a nobleman. Alongside him walked Koyla; his hatred for Sonja's mother had found its opportunity.

The troops stopped in front of the church. Father Chkalov emerged from his cabin and hurried toward the newcomers while a curious crowd gathered.

"Are you Alexsey Chkalov?" the officer on the horse demanded.

The priest bowed. "I am."

"I am Major Sergey Vasil'yevich Zubatov of the Imperial Guard. I seek the girl named Sonja Gladkov."

"Why, sir?"

The Major looked down sharply. "Are you an Old Believer, too?"

Chkalov immediately shook his head so violently that he might have easily sprained his neck. "No, sir. No, sir."

"We shall see." The officer turned to his soldiers. "Search the village. Bring all books and papers to me. I will be in the church."

The soldiers acted like they had done this before. They split up into pairs, with one searching while the other stood ready with his musket. When they returned, they had only the priest's Bible and a few devotionals from the baggage of some of the more wealthy.

As the officer leafed through these books, I moved in closer and touched his leg.

- - - - -

His grandmother did not like cemeteries, so he was eleven before she took him to one. His ancestors were buried in the plot behind the north church. This church was only for use by his family; the serfs used the west church. His parents resided in a mausoleum behind a locked door. His grandmother did not take him in there.

"I will soon be sending you to join the family regiment and serve the Motherland and Czar," his grandmother said. "You are now old enough to know."

Becoming a cadet was expected. "Know what?"

"In this cemetery are buried six generations of Zubatovs, ever since we took this land from the Tartars."

"Yes, ma'am." Sergey knew the story of how his ancestors drove the infidel back across the plains and the Czar gave them this vast land and ten thousand serfs as a reward. The Zubatovs were powerful and wealthy. Sergey himself was the third cousin to the heir to the throne, Peter III.

His grandmother sat down on a stone bench near the church and stared out over the recently cut grass and mossy stones. Sergey waited. He was used to her melancholy. The physician said it was to be expected of a woman as old as her.

"I used to go to the grand balls in Moscow, where orchestras played the latest waltzes from Vienna and we wore such fine dresses."

Sergey shifted on his feet and waited for her. Experience had taught him that she eventually came back to the point. She might wander, but she was not senile.

"You may have noticed that my husband is not buried here."

He hadn't, but that was a surprise. "Where is he buried?"

"Nowhere."

Was he alive? He had never known any relative other than his grandmother.

"Your father promised to name you after your grandfather before he died. This was done, but your namesake did not die a normal death." Then she blurted out the awful shame. "Peter executed him and left his body for the wolves to take."

"Why?" Sergey cried out.

"Because the man—my husband—was a fool. He joined the Raskolniki, a group of those Old Believers. Even worse, he told everyone about it and tried to convert them too. His cousin, our Czar, could not tolerate this attack on the Mother Church by such a great noble."

Sergey only vaguely knew what Old Believers were, but he did know that they were heretics. Now he understood why people so rarely came to visit his grandmother, and why he never remembered her ever going to Moscow.

She looked up at him, her eyes hard. "Sergey, you are the remaining Zubatov. You must reclaim our name. The only way to do this is to be totally loyal to our Czar, the Mother Country and her Holy Church." She crossed herself.

Now, two decades later, Sergey Vasil'yevich Zubatov served his Czar here in the north country. In order to expedite justice on the frontier, Zubatov was also a magistrate, making him judge and executioner. When reports of heresy came in, his regimental commander always gave the assignment to Zubatov. The other officers did not like such messy work, while Zubatov considered his diligence to be his true calling.

Three months ago he had gone to the village of Parisk. The whole village was infested with heresy. Most of them recanted and he only whipped them. Two did not, a brother and sister, both in their fifties and both without further family. He burned them and he still keenly remembered the charred scent and awful screams. He regretted that the heretics brought such punishment on themselves.

Now he was in Krist. The books in his hand were not heretical. A commotion on the other side of the crowd caused him to look up.

A young girl in a simple dress, with long blonde hair, approached him.

"You seek me, sir."

"You are Sonja Gladkov?"

"I am, sir."

He motioned to his soldiers and two of them grasped her by the arms.

The crowd gasped and a few cheered as the major toppled from his horse in a stupor. My fragmental within the officer did not know what else to do, so it had caused a paralysis of thought within him. I could not let him send her to the flames also.

CHAPTER SEVENTEEN

Sonja wants a trial. She needs to prove her faith in God. I consider this to be complete madness. She has a greater faith, a greater certainty than anyone else I have met in the last century. How could she doubt herself? Of course, she is not like me, she does not know the innermost thoughts of others. She does not know how extraordinary or unique she is.

I sit with her, holding her hand, the fragmental within her and myself communicating. She is unaware of us, lost in her own thoughts. We are in a small hut that the soldiers have commandeered to use as a holding cell. The major lies in the priest's cabin, still slack and voiceless. The sergeant in charge of the soldiers is paralyzed by his lack of authority. He has sent scouts to find the nearest physician and a runner back to the garrison, but it will be at least two days before another officer arrives.

What am I to do? I do not want to see this angel die. She touches so many people and conveys to them the grace of God. She is not insane. In fact, she is more sane than most. She knows which impulses to nurse and which to shunt aside. The ability to control and direct the impulses of the hidden mind is the basis of strong character. Such control, such compassion. Even though only fourteen, she has the wisdom and maturity that most old people never come close to acquiring.

It is ironic that a girl who still experiences the old pagan ways of forest spirits is defending the old orthodoxy. For hundreds of years, the Christians have striven to stamp out the old ways of superstition and pantheism. I perceive this irony because of my detachment, but I do not want to feel objective and detached, I so much want to be engaged with her, to feel all that she feels, to be inspired and loved by her—to literally be her.

The central fact is that though she is young, she is fully aware of the consequences of her actions. I know that it is not my place to manipulate events and deny her this choice.

I decide to release Zubatov.

The next day, in front the church, a trial was held. A mockery really, since Major Zubatov served as prosecutor and magistrate. He called forward only Sonja to testify and she was the best witness that he could ask for. Soldiers were positioned on either side of her, guarding a fourteen-year-old girl whose hands were bound. She stood facing the officer while he sat. The villagers and pilgrims clustered around, kept back by the other soldiers.

"Are you an Old Believer?" he asked.

"That is what you call me. I am a True Believer."

Zubatov dutifully wrote down this answer.

"Who taught you these ideas?"

"Our Lord."

The Major found this answer insufficient. "Who taught you these ideas?"

"Do not mock Our Lord!" Sonja cried out. "Our Lord has spoken. He desires the old words. Our words. Glory be to God!" Sonja crossed herself then, using two fingers instead of three. This action condemned her, for it was the old way.

Zubatov let anger break his impassive judicial front. "You damn yourself!"

Sonja bowed to him, a slight smile creasing her mouth.

"There is no need for further questions." He scribbled in a logbook for a bit longer, then stood and ran his gaze across the crowd.

"Does anyone wish to speak on this heretic's behalf?" the Major asked the crowd.

"I will." Mariia Gladkov called out and stepped from the crowd.

"And you are?"

"This child's mother."

"Your name?"

"Mariia Gladkov."

"And your statement?"

"She is a child!" Mariia cried out.

"Is she not fourteen years of age?"

"She is a girl! She has not bled yet. She is not a woman. You cannot punish her."

The Major was quiet for moment, caught in thought, then he decided. "That is not relevant."

After a long recitation of legal precedent and other formalities, he pronounced the inevitable decision. Soldiers immediately went to the nearest woodpiles to collect firewood. A sturdy young pine was chopped down, brought to the empty space in front of the church, and placed upright into a hole. The soldiers stacked the firewood around the pole, like a splayed skirt.

Sonja waited in the improvised jail. Father Chkalov was in such shock that I went to her and administered the last rites. Her mind was like a calm sea, unruffled by any wayward impulses. Her hidden mind was in harmony with the conscious mind, a most remarkable occurrence.

We prayed together and I cried and she was the one who comforted me by placing her arms across my back and murmuring that Our Lord loved me too. Damn Our Lord, I wanted to cry out. How could He allow her to die in such an awful way? I did not speak though, out of respect for her. Such blasphemy was unworthy in her presence.

That evening the soldiers came to lead her to the pyre. The major stood before her and read a long, wordy pronouncement while the solders lashed her to the post. There were not many people around. A burning usually incites a grotesque fascination within people, a brutal slap of that mortality that is within us all and that we spend so much of our lives trying to flee. This time though, most of the pilgrims had left, driven away by a mixture of shock, sorrow, and anger. A few stayed behind, yearning for a miracle, just as they had hoped for a miracle when they first heard about Sonja.

As I walked with her, I retrieved my fragmental. There was no purpose in sharing her death, since my own fragmental would cease with her death and I would not be able to reabsorb its memories. Alone with my thoughts, I reflected on the sadness that I found everywhere, in so many of the lives that I touched. While sadness leads to misery, that misery is not an excuse to rationalize selfishness and cruelty, and thus increase the sadness of others. Rather this sadness demands unfailing kindness from us. Though she never thought those thoughts, Sonja lived them.

Her mother approached, supported by two other village women. Mariia looked at her daughter through a sheen of tears. Her hands clawed at her skirt, but found the fabric too tough to rip. She began to sob, then collapsed into screaming.

Sonja called out to her softly. Her mother did not hear her. Again and again Sonja called out and finally her mother listened and quieted.

"Love Our Lord, Mother," Sonja instructed, providing strength for all others when theirs failed. "Love Father and my brothers. We will all meet again in Heaven. And Mother, if I cry out, it is because the faith of my flesh has failed, not the faith of my spirit, for it can never fail."

Behind us, the villagers gathered into a crowd. While becoming intoxicated on the potent beer made from potato peelings, they had talked among themselves. Their thoughts had come together. If the girl died, surely the plentiful harvests and good will of the Lord would go with her. Remember the warnings of the priests. Why did God hate Jews? Did not God punish the Jews for crucifying the Christ? Are we to be the new Jews? Taking up scythes, hoes, and clubs, they approached the soldiers.

Major Zubatov reacted quickly and competently to the threat. There were not enough soldiers to surround and protect the pyre, so the officer ordered his men into a tighter circle next to the pyre. Fixing their bayonets on their muskets, they faced outward like a porcupine, ready to fire.

The mob surrounded them, but did not rush. Several of their number went to release Sonja. The Major was yelling something, threats or exhortations, but no one was listening, instead Sonja held their attention.

"Do not do this, my brothers and sisters!" she cried out. "Our Lord will welcome me into His arms. Do not shed the blood of each other. Did not Our Lord say in His holy scriptures, thou shalt not kill?"

The villagers hesitated.

"Please go home and put away your tools. Do it for Our Lord. Do it for me. He will bless you. I will bless you."

Then on May 2, 1765, Sonja Gladkov died in the flames. She did not cry out, though she may have whimpered; if she did, the crackling of the flames covered the sound.

Even after everyone else returned to their homes, I remained kneeling before the pyre. The fading embers warmed the air and the stench of her burnt flesh polluted the air. I did not and do not have the courage to face death. She had the faith, willing to die for God. I did not and do not have that faith. I prayed for that faith, but it did not come. I am worse than a weak coward, because I know—even though I suppress the memories—that I will take anyone as my host if my own mortality is threatened, whether they are innocent or not. My guilt condemns me.

All the next day, I continued to pray. Major Zubatov ordered that the bones and ashes be left where they lay, to serve as an example. Then he mounted his horse and left at the head of his column of soldiers.

When dusk came, I gathered all of my fragmentals back into myself and ate a meal. Tomorrow I would return to Kerga and then head south. I no longer wanted to stay in the northern forests.

Later that night, the church burned and no villagers approached to try to put out the flames. The priest had set the fire.

CHAPTER EIGHTEEN

When I slip back into consciousness, I find my face streaked with tears. Mourning Sonja or pitying myself? Her faith was so strong, so intimidating. Back then, before the French philosophers and their Enlightenment, everyone had some form of faith. It was unthinkable to not believe in God, or at least a supernatural world where benevolent and malevolent spirits worked their influence. Considerable philosophical finesse is required to reject the idea of the spirit world. The jury of my mind is still in recess on the issue.

What about the healing that the icon brought? It was said that people learned to walk and work again. Did that not show the presence of His Spirit among the common people?

But the power of the mind to heal is extraordinary. Certainly there is something within the mind that can occasionally be released and promote a cure, even when deceived by a placebo. I can only know a person's thoughts, not the inner chemistry of the body, so I do not know how this works. But who can prove that this inner healing is not a result of a divine touch? I could spend lifetimes justifying and defending either position. In years past, I did not question His or Her existence; now I hope for it.

A profound song once said that grief is an emotion to describe the absence of feeling. That is true, and I still do not know how to feel about Sonja. She exhilarated and humiliated me. I like to think that I am like her, giving comfort to the miserable. But she is greater than I am, she faced death with an unclouded conscience and she gave comfort without manipulation.

A sound distracts me from further recriminations. I realize that the sound has been there all along, or at least the last five minutes, and I was too preoccupied with myself. Some people are talking loudly on my front porch. I freeze and listen more closely. A man. A woman. Arguing.

The words are muted by the door. One sentence from the male comes through clearly. "Screw the warrant, we got probable cause. This guy has killed—" The figure is lost as he lowers his voice.

Law enforcement.

Before I even have the chance to react, the door bursts open. The strip of molding next to door handle falls to the floor with a clamor, raising a cloud of dust. The open door hangs at an odd angle, the lower hinge attached by a single twisted screw.

"Freeze! Right now!" a voice roars. A figure with hunched shoulders is silhouetted against the sunlight streaming through the doorway.

I do not move, waiting for a volley of bullets to shatter my body. It had been centuries since I was so vulnerable, with all my fragmentals in one host. With no fragmentals to continue on my life, I was really going to die.

"I surrender," I cry out in terrified desperation.

The silhouette moves inside and another one takes its place. Smaller, feminine. Her shoulders are also hunched into a police stance.

"Cover her, Lauren," the first orders. He comes closer. I can still watch him out of the corner of my rigid eyes. Well built, wearing a suit, carrying a semiautomatic pistol in his right hand. Handcuffs appear in the other hand as he moves around me.

"Got it, Dave," the second says, a soft voice that contains an edge that demonstrates her willingness to use her weapon.

"Slowly bring your hands behind your back, Miss Prall," the first, Dave, says.

My hands had remained frozen, as instructed, suspended in a defensive posture in front of me, fingers splayed, palms outward. Futilely warding off a threat. I drop my hands and bring them behind my back. Miss Prall. They knew the name of my host. This is not a random arrest, not that there had been much hope of that.

He touches my hands and professionally clamps the handcuffs around my wrists. I cast a fragmental into him.

- - - - -

This was the opportunity of a lifetime. For twenty-two years, obscure assignments of no distinction. Even this assignment was only grunt work, checking every house in areas where James Barash had used a credit card or cashed a check. The credit card receipt was from two years ago at a gas station a mile down the road. A foolish search, considering that the good doctor's body had been found less than a day after the assassination of the senator. Of course, that had not been released to the press while the hunt for the other conspirators continued.

The neighbors had said this cabin was empty, yet when peeking through the window he saw someone lying on the couch. Since there was no car outside, he suspected that it was a vagrant taking advantage of the shelter. But when he entered, he found the prize, Joanna Prall.

Having cuffed his prisoner, Dave Fisher asked his partner, "Lauren, will you take her to the car while I search the place?"

He had not wanted to say those words. He wanted to take the prisoner to the car himself. This was his collar, not Lauren's, he protested to himself. He tried to take back the words, to thwart his approaching partner, but his voice refused to obey.

- - - - -

When Lauren Yalom grasped my arm, I cast a fragmental into her. She immediately turned around and went to the door to see if anyone had noticed the arrival of the pair of FBI agents.

Dave used his key to release the handcuffs and stepped back

respectfully. As he touched me, my fragmental within him relayed all that it had learned.

I sat down and rubbed the aching area on my right wrist where he had slapped the cuffs on. It was bruising quite nicely.

Using a two-year-old credit card receipt? My adversary must be desperate. That meant that it did not know where I was. FBI agents were being flown in from all over the country to help in the search. Dave had heard a rumor that half of the Bureau's agents were taking part in the hunt. It was as if the president had been shot, not a mere senator.

- - - - -

Lauren Yalom watched out of the door. A nice place. Green trees provided shade. Shrubs and grass flourished where the sun reached the forest floor. She could see parts of two other cabins through the trees. A squirrel ran down a tree and met another squirrel. After a short conference, they dashed back to their respective trees. The low hum of insects provided background music, so different from the city life that she knew so well.

The Avis four-door rental that she and Dave had driven was parked in the driveway. She thought of the Bureau car that she drove back in Memphis. There were no Bureau cars, or even GSA cars, still available in Ohio; all were in use in the grand manhunt.

And they had captured her. Yet Joanna Prall was in the living room, sitting uncuffed on the couch. This did not make any sense.

She strove to continue that line of reasoning, but successive thoughts refused to form. Fuzzy grey cotton surrounded each thought, inhibiting its ability to connect to other thoughts. Without coming together, a concept could not be formed.

Her eyes grew blurry, forcing her to lean against the door frame. A sliver from the damaged wood cut into her shoulder, causing her to start. The grayness faded for a moment and a clear thought surfaced. *I've been drugged.* Before she could continue any further, she slipped to the porch and slept.

- - - - -

What am I to do? Two FBI agents asleep in my home. There are only them, since they have not contacted any others. I pull the sleeping woman into the living room and make her comfortable with a pillow under her head. The man lies down on the couch and my fragmental sends him into sleep.

The door will not fit back perfectly, so I lean it up against the door frame and prop it with a chair. From a distance, the door looks normal.

I need to think. Briefly touching each of them, I pull in the information that the fragmentals within them have learned.

Brief life capsules of my hunters. Dave Fisher is from Chicago and Lauren Yalom is from Memphis. He is a dull man, lacking in ambition, happiest among ledgers, divorced from his wife because he could not sustain an interest in her. Lauren is a most interesting woman. Raised in New York in a Jewish Orthodox family, educated in accounting at Columbia. She had divorced her abusive husband and left with their two children. Highly intelligent, she graduated from Yale Law summa cum laude. She is determined to prove to her distant parents that she can raise her children alone and be the best Bureau agent at the same time. She was not going to stay home like her mother.

While these two hunt me, they are not bad people, and I feel responsible for them. Dave has just been going through the motions on this case, recognizing that they were just more manpower to perform legwork. Lauren is different. Her habit is to be thorough in all things, so she attempted to learn all she could about their assignment.

A psychiatrist named James Barash assassinated a patient of his, Senator William Handlin, with a blow to the head. This federal crime brought in the FBI. Local authorities were already hunting for the doctor, and the special agent-in-charge for the Cleveland office had quickly concluded that a conspiracy was involved. Barash had also slain a janitor in his office building and a police lieutenant had also been found dead. The causes of death were as yet undetermined, though poison was suspected. Blood workups from the autopsies had so far proved inconclusive.

A nurse at the mental hospital were Barash was employed was found beaten to death, as was her husband. Two others at the hospital were also killed, all by possible poisoning. The body toll was climbing steadily. It was obvious that the good doctor was not working alone, since two of the deaths had occurred after Barash himself had died.

That was the really curious part of this case. Barash had been found on an isolated road, dead in his car, again of apparent poisoning. Now they were pursuing Joanna Prall, only a woman of eighteen, yet thought to have killed the good doctor. A bulletin from the special agent-in-charge informed all other agents that he suspected that even more people were involved, whose identities had not yet been learned. The body count so far, including Barash, stood at eight. The press was avidly following the supposed exploits of Barash and Joanna. A psychiatrist and his patient make juicy reading. Already they have a name for our conspiracy: the Psycho Ring. James Barash was the ringleader and Joanna Prall was a follower. Other followers were suspected, but not known. When they found Barash's body in his car, they suspected poisoning and assumed that Prall was now the leader.

So many questions, so little time to ponder them. The janitor of my office building had been killed? That hardly made sense, did it? After a bit of contemplation, it did make sense. The adversary had been in a dying body. The janitor was probably the first to find the senator. The adversary took the janitor as his host. But then why did it leave the janitor? It must have wanted another body as its host.

Now is not the time for considering my dilemma. I roll up my sleeping bag, and fill a large gym bag with cans of food and fruit juice. Don't forget a can opener. A gallon-sized insulated water jug is under the sink, which I fill with water.

Tugging the fridge back from the wall, I remove a wallet full of hundreds, twenties, and tens. Another wallet is retrieved from the attic crawlspace. The third cache is buried out back in a can, and I cannot afford to the spend the time digging for it. I have about three thousand dollars now anyway.

Lauren has the car keys in her pocket. Popping open the trunk, I find their luggage. I place my water jug and gym bag in the trunk, and lug the suitcases into the house. A thorough search reveals nothing of use, other than another two hundred dollars. I take the money, then realize that Lareen is about my size. I select some of her clothes to replace the oversized sweats that I am wearing. Underwear, a pair of jeans, running shoes, and a blouse make a more presentable appearance. I also select a jacket to take with me.

Then I search through the rest of the car. A set of maps are on the front seat. Someone has marked various roads with red slashes. The memories that I drew from Lauren inform me that these roadblocks are staffed around the clock.

How do I get out of this? I scan the map, urging my sluggish memories to yield up information, all that I have learned from personal experience and the experiences of those I have touched. My attention is drawn to the Ohio River. A couple of years ago, an old man had been admitted into Jenkins State Hospital. He should not have really been there, since he only suffered from an advanced dementia caused by old age. A nursing home was more appropriate, but occasional violent outbursts sent him to our dumping ground. There was nothing I could do to help him, but during those occasional times when his mind cleared, my fragmental learned of a long life spent pushing barges up and down the Ohio, Mississippi, and Missouri rivers.

Yes, that was the answer. I trace the river with my finger. Wayne National Forest borders the north bank of the river before reaching Marietta. I count four lock and dam combinations. Each of them stops the river traffic. Best of all, they are only an hour's drive away.

I start the car, then return to the house. I take Lauren's automatic pistol, its holster, and two extra clips of ammunition. My fragmentals push the two agents as deep into sleep as possible, then I retrieve my fragmentals and leave.

CHAPTER NINETEEN

Two hours later I stand on the bank of an estuary that feeds into the Ohio river. The surrounding trees and setting sun cover the forest glen and water in deep shadows. The rental car is disappearing beneath the surface of the water.

Using a branch, I do my best to erase the tire tracks leading to the water's edge. The Willow Island Lock and Dam is only a mile away through the forest. Picking up my jacket, gym bag, and water jug, I hurry through the woods while there is still enough light to see my way. The pistol is tucked into its holster on my waistband. I have been in men and women, even children, when they were shot. I know the pain and the savage damage done to the body, yet I feel it prudent to keep the gun. The implications of using it are deliberately repressed.

The darkness becomes twilight as I break out into a meadow. Like whitened bones, the bare trunks of heat-killed trees dot the meadow. A hot fire had come through some time ago, leaving a graveyard. The light is sufficient for me to glance at my wrist. There is no watch, just habit.

An unbidden memory surfaces. I saw my first clock in Antwerp in 1581. Marvels of mechanical mechanism, inconsiderate bastard machines, little did we know that the tyranny of time, the hour, the minute, and the second were being introduced.

Now that I have broken the seal on my past, these memories flit about in my subconscious, anxious to push themselves forward. I am more like a normal human now, where a scent, a tune, or simple nostalgia provokes the retrieval of memo-ries. One can make a shopping list of the many different types of memory cues. I have often experienced these cues in my carriers, but not in myself.

The sounds of the lock come to me first. The clanging of metal against wood, the shrillness of a whistle, the murmur of voices. The quay along the river bank is made of poured concrete. Two towboats and their brood of barges are drawn up to the side, secured by lines. Another towboat moves slowly past, its powerful spotlights sweeping the river as it heads into the lock.

The air is a mixture of the scent of diesel and the smell of river, tangy with a touch of vegetation decay. The river provokes a memory. Not my memory, but that of a person that I once touched in Toronto in 1851.

Billy Motubo, captured as a youth on the Gold Coast, was smuggled into Texas after the slave trade was supposed to be over. He tried to escape and received the raised ridges of lash scars across his back as a punishment. The overseer ordered him to take one of the other slaves as a wife, but he spilled his seed on the ground rather than make her pregnant. He knew that he could never leave children behind.

He fled once more and spent days creeping northward, catching fish in streams and rivers that he ate raw, since a fire might attract attention. On the grand old river, the Mississippi, he watched stern-wheel steamboats go past, decks crammed with bales of cotton. He yearned to hide among those bales, as he often hid among the cotton fields, but the paddlewheels were usually heading south toward New Orleans.

Finally, he made it to Canada, where he worked in the fields as a laborer. Similar work, though the dry Texas heat was gone, but at least he was paid in coins. In the evenings, he struggled to learn to read, and I helped him. He had a fire of righteous ambi-tion in him that endeared him to me. Before I left him, I gave him enough money to book passage back to Africa. I do not know what happened to Billy Motubo, whether he returned to his tribe on the Gold Coast, or settled in Liberia. And now I was running too, finding refuge in the south instead of the north.

The forest comes directly up to the quay. I carefully examine the lock from behind the cover of a tree. The control room is lit up and I can see two people in it, one working the controls while the other writes in a log. There do not seem to be any police or other uniforms about. A middle-aged woman is walking towards the lock, her work boots making her steps heavy. As she passes, I reach out to touch her.

"Oh, excuse me," I mutter, ducking my head.

She looks at me with confusion on her face, but continues on her way with my fragmental inside her.

I withdraw back into the shelter of the tree.

- - - - -

Rose Gardner walked along the quay, grateful that this isolated lock had no nearby businesses. No taverns, no liquor stores, not even a convenience store that sold beer. She didn't care for beer much anyway. Too mild.

When a young woman emerged from the trees, she was startled, but she did not jump back at the touch. The damage from alcohol had robbed her of her reflexes. Nine years, six months, and three days since her last drink, but she knew that her nervous system was permanently crippled.

She took her first sip when she was eleven. Her mother was in her own drink-induced haze, and her father was on the river. It was just a little sip, but straight vodka caused her to vomit. Her mother whipped her when she found out, but Rose persisted. When she was twelve, she got drunk for the first time; at thirteen, the blackouts started. Her teens and twenties were a blur in her memories. Her mother died in a car accident sometime during those years, killed by a drunk driver, ironically enough.

After several attempts at rehab, her father stepped back into her life. He dragged her aboard his towboat and would not allow her to leave. As imaginary spiders crawled over her skin and the shakes made the world around her vibrate, she contemplated jumping overboard and swimming for those beckoning lights on the shore. But she could not swim and her fear of the water was stronger than her need for a drink. She thought about suicide, but a Gardner never took the easy route; contrariness was in their genes.

So she came to love her father's boat, and even him, a little anyway. She was named after the boat, the *Rose Marie*. Two hundred and six feet long, forty-eight foot beam, almost four thousand horsepower from quad diesel engines. A towboat, a silly name, since all towboats actually pushed their flocks of barges. She was proud of this boat, and after her father died and she assumed ownership, it became her home. She did not have a base on land, and even stayed on the boat during dry dock inspections and maintenance. No liquor was allowed on the boat. Any crewman who violated this rule saw his drink spilled into the river and was put ashore at the next lock.

This was a long run, bringing a load of concrete culvert pipes from a factory in Pittsburgh down to New Orleans. There was paperwork at this lock, which she quickly disposed of. Returning back up the quay, she saw the young woman again. Long blonde hair, unlike the short-cropped gray hairs on Rose's own head.

The woman smiled at her and held out her hand. Confused, thinking that a stranger wanted to shake her hand, Rose reached out to touch me.

- - - - -

This is the perfect path for escape. After a quick exchange of information, I watch the towboat captain continue on her way. Rose Gardner is a strong woman, and I admire strength when it is built on top of weakness. A fragmental is in her to provide me with extra protection.

Retrieving my bag and jug of water, I follow at a discrete distance. The *Rose Marie* is pushing fifteen barges, arranged three across. I pick a barge on the second row from the front.

A hawser secures the barge to the quay to prevent drifting. A tarp covers the cargo so that rain will run off the tarp, not into the barge.

Normally, the towboat had powerful searchlights turned on to scan the barges and the river ahead, but they are turned off, so I am in shadow. Tossing my pack and the water jug across, I grab hold of the hawser and inch myself across, hanging like a insect under a twig. My arms and legs complain from the unusual activity as the brain rediscovers muscles long unused.

Only ten feet, but my arms are shaking when I crawl onto the tarp. No time to rest, the tugboat in front has already entered the lock. The whine of the lock machinery, shivers of high notes, echoes across the water.

The concrete culverts are some six feet wide and the same high. They are arranged vertically, with the tarp draped over them like a tent. I crawl over the circular bumps and collect my bag and jug, then I return to the edge of the tarp. There is room to slip in under the tarp and down inside the gunwale of the barge.

The tarp is loose enough so that I can climb over the lip of a culvert and down inside. This will be my home for a while. Wrapping myself inside my jacket, I settle down to sleep, even though I know that my memories wait for me, like a prosecutor. I am so exhausted, and it is six days to Memphis.

CHAPTER TWENTY

I lived for a over a century in Spain. In 1409, I was a brother of the Order of Mercy, Father Juan Gitabert Jofré, living in Valencia. The Moors still ruled the southern part of the peninsula. One fair morning, as I walked to Mass, I came across a crowd of children in the street. The cruelty that comes from the ignorance of youth had possessed them. They danced around a pitiful creature, crying, "The madman, the madman, here comes the madman." They kicked at him and pelted him with stones.

He cowered, sobbing, croaking incoherent cries of misery.

I drove the children away and took him with me to the cathedral. During my sermon, I brought the madman to the front of the assembled congregation. Filthy rags served as his only clothes and caked blood covered his right ear. A fragmental of mine had examined him and found him not whole, a permanent three years old.

I persuaded the city fathers to fund an asylum. Only a little prompting by my fragmentals was necessary. There were asylums elsewhere in Europe, designed to protect the good citizenry from the ravings of madmen and the embarrassment of imbeciles. In Finland I heard that the mad were sent to live with the lepers in their colony.

My Hospital Sancta Maria dels Inocents was different. I wanted to protect those inside from the masses outside. Some of my charges were simpletons; not much that I could do for them other than protect them from the cruelty of others. Others were mind-sick, but I was able to heal them of poisonous thought structures. And some were completely estranged from reality. I prayed for them.

Later, I started to take in abandoned children, since they needed protection as much as my other charges. We were a community, taking care of ourselves as much as we could. The idea spread to other cities. They built hospitals and cared for the mad and the abandoned, pushing Spain to the forefront of tolerance. Then came the Inquisition, priests with hate in their eyes, and attitudes turned sour. Tolerance is always a fragile flower.

The end of tolerance happened around the time that I left. The discovery of a new world across the ocean fascinated me and I paid attention to the stories that came my way. Eventually I decided that I would go to see this wondrous land for myself. I left the hospital in Valencia in the capable hands of other brothers within the Order of Mercy.

But I feared the ocean. What if my host drowned? I would certainly die with my host. I had lost hosts before. When that happened, the host fragmental dies also and I lose all that I had known since the last joining with another fragmental.

I decided to send my host across the ocean. As a precaution, I left behind a couple of fragmentals. One of these carriers was a petty nobleman named Alonso de Aux. He was petty in rank and in demeanor. While inside him, I stopped his cruelties and felt comfortable with taking him as a host if the need arose.

In the summer of 1507, I set sail from La Coruña. A month later, my fragmental in Alonso thrashed awake. I knew that my core's host had died. Some storm probably; I will never know, since all that it had experienced since he left was also lost to me, as if it had never existed.

I felt the essence of life seeping from my fragmental. A tapestry coming apart, stitch by stitch. Frantically, fueled by desperation, I pushed Alonso out of his body and took full possession. I was whole again, my core centered in a new host. After some rumination, I realized that my core is reasserted in the most recent fragmental to have touched the core. That is why my Alonso fragmental became the core rather than one of the others that I had scattered about.

It was not until the summer of 1521 that I collected the courage to try again. The newly named Americas called to me. I left a couple of fragmentals behind in potential hosts, and Alonso de Aux set sail in the caravel *Santo Domingo*.

I had never sailed across the deep ocean before. Little jaunts about the Mediterranean and along the coasts of the world had not prepared me for the isolation of being thousands of miles from land. Alonso had never been to sea and a bout of seasickness was necessary to get my sea legs. The ability to tolerate the roll of the ship is a skill squirreled away into the hindbrain and nerves. Even though I had sailed before, my current body needed to acquire those skills. A momentary respite was provided by landfall on the Canary Islands, then we set sail across the watery deep.

Shipboard life, with a crew of thirty and ten passengers, was a very confined environment. Within a couple of weeks, my fragmentals had examined the entire complement. The captain and navigator, an uncle and his nephew, were the most interesting. Standing on the stern every day at midday, they used an astrolabe to measure the altitude of the sun from the horizon. That told us our latitude. A compass kept our westward course true.

Their years of experience and knowledge gave me a sense of mastery over the ocean. For over three decades, the captain had sailed across the sea, a dozen times to the new world. He wore a fashionable floppy hat with moldy feathers in it to protect his bald head from the sun. The nephew was in his twenties, almost ready to command his own ship. They proved that the ocean could be tamed. We made good time, even through the doldrums, with only a couple of squalls to mar perfect days of ocean and bright skies.

Despite the wonder of the voyage, we shared a common misery. At night, we were packed in the ship's hold shoulder to shoulder to sleep. We drank foul water from casks until we could stomach it no longer, then we turned to the precious supply of wine, which was rationed. The cook used an open fire to make simple meals of hard biscuit and beef pickled in brine. Most of the crew and passengers had brought along a few amenities to supplement their own diets. For myself, I had brought onions and dried fruit, which lasted for little more than two weeks.

We sighted land after fifty-nine days at sea. We went ashore to obtain fresh water, and an enterprising sailor speared a couple of sharks. We feasted that night. The captain recognized the island from a previous crossing and we pushed on towards Cuba. Two nights later, a strong wind began to push against our stern. That morning revealed dark skies and an even harsher wind.

The captain ordered the passengers to stay below. The crew secured the ship. After a day of tossing among the swells and crests, smelling the vomit of other passengers, I grew fearful. I scattered my fragmentals among the crew, reasoning that they had a better chance of survival than the passengers. I chose those that I was most comfortable with taking as a host if the need arose. The instinct for survival is too strong to deny. It damns me.

All the choices could prove to be fruitless. Even with my extraordinary abilities, I am as vulnerable to nature as anyone else. When the waves close over me and I gasp for air and find only saltwater, I will be dead too. True, my fragmentals back in Spain would carry on, but that did not keep my fear of death at bay. I fear oblivion.

I lost track of time. The rolling of the ship seemed endless. The cook passed around some hard biscuits, but few could eat.

Then the storm began to subside and we knew hope again. The exhausted crew rested while the passengers carried buckets up from the bilge. I joined in, happy to feel useful. The wind had subsided to a light breeze. A steady rain poured from a dark sky, so thick that you could not see the individual drops splash down on the layer of water that covered the wooden planks of the deck. Even though it was day, visibility was poor, no more than a ship's length.

The captain stood on the poop deck, hand firmly clasped on his hat, peering into the storm. When I passed him, I brushed lightly against his arm, taking the fragmental and putting another in its place. My retrieved fragmental reintegrated and passed all its knowledge to me, memories of the days just past. The captain had known fear as the storm battered the ship. His brother had disappeared in a storm such as this.

But now the Captain had a new concern. The waves did not look right; the swells were too shallow. He feared that we were in shallow water, near an island or maybe some rocks. He was considering dropping anchor, but his instincts told him that the storm was not over, just resting.

I went below for the next bucket of bilge and had returned to the deck when a gust of wind hit our topsails. The ship twisted a bit, then ran aground. The deck tilted dramatically and I found myself flung into the sea. As the cold water closed over me, I frantically struck out with my arms and legs, scissoring wildly. My hand touched sand, then I was bursting up through the boundary between drowning and life.

Gasping for air, I treaded water. Other people were in the water with me. Above us the caravel loomed, canted at a crazy angle. The bulk of the ship protected us from the waves coming into the beach by creating a calm spot.

Some of the others were swimming away. A shout came through the rain, "Land! Land!"

I turned and swam away from the ship; within moments my feet touched shore. What a wonderful feeling. Humans are land creatures, not water creatures. We belong on land.

Others came from the ship. Those that could not swim were helped by those that could. No one was lost. The wind picked up and the waves pounded at our ship. In the darkness I stumbled across the captain and learned that he thought the ship would be lost by morning. I found shelter behind a dune and huddled against the storm.

I awoke next to a dying man. His wide eyes slowly lost their luster as his life gushed from his torn throat. A hand grasped my hair and pulled my head back, baring my own throat. I cast a fragmental into the attacker before the bloody chert knife descended.

The attacker froze in place as I scrambled to my feet and climbed the dune behind me. Storm clouds still dirtied the sky and the sand was still soggy, but the rain had stopped for the moment. Driftwood, including planks and timbers from our ship, littered the beach. A short, brown-skinned people roamed the beach, slaughtering the exhausted European men. I saw one sailor try to fight back, but for naught.

I went back to my attacker and touched him. His language was foreign, but I quickly absorbed understanding and proficiency as my fragmental trolled through him.

- - - - -

His name was Yaki, a young farmer and fisherman who lived in a village nearby. The white demons had come during the storm, and they did not have horses, so the villagers poured out to take their lives. The gods had given them this gift, a way to strike back without bringing the metal men and their terrifying horses.

Yaki had already taken the life of one who was still moving. He had cut the throat of another who might have already been dead, since the skin was even whiter than normal, if that was possible. He had only seen a white man once before, when he went to Izamal to sell dried fish last year. The large man sauntered through the market, his face bushy with a red beard, a metal axe slung casually across his shoulder. From whispers among the throng, he learned that this feared man had helped the priests of the dead god destroy the temple of Ixchup.

Yaki had only known the time of sorrow for his people, when the metal men took the Mayans away as slaves and herded them into the waters of baptism. Many resisted, but cotton armor and war clubs edged with obsidian were no match for armor and well-wrought steel blades. It was even whispered that women were smothering their newborns rather than let their children grow up in such misery.

Yaki was no warrior, though the hot blood of youth sometimes sent him daydreaming about glory. Killing the sailors made him feel like he had done something to strike back at the foreigners. Yet, even in his elation, he feared the retaliation that would surely fall if their deeds were ever discovered.

And now the white man that he had tried to slay was standing over him.

"Yaki, where are you? Yaki!" His grandfather, the only relative of his still alive, called for him.

"I am here," he said, mounting the top of the dune. For some reason, he had not wanted to kill this white man and that terrified him, for surely this man would tell the others and the villagers would perish.

- - - - -

"Yaki, why have you left this one alive?" Ulán demanded of his grandson. Ulán was an *ah men*, a maker of prayers and caster of sooth stones. His seventy years gave his wrinkled face a touch of dignity, and his body was still as wiry and firm as when he had taken his first wife. His long silver hair lay in wavy curls against his shoulders.

When Ulán approached, the white sailor reached out to touch the old man. Ulán's anger drifted away, to be replaced by a plan. This white man was the only one that he had ever heard of being taken prisoner. It occurred to him that this was an answer to his prayers. As a child, he had witnessed the sacrifice of a virginal pair of twins, a boy and girl, on top of the tallest pyramid temple in Izamal. Such a dramatic sacrifice was occasioned by the approach of an Aztec army. The sacrifice worked and the Aztecs returned to their cities.

Now the Aztecs were subject to an even stronger people.

Perhaps it was time for another sacrifice. Ulán doubted that the sailor was a virgin, but his skin was white and his face covered with a brown beard, a fitting offering to the gods.

After the horror of the sickness that had taken all his kin except Yaki, Ulán faced the wasteland of despair. Though their village was small and he only an *ah men*, not the priest of a temple, he had fought the sickness with all the lore that he knew. In the end, the sickness left of its own accord, leaving only two of every ten behind.

Only his constant prayers allowed Ulán to cling to a remnant of hope. He now directed his prayers and ritual offerings to Itzamna. Few people prayed to Itzamna, son of the Hunab Ku, the supreme creator. Itzamna had taught the Mayans to grow food, to find medicines in the jungle, and how to write, but he was a distant god. He was not the one to present offerings to if you wanted a good crop or the affection of a maiden. Yet the other gods, of the maize, the spring, the storms, were limited. They could not save the people, only the power of Itzamna could do that. So every day, morning and night, Ulán prayed at a shrine behind home. Offerings of fruit, an obsidian knife, and pieces of clothing surrounded a statue of Itzamna, with his bearded face, and wise eyes, on the body of a sacred lizard.

Itzamna demanded a human sacrifice.

CHAPTER TWENTY-ONE

The Indians kept me in a small hut under guard at all times. I was the sole survivor; even the other sailors with my fragmentals in them were dead. My new home was a building typical of the tropics, a wood structure with woven walls. A hanging cotton blanket served as a door. The real purpose of the long house was to keep off the rain and provide the privacy and personal space that all humans crave.

In the morning, the villagers brought me corn gruel to eat and in the evening I ate fish and tortillas. My arms and legs were usually bound behind me, and loosened for each meal and calls of nature. My bed was a straw mat with a cotton covering. I had certainly suffered through worse physical discomforts. My captors were not cruel; they just did not want to lose their prize.

Few had ever seen a European, and so they came to gawk. Many were bold enough to touch me, especially when I was bound. I rewarded them with fragmentals and within a couple of days was quite familiar with the village. Fewer than a hundred people lived here, divided into two major kin clans. They went to other villages to find brides. They lived off corn fields that they burned from the jungle, and fish that they caught in the swampy waters.

I looked for someone who was corrupt enough that I might take him or her as a host, and leave Alonso de Aux to be sacrificed, but there were no corrupt ones. Plenty of pettiness, but no true evil. Even the gossipy wife of a village headman tattled with foolishness, not malice. It seems to me that corruption requires a power imbalance or anonymity. The village was too small to have significant differences in social status and no one could conceal their crimes.

This village had seen its share of misery. I did not have to use my fragmentals to see the pockmarks on almost everyone's bodies, especially their faces. Smallpox. The disease usually did not kill so many when it visited European villages and cities, but it devastated the Mayans and other New World nations.

Like others, I assumed that Indians were weaker in some way and smallpox killed them more easily. It was not until this century that scholars began to understand why smallpox was so devastating in the New World. The Indians were just as strong as the Europeans, but they were virgin territory for smallpox. When the pox arrived, often before anyone had yet even seen a white man, everyone got sick. Most people will survive the ten-day-long ordeal of pox if they are cared for. But when everyone is sick, then no one is left to do the nursing. When there is no one to gather food or to cook it, most die.

Yaki considered me his own special trophy. He often came to the long house after working in the fields. He sat in the corner, allowing me to marvel at his talent. Taking a raw hunk of black obsidian, he chipped away with a stone. Instead of creating a knife or a scrapper, he crafted a work of art. He made trees, corn husks, and symbols of gods and spirits crowned with feathered headdresses, all intricate, so fragile, yet so full of grace. His father had taught him the skill, and when his parents died of the pox, a horde of obsidian was left behind.

One evening, a couple of weeks after the shipwreck, I watched him tap away. The sunlight of the setting sun came through the door, partially blocked by the hanging blanket, illuminating the room in dark red. After only a half hour of work, he had two figures, a man and woman, facing each other, still connected by a fragile bridge of stone.

"I will marry soon," he said. "And this will be a gift for her."

I knew their language because my fragmentals brought that knowledge to me, but I pretended to learn it by degrees. Even so, the villagers were astonished at my seemingly quick progress.

"Who?" I asked.

"She is called Malia. She is from the Quic village, down by the Tzolaab river," he replied. "She is of the Water clan. My grandfather married into the Water clan with a girl from that same village."

"You are of the Corn clan, right?"

"Yes."

"Is this a good match?"

"Yes, grandfather threw the stones and found that Malia and I will mix well."

"Have you ever met her?"

"No," Yaki replied ruefully. "But grandfather says she is pretty and a hard worker. She has already had the sickness and survived."

I listened to him describe his plans for her. A long house to be built. Many of the villagers would go to the other village for the wedding feast. Grandfather would determine the auspicious day.

"You are waiting until after I am sacrificed, aren't you?" Ulán had decided on the autumn equinox, which left me with another month to select a new host or escape.

Yaki flushed. "Yes, we are." He hurried to speak further: "But you should not fear the sacrifice. Grandfather says that sacrificial victims are like warriors who fall in battle or women who die in childbirth, they all are guaranteed a place in the thirteen heavens. You will be in paradise, where there is no war, always enough food, and everyone is happy."

"You think so?" I asked.

"Well, yes. Even though you are from across the sea, you will probably go to the thirteen heavens." His mind reached out for new thoughts. "Or maybe you will go to the heaven that your dead god has provided."

I smiled. My dead god—that is what they had learned of Jesus Christ. The stories that priests and monks taught were filtering through the continent, seemingly faster than the conquistadors.

One day when Yaki took me outside so that I might urinate, he pointed to a nearby long house. Holes in its thatched roof and a collapsed wall indicated that it was one of the many abandoned homes in the village. "That is where I used to live," he said. "My mother, father, sisters, and brothers all died in there. They are also buried there."

I touched him and felt his sorrow. Among the mix of memories, I also perceived his fierce determination to live. And to live is to take a wife and raise children, to continue on. Such an earnest youth; I grew quite fond of him.

During later conversations, he told me of the ruins not far from there. Great stone walls, a pyramid even taller than the temple in Izamal, all overgrown with jungle. These were the homes of his ancestors. The Mayans had once been a great urban civilization, but were now little more than a rural shadow.

One day he brought me a book. He did not know how to read, but the painted drawings enchanted him. The pages were made from bark, smeared with bitumen, and stretched into sheets several feet long. It was like the illuminated manuscripts that were produced only a century ago in Europe, rather than the new books of the printing press.

"Where did you get this?" I asked.

"A priest of the goddess Ixchup came through here five years ago and left it with us. He said he would return for it, but he has never come back. I have heard that the priests of the dead god burn every one of these that they find."

CHAPTER TWENTY-TWO

Two days before the equinox, when the day was still longer than the night, a conquistador arrived unannounced in the village, riding a worn-out horse. A dozen soldiers walked behind him, wearing chain mail and carrying swords and crossbows. Ulán came from his hut to stand before the Spaniards.

Yaki was watching from the shadows of a hut. My fragmental in Yaki prompted him to worry that the white man should be hidden. If the Spaniards found me, they would slay the entire village. He rushed over to my prison and touched me, and I learned what was happening.

I cast a fragmental into my guard to free myself. He and Yaki untied me and I left the hut, walking to the edge of the village.

The solider on horseback saw me first. "And who are you?" he called out, raising his hand in astonishment.

Ulán turned and I saw desperation in his eyes.

I spoke to Ulán in his own tongue. "Do not be afraid. I will not betray you."

To the soldier, I said. "I am Alonso de Aux, the sole survivor of the *Santo Domingo*. The ship wrecked near here some months ago."

"I am Don Roberto Protilla, in the service of Hernán Fredrico, governor of this province. A captain in his guard."

I reached the captain and reached out my hand. We clasped each other's forearms and I put a fragmental inside.

- - - - -

Don Roberto Portilla had never entertained an introspective thought in his entire life. I did not have the time to go through thirty-six years of memories, but a cursory glance did not reveal a hint of malice. He was a soldier, nothing more. He was not unnecessarily cruel in his duties and went about pillaging as a duty. The Mayans had been defeated, and by right of conquest, they could be enslaved.

That was his purpose in this obscure village. He needed ten slaves, preferably strong, young men. On the way back, he intended to visit four other villages. The governor needed slaves to work in the silver mines in mountains many days' travel from there.

- - - - -

I saw what the future held for these people. The continual drain of slavery by overlords who saw the Indians as cattle to be exploited.

"You seek slaves," I said.

He nodded.

"Don Portilla," I said. "What you are doing is not only wrong, it is foolish. These people are used to paying tribute and giving their loyalty to a lord. They will give a limited measure of their labor, just as they have traditionally done. Do not push them into slavery."

"They are a conquered people. We have a right to use them as we see fit."

"You will provoke them to a revolt," I protested.

"Then we will crush them, just as we have crushed them before." The captain smiled sardonically. "They are not much in the way of fighters. We have steel, they have stones."

"I ask you to leave and convince your governor that this is wrong."

Don Portilla opened his mouth to object, but then a quizzical look crossed his features. He nodded in assent. My fragmental was asserting its influence.

Turning his horse about, he led his men from the village. His soldiers obeyed out of military discipline, but their perplexed expressions showed their true confusion.

The villagers were ecstatic. Though they did not understand Spanish, they saw the effect of my conversation with the conquistador. I had not betrayed them, I was their savior. A human sacrifice had not even been necessary.

My captors became my hosts. Three pigs were slaughtered for a feast. Pulque flowed freely, leading to antics of drunken behavior in some and melancholy in others. I puffed on my first pipe of tobacco and vomited when the smoke mixed with too much rich food.

These Mayans believed in cycles. They saw cycles everywhere. The rising and setting of the sun, the rhythm of the growing seasons, the birth of girl child to replace the death of an old woman, or the birth of a boy child to replace a fallen warrior. What happened long ago, and does not now happen, will happen again.

They also see endless cycles in history. Life repeating itself, over and over. I had come from Christendom, an eschatological faith. Christians think that history has a purpose and that history will end. The Christ will come and the purpose of the Earth will be fulfilled. Marxism, not to be born for another three centuries, is a religion without a god parading as ideology. Marx preached that the final climax of civilization will be communism, where the worker will have no master and all will be equal.

The search for the end of time has caused so much damned pain. Is the Mayan belief in cycles a better way to believe? I don't know. Ironically, for such seemingly polar views of reality, both paths lead to the same emotions. Fatalism comes from believing that the end of time approaches and nothing can done, or fatalism comes from believing that this cycle is against your people. Either way, hope is lost.

You are conquered now, but maybe during the next cycle, you will be the conqueror. Sometimes the gods ordained captivity, others times conquest, or maybe the gods were deaf and blind and powerless.

These Mayans were great once, they would be great again. A new cycle was beginning, or so they thought.

CHAPTER TWENTY-THREE

Four days later, a troop of one hundred and four soldiers came walking down the road. The governor of the province, Hernán Fredrico, rode a frisky spotted horse at the head of the column. Don Portilla, bound in chains, sat in a cart pulled by another horse. When they reached the center of the village, the soldiers formed a rough ring around the governor and cart.

The governor called out for me. "Don Alonso de Aux, I have come to see you."

I emerged from behind a long house and approached. Ulán trailed behind me, wearing a fine feathered headdress, carrying his precious statue of Itzamna.

"I am Don Hernán Fredrico, governor of this province, by the authority of Cortés himself."

"Don Alonso de Aux at your service, my lord."

"You have put strange ideas in the head of my captain of the guard." The governor spoke with the strong, confident voice of a natural leader.

"Strange, my lord?" I desperately wanted to get close enough to touch the governor, but a screen of soldiers shielded him. To push through them seemed socially awkward at the moment. The governor obviously desired this physical separation in order to accentuate his social separation from a lower nobleman such as myself.

"These people are our slaves, and you will not get in the way."

"Are you a Christian, my lord?" I asked.

"Of course," he replied in anger.

"Then follow Christ. He would never have enslaved these people. These people are heathens, they need the Gospel, not the lash."

"Yes, they are heathens, and we will baptize them at the mines. The friar there will teach them the Holy Sacraments."

"But you will make them slaves, nevertheless."

"Yes," he spat. "Christian Indians work as well as heathen Indians."

My approach seemed to be failing. I had to touch him!

"I implore you, my lord." I moved forward, my hands held out beseeching his favor. My arm touched a soldier and I sent a fragmental in him to move him away. "In the name of Jesus Christ, leave these people alone. They are children of God too."

The governor lost control of his wrath. "No! Kill him! Kill them all! Now!" he shouted to his soldiers.

Bedlam erupted. Shouting by the soldiers, screaming among the Indians. I lunged forward and touched the governor's foot as a sword pierced my back. It went through a kidney, paralyzing me with pain. Vomit rose in my throat, stopped by the clenching of every muscle in my body. I blasted my way into the governor, to take him as my new host.

As the essence of Don Hernán Fredrico died, he jerked back off the horse. He fell to the ground and I took complete control.

As I pushed myself to my feet, a spasm stabbed through my shoulder. I had broken my collarbone. A soldier in front on me swept down with his sword, cutting the life out of an Indian who had tripped.

"Stop!" I yelled. "Stop! I order you all to stop!"

The soldiers seemed not to notice. The bloodlust necessary to overcome the innate human reluctance to kill clouded their minds. Pushing aside my pain, I shuffled over to the soldier that was now taking another swipe at the prostrate body before him, making sure that the Indian was dead.

I touched him and placed a fragmental in him. The fragmental took control, though it did not kill his soul. The soldier dashed off after the other soldiers, shouting for them to stop.

Moving as quickly as I could through the village, I passed out fragmentals, trying to regain control of these troops. Each fragmental-controlled soldier aided me in my effort. Sometimes they were forced to attack the other soldiers in order to bring them to their senses.

Passing a long house, I heard a scream inside. When I pushed aside the doorway blanket, I found a soldier on top of a Mayan woman. The neural connection between sex and violence, making rape, is something that I have never been able to fathom. The penis serves as another type of sword, imposing another type of death.

"Stop!" I shouted as I stepped forward to place my hand on his back.

My intention was to place a fragmental in him, but when I attempted to do so, I felt the fabric of my being begin to fray. I had reached my limit. No more fragmentals left within me.

"Stop now!"

The soldier jerked back, his face screwed up with frustration and anger. "Why, my Lord?"

"Because I have ordered the attack to stop," I said. "Go tell the others."

He adjusted his pants. "Yes, my lord."

After he left, the woman stared up at me, her eyes filled with foreboding. I did not need a fragmental inside her to understand her feelings. She knew me as the leader and did not know my language, so she assumed that I wanted her for myself. I recognized her. A mother of six, only one of whom had survived the pox. She was past forty, her face worn by too many years of work in the sun; not young and pretty, not desirable in any way. I yearned to place a fragmental in her to ease her pain, but the best I could do for now was leave her.

Outside the hut, I found the soldiers coming back from their rampage. Many of them carried bloody swords and just as many carried booty, a piece of jewelry or a fine blanket. War mixes so well with greed.

"Assemble the men," I ordered the sergeant.

Back at the center of the village, Ulán lay on the ground, his stomach cut open and his head almost severed from his body. A sticky pool of red soaked the hard ground around him. His idol of Itzamna lay in pieces among his blood. Perhaps this was a sufficient sacrifice.

Yaki sat on the ground next to his grandfather. A cut across his cheek dripped blood, but he had survived somehow. I was glad of this. He did not cry, but when the soldiers returned, he looked at us with a determination in his eyes that spoke volumes. He was ready to die and he would not give us the pleasure of his fear.

As I brushed through the throng of soldiers, I found two of my fragmentals and retrieved them. I moved toward Yaki with the intent to touch him. He recoiled back and I stopped. To him, I was not the stranger from the ship, but the governor of the province. I reached forward and touched him anyway. My fragmental would comfort him.

Having taken care of Yaki, I turned to survey the soldiers. These were my soldiers now. I instructed them to bring water for the wounded and provide care as well as they could. Though confused by the governor's change of heart, they moved to comply.

Half of the villagers were dead. The soldiers were too efficient, leaving only a few wounded. Most of the rest of the Mayans were still hiding in the fields or the jungle. Those few that remained, I placed fragmentals in to help ease their pain and grief.

I was such a failure, unable to protect these people. Further contemplation induced an even deeper sense of helplessness. I planned to lead these soldiers away and do my best to see that more did not come, but I knew that I would fail. Even if I went back across the ocean and took possession of the King of Spain and used him to order the conquistadors to stop, adventurers from other countries would fill the void. Even if I took possession of the Pope and issued a Papal Bull prohibiting contact with the New World, greed would cause some to still come. The

Protestants would consider such a Bull an open invitation.

I cannot stand up to the forces of history. It is all so futile, I feel like a shepherd of the winds. No one can control the random movements of the wind and I cannot heal a civilization. I can only heal individuals, one at a time.

CHAPTER TWENTY-FOUR

When I wake, it is chilly, and I am grateful for the wood planking that protects me from the metal bottom of the barge. Even so, the cold touch of the river has made my buttocks numb. The patter of raindrops beats against the tarp. I stand and walk about, wiggling my arms and body to get the blood flowing. Some unwarmed food from a can helps.

God, the horror of my memories. Though my body is firmly anchored aboard this barge, I feel as if I am loose in time, floating through different bodies, experiencing different people, living the joy and the pain. Mostly the pain. Why do I punish myself so much?

Sleep and my regression through time returns....

Her baby died before the sun came up. The labored breathing stopped, stilling the chill-racked body, quenching the internal blaze that burned the infant's skin, and she knew. A small cooking fire warded off the night as she held the slowly cooling body in her arms. She mumbled words in Latin, the magic language of the priests. Jesus and Mary understood only Latin.

She pressed her eyes tightly together, shutting in the swollen tears. She did not know Latin. Sometimes she wondered if the priests even knew it. Maybe St. Gerlac would listen to her. He had lived in a city not far away, and he knew her tongue.

She prayed to him. Please let my baby go to heaven, even though the priest has not had the chance to baptize this precious angel.

Surely no God would allow such pain without future reward. Heaven was the absence of pain. Please, Jesus...Mary, let me see my children again.

Shouting and general tumult from down the street attracted her to the doorway. She watched.

A soldier, sword stained with blood, ran down the street. His coat of mail slapped against his bare legs. The grin on his face seemed maniacal, almost insane. His eyes were round with fear. He faced a foe that no blade or stratagem could conquer. His bravery and prowess were for naught. Slipping in the mud, then righting himself, he ran past her, chasing an unseen foe.

She returned to the baby. She wanted to bury him in hallowed ground, but he had not been baptized. Those who carried the carts of dead out of the city walls did not care who was baptized. They buried them all in a common pit, which a priest hallowed then with his blessing.

Cradling her child, she went into the street. Last night's rain had turned the alley to mud. She slogged through, her bare feet making sucking sounds with each step.

When she was only a child of seven, the plague had come through this city for the first time. She sickened, but did not die, so now the plague could never take her. This was the second visit of the Black Death. Some said that it came every generation to chastise the bad and provide opportunities for the good to show their faith.

Her husband succumbed four days ago, then her four-year-old son a day later. She had hoped that the suck she gave the baby would protect him.

The buzzing of flies, the sound of the plague, filled the air, as descriptive as the stench of decay, each well remembered from her childhood. She walked by the slumped form of a man on the street and a cloud of flies lifted from him. They swarmed around her, attracted to the moisture of her eyes and her nostrils. She kept her lips pressed tightly closed, fearing that a swarm would get inside and she would never be rid of them.

As she left the body behind, the flies broke away, returning to their task of hastening decomposition. She slipped in the mud, reacting instinctively to protect the baby as she fell. She twisted herself to the side, allowing the baby to land on her.

She heard their singing and crying before she saw the procession. A ragged group of people moved down the street, wearing scratchy woolen tunics, flagellating themselves with whips. They sang hymns and cried out to the saints to be saved from this horror.

She found an oxcart, bodies stacked on it like sacks of spoiled grain. Two men, with cloths covering their noses and mouths, carried a woman from down the street. Her rigid form, which dipped only slightly between them, was bloated with putrefaction. They heaved the body on top of the pile. Blank eyes passed over the mother. One took hold of the ox's halter, and the other flicked its flank with a switch.

The cart began to creak forward. She stepped after it and gently laid the baby on top, snug between the putrefying woman and a bare leg that protruded from deeper in the pile.

My fragmental within her stroked her, attempting to soothe her loss.

The memory of the mother leaves me shaken, thankful for the new drugs of the past two centuries. The plague is a footnote in medical textbooks now, of interest only to historians. My head is groggy with strands of memories. I am in a half-awake dream state, aware that I am on the barge, but still feeling so intensely the memories of my lifetimes. I need to pee, so I climb out of the concrete pipe, rubbing my back along the tarp. Squatting over the wooden flooring brings on the another time when I assumed the same stance.

I was once a whore in Greece, stricken with venereal disease and pissing pain. Before the story unwinds, I force a stop to the remembering. Why do my worst memories seem the most vivid? My mind, seemingly of its own volition, skims over the joyful times. I am reminded of my failures and of the fear that we all experience. Perhaps this predilection can be traced to my current state of fear. Unfortunately, I am as handicapped as any normal person when it comes to introspection. It is so difficult to see ourselves as others see us, or even come close to an objective view.

Climbing back into my nest, I huddle with my arms around my knees. Before the Black Death came to Europe and laid Christians low, it visited the Moslems. I was there, in Egypt, on my way back from my sojourn in the eastern part of the world. Everyone faces death, all people (save myself) are born with their genes ticking down towards the end, but the plague is a particularly ugly face of death.

I remember a peasant woman named Nabi who lived in a village along the Nile. Three decades of desert sun had cracked her face into a network of lines, but her long, dark hair still held its luster.

The plague took her husband and all her children, except a nine-year-old son. For Nabi, this was not a divine punishment, but a consequence of life, like floods, droughts, and sandstorms. She pushed on, praying to Allah, trusting in her amulets, and performing her communal duties. She went to the fields every day and tended the crops.

She mourned for the rest of her life, remembering in particular her two-year-old daughter. When parents normally remember their children, they recall episodes from different times, when the child was an infant, or at eight, or as a teenager. She always recalled a child caught in time at the age of two.

I lived among the people of Nabi's village for a generation and learned to love Allah. I even traveled to Mecca on my own Hajj. Islam is another set of ideas about God that encourages people towards good and sometimes provokes them towards evil. The idea of jihad, which is striving for the good of Islam, often turned towards holy war, which seemed so contrary to the pacifism that I tried to practice.

The Moslems did not blame the Jews or Christians for the plague. In Europe, the Jews were slaughtered for spreading the plague, and in Spain, the Christians slaughtered Moslems. For

Christians, the plague was the beginning of the Apocalypse, the final punishment of God.

Christians feared death, and only found martyrdom when dying at the hands of fellow humans. Many Moslems welcomed the mercy of martyrdom in the plague. In Egypt, while I did find rampant fear and group madness, no group of outsiders was blamed, and everyone struggled to continue living their lives as normally as possible.

Praise be to Allah.

I have seen so much, experienced so much. I am the sum of the lives that I touch. Closing my eyes, I seek a path to sleep, and my memories move further back into time, leaving the Muslims and going east to the land of the Middle Kingdom.

CHAPTER TWENTY-FIVE

She had the hands of an old woman, cracked and worn, and the face of a prepubescent girl of twelve. A slight body with dark hair cut short completed the physical packaging. She wore a simple shrift of hempen cloth. There was nothing to distinguish her from the other children in the village.

Finishing my drink from the village well, I strolled past her on the way back to my sedan chair porters and brushed her skin out of idle curiosity. She looked at me oddly, shocked that a noble such as myself would even touch a nobody such as her. After ensuring that my party was ready to leave, I returned to where she sat and took back the fragmental.

The power of her intellect stunned me and my hand stayed on her shoulder. Cascading thoughts, so active, so creative, rushed through me. This little girl was the brightest person I had ever met; not the smartest, but the one with the greatest potential. Being smart is the result of discipline and learning how to reason, combined with innate ability. This girl, simply named Qui, had never been given the time for simple reflection, let alone the opportunity to learn how to think.

- - - - -

She was a slave, bonded to the Huang family, which owned most of the land and villages along that stretch of the Yangtze River. She knew her own history, having been told it by an aunt. Qui was born the third daughter of Wang Lien, a poor peasant who worked the rice fields of Huang Chow. Two older brothers also preceded her in the family. Third daughters were unheard of in her village of Ple, since second daughters were bad enough. The midwife wrapped the baby in a rag and murmured that she was taking a walk. The mother, still drenched with sweat and oozing afterbirth, lurched to her feet and grabbed the baby away from the midwife. I regret never having met that mother, for she possessed a tenacious fire within her to resist the lure of abandoning her infant.

When she reached three years of age, Qui could speak as well as the adults. Her mother exclaimed loudly what an extraordinary child she was. Her father ignored her.

One day Qui saw the daughter of Huang Chow, who was the same age as herself. Huang Wei's painted face looked like that of a goddess, and her petite feet, bound by strips of silk, indicated that she would never labor in the fields like Qui. Qui looked down at her calloused feet and felt ashamed that she was a nobody.

Her mother died giving birth to her ninth child, a fourth daughter. The villagers murmured that it was an appropriate punishment for a woman who kept her daughters. Qui was eight years old. Her father came and took her to the house of Huang Chow, where he offered her as partial payment of a debt. She was sold.

She was not a house servant. For the next four years she cleaned the privies, weeded the garden, and carried wood and water for the kitchen.

Now this traveling wellborn gentleman was detaining her with his touch. She so much wanted to leave with her pot of water, but feared to offend one so noble. She resigned herself to a beating by the cook for being tardy.

- - - - -

I allowed the girl to leave, then went to the house of Huang Chow. We engaged in the required pleasantries, a social dance that I found wearisome. I am quite sure that I would never have learned the Chinese social graces on my own, but my host had been trained as a classical scholar, a scion of a noble family, and I took advantage of that.

I offered to buy the girl, and after some polite bartering he accepted some paper currency that could be redeemed for salt at the local government storehouse. Paper currency was one of the more interesting innovations that I had encountered in China.

My intention had been to leave the eastern half of the world and make my way back to Europe. I had spent the last couple of generations in Japan as a Buddhist monk, serving at monasteries and at the Imperial court. Encountering this girl prompted me to readily abandon such plans. Such a jewel required careful nurturing and the finest education that I could find.

While I returned to my sedan chair, Huang Chow sent word to the girl of her new owner. When the girl—now my property—came out of the house, she carried her only possession, an old blanket, in her arms.

- - - - -

Qui carefully looked over her new master. Why would someone buy her? She was a hard worker, but not strong or skilled. She wondered if this strange man, a merchant of some means by the looks of it, wanted her for a concubine. But she was not pretty, and her feet were flat and ugly.

She bowed her head. "I am Qui, my master."

"I am Li Jiang," the man said. "And you are an extraordinary girl. You will become an extraordinary lady."

Lady? "I do not understand, my master."

"Come, sit with me here." He patted the sedan chair next to him. She climbed up and sat, feeling small and awkward in such a place. A girl of her station never rode in a chair. The porters picked up the chair and trotted out of the village. Qui grabbed the railing of the chair, fascinated by the sensation of movement. It was like riding an ox when she was younger, back before her mother died. This was fun, and in spite of her apprehension, she giggled.

Her new master placed his hand on her shoulder and left it there, remaining quiet. His gaze roved over the countryside, the green fields of ripening rice, the vast expanse of the river, and the path that passed for a road in this area.

She looked back at the village of her birth. The villagers treated her as a stupid mistake by her mother. She would miss her sister and her aunt, but no one else.

She had never been more than a couple of leagues from the village of Huang Chow. When the porters carried her through another village, she watched everything with curious intensity, missing very little. This village was much like hers. The next three villages looked the same and she wondered if the world was just a vast number of villages and peasants working in the fields. Then she saw on the horizon the faint outlines of mountains. She had heard people talking of these, and of the bandits that lived there, but never expected to see them, even from a distance.

At the end of the day, they came to the town of Hsin-wang. Even though the setting sun cast long shadows, the market was still open. The smells of a kitchen permeated the air, reminding her of her hunger. Her master led her into a small stall. Silk and cotton clothes hung on the walls. Her master displayed his money and clothes were brought to her. She was given a cotton dress and knitted shoes for traveling clothes. The cloth was softer than anything she had ever touched, smooth and comfortable. Her master also presented her with a round parasol of blue-green silk to shield herself from the sun. When they left, he carried a satchel, which contained a silk dress and a silk robe, embroidered with flowers. Those were for more formal occasions.

Her master was an important man. They stayed in the house of the local magistrate that night, a guest of his hospitality. A servant girl her own age subjected her to the bizarre experience of a bath. The girl picked the lice out of her hair, popping each one in her own mouth. Qui usually ate her own lice and felt annoyed that the other was enjoying this treat.

Her master introduced her to the magistrate, a distinguished gentleman who wore an intricately embroidered jacket. "This is my long-lost daughter."

Now it all made sense. Her master was insane, and thought that she was his own blood. What would he do when he figured out the truth? She was only a peasant.

She wore her new silk dress to dinner that night. The magistrate's family chatted politely as they ate the richest meal she had ever seen: balls of rice, silkworm pies, mutton strips, and wine. The family of Huang Chow never allowed her into their home while dining, and she knew from what help she had given in the kitchen that they rarely feasted so well. Embarrassment simmered just under the surface of her faltering smile and she ate very little, afraid to make some blunder that would reveal that she was really only a garden girl.

Later that night, as her stomach growled from hunger, her master slipped into her room. She lay on the mat, rigid with apprehension. She hoped that this insane man knew the difference between a daughter, even a fake daughter, and other girl children.

"Here, I brought you some food," he said, thrusting a folded cloth into her hands.

"Thank you, master," she murmured, unfolding the cloth and finding rice flavored with chicken. She ate quickly.

Her master touched her on the shoulder briefly, then sat down on the other end of her mat. He moved with such grace, a well-born sophistication that she envied.

"Qui, I know that you are not my daughter. You are a peasant girl, but you are so much more. I want to take you away with me and educate you, make you into a lady and a scholar. I know that you felt out of place tonight at dinner. That is an awkward feeling. I will teach you how not to feel out of place. Would you like that?"

"Yes, master," she said. He was offering her a life she had

never thought to even dream of, but she was quick enough to recognize the opportunity being offered.

"I do not want you to call me master," he said. "I am not your master. I free you as my slave, but I ask that you remain with me and call me father."

She thought about this and answered. "Yes, father."

CHAPTER TWENTY-SIX

This was the twilight of the Sung dynasty, though few people seemed to notice. The barbarians had already taken the northern half of the country, driving the throne of the Son of Heaven to the southern city of Hangchow.

Hangchow lined the northern bank of the river Che near where the river emptied into the great ocean. Because the tide pushed saltwater up the river to the city, the artificial Western Lake provided water for the city. As the capital of Middle Earth, Hangchow was greater and richer than any other city in the world, or so I had been told. Certainly it was larger than any city I had seen since Rome in its grandeur.

Shops in the paper district used wooden blocks to print books of the classics. The National University was here, as well as the Military Academy, and the Imperial Academy. Numerous other smaller colleges and places of learning thrived. Among these cultured scholars I hoped to see Qui flourish.

My host had been a wealthy merchant inclined towards cruelty before I occupied his body. I used that wealth to set up a fine household on a side street near the Imperial Way. A retinue of servants tended to our mundane needs and kept the garden a beautiful and contemplative retreat. Qui grew to accept the servants' ministrations, but she always treated them with kindness and respect. She had not yet learned arrogance, and like a good father, I hoped to steer her away from any sense of haughty self-importance.

Tutors that I hired came to teach Qui every day. The tutors

were university or academy students who liked to have some extra money to spend in the singing-girl houses. They taught Qui to read and write characters. Within months she had the command of her language, then she began to learn the Classics, law, history, and medicine. She sucked in this information at a pace that bewildered her tutors. Her fingers were stiff from years of hard work, so learning proper calligraphy, how to paint, and strumming a four-stringed guitar took longer.

The wisdom of Confucius dominated Chinese thinking. Confucius taught that morals and ethics should guide a person's individual and family life, as well as the lives of an entire nation. He said, "By extensively studying all learning, and keeping himself under the restraint of the rules of propriety, one may thus likewise not err from what is right." So Qui learned the sayings of Confucius, readily memorizing his Analects. Her favorite: "Is it not pleasant to learn with a constant perseverance and application?"

Qui required training in the social graces so that she might know how to function in high-born circles. I sought out someone with the right attitude who could work with her. I did not want someone who had learned their skills from birth into a noble family, but who had been forced to learn them later in life. My discreet inquiries led me to Lao Ning, a woman in her fifties who used to be a singing-girl. She had actually sung with a talented voice, rather than earning her living only on her back. Her skill and fame rewarded her with a marriage into the family of Lao, though the family of scholar-magistrates was on the decline. Not one person in the family had passed the examinations in two generations. They struggled to live on their meager inheritances, since pride prevented them from becoming merchants or entertaining the thought of any other profession except the role of a government official. Of course, because of the examinations, none of the family had served the government for two generations.

When Lao Ning first came to our home, she was dressed in all her magnificence. Cosmetics highlighted her features, which were still beautiful after all these years. She smelled of tangy flowers and multiple combs guided her hair into an elaborate arrangement. A pearl necklace lay draped about her fine throat. She walked with dainty small steps that came from binding. I knew that each step was painful, a throbbing that she had gotten used to over the years.

Lao Ning taught Qui how to dress, how to arrange her hair, and how to behave in public and in private. The proper forms of small talk, every move of the body, were so important in that ossified, class-conscious society. If Qui was to feel comfortable, she needed these skills. The old courtesan was occasionally too harsh with my daughter, so I put a fragmental in her to encourage her to exercise patience. Since Qui was living the life the courtesan had always wanted, I was also forced to moderate the older woman's jealousy.

One morning we summoned a sedan chair and went out into the countryside. At a village near the Che river, we stopped. Lush rice fields and prosperous houses surrounded us. The village was wealthy beyond its means, my donations of money serving well their purpose.

Qui's aunt stepped from a house, wearing a fine cotton dress. A comb held up her hair in a stack and she looked years younger than her real age. Happiness has a way of making the wrinkles of worry fade.

Qui reacted with joy, hugging her aunt and chattering away happily. I observed closely as her sisters, brothers, and their families emerged from the other houses. The younger children, nieces and nephews, goggled at Qui's silk robe and babbled about the "Lady Qui." They treated her like a queen.

During our meal, her father entered the room. Like other peasants, he was prematurely aged. Though only forty years old, he looked sixty. His hands were calloused and puffy from years of pulling at rice. His eyes rested on Qui and guilt crossed behind those eyes. I felt sympathy for him: to be married to a woman who insisted on keeping her girl children, as well as the constant strain of trying to feed his family while coping with the debt that all peasants labored under.

Qui introduced me to her biological father with the words, "This is my father."

"I am honored, my lord," he bowed to me. "I thank you for all that you have done for this family."

"It was my pleasure and my duty," I said, touching him to put a fragmental in him. He was a good man in his own way, a victim of a culture that considered daughters to be liabilities. I eased his pain, then retrieved the fragmental before we left.

After dinner, she delighted her family by writing each of their names on separate pieces of rice paper. This skill poignantly accentuated the gulf that now existed between them and her.

During that visit, my fragmentals trolled through all of Qui's relatives, seeking any duplication of her talent. There was none. These were ordinary people. Qui was unique, an anomaly.

As we left, I contacted my fragmental in Qui and was gratified to learn that she felt only sympathy for her family, not arrogance, or a sense of superiority. They felt alien to her now, and I was astonished at how well she had reconciled the two different phases of her life. So many other people would have been tormented by guilt, or sought refuge in a distaste, bordering on loathing, for any reminder of their past.

Upon our return, Qui began to write poetry. Her first faltering efforts were not very good, and her tutors smiled indulgently, but she rapidly improved. She wrote about common things, the flowers in our garden, the relaxation of an evening walk, or the song of a bird. She also wrote about her life as a slave. One poem, which she particularly treasured, and did not read to me or anyone else, was for her mother. She expressed her sorrow, her regrets, and explained her new life to the woman who had given her life.

She also wrote several private poems on another topic: her filial love for me. She considered me to be her true father. She even had strange fantasies where I had been the one to impregnate her mother during a nocturnal visit, rather than her own father. Every day I tried to live up her expectations and be worthy of her love. Never had my own life been so intertwined with another, and I realized that my long life had been a solitary one, even with my fragmentals and the intimacies that I shared with others.

One day, when she was fifteen years old, after another visit to her family, she asked, "Do you think my family is happy in their new village?"

"Oh, yes, I am sure they are happy," I replied.

She sat in thought for a while. "Yes, they seemed quite happy. You have blessed them." She paused. "I have a strange thought that I want to discuss."

I encouraged her to continue.

"Well," she paused. Qui was not normally at a loss for words. "I have been thinking for quite a while and I have come to the conclusion that you have a special gift."

My fragmental had warned me that this was coming. It had watched the suspicions begin as a mere kernel, then flower with the collection of evidence. She would have made a fine lawyer or detective.

"What gift is that?"

"Father," she said. "You can see into other people's minds, read their thoughts as if they were a book."

"That is an interesting theory, Qui," I said. "Do you think I can see into your mind?"

She avoided the question and launched into a long description of her reasoning. As a keen observer, she remembered the times that I knew an unusual detail or some private story about another person. One or two such incidents were easy to explain away, but not such an accumulation. I was proud of her; of all the people I have ever known, she alone approached the potential of my own eidetic memory. As her suspicions bloomed, I could have diverted her with gentle nudges by my fragmental, but I had resolved to never tamper with such a jewel.

"Yes, my flower, I do have a gift, a way of discerning the minds of others," I said. "It is that gift that showed me how special you are. It is why you are here."

She nodded, satisfied with the answer. My fragmental informed me that she suspected that I knew her thoughts. This did not disturb her. She trusted me with the trust that is only found in children for their parents.

I felt so good.

CHAPTER TWENTY-SEVEN

Two years after I first brought her to Hangchow, Qui began to menstruate. She was a woman now, able to bear children. The thought of children intrigued me. If her husband was healthy and intelligent, would their children inherit her brilliance? If so, then I could stay around, nurturing them also. In a couple of centuries, humanity could be blessed with a whole nation of geniuses.

That vision exhilarated and nauseated me. I felt like a dog owner, breeding for certain characteristics. Was I being too controlling? This was a difficult dilemma, respecting my daughter as a person as opposed to the potential benefits to all humanity. I resolved not to interfere with her ability to make choices. She was so eager to please, though; a result of her childhood. She knew gratitude in a way that most people can never achieve; that is, without a trace of resentment. She truly loved me as a father, and I loved her as the child that I had never had.

I could take a woman as my host and become pregnant, but I had no idea what the result might be. Would he or she be a natural child, with a mind of his own, or would the baby be another me? Until I knew the answer to that question, I would never try the experiment. And without an experiment, the answers were impossible to find.

No doubt Qui would one day want children. My intervention or encouragement was not necessary. Still, I kept my eye out for a suitable husband; by tradition, an arranged marriage was expected.

I recognized that the scholarly learning of the Chinese was only a small slice in a globe of possibilities. So much of their learning was rote memorization of classics, a trivial task for her. The intellectual climate was stagnant, not a fertile ground for great ideas or new thoughts.

Trading colonies of Jews, Moslems, and Hindus lived in the city. We became friends with these merchants and Qui learned their languages. I bought books and scrolls from them and she devoured different ways of thinking. This violated an analect of Confucius, "The study of strange doctrines is injurious indeed!" By this time, Qui had graduated beyond the preconceptions that limited most of her fellow scholars in Hangchow; she understood that the world was much more than just the Middle Kingdom.

She wanted to know more about the world, and during one evening, as we sat in the garden sipping tea, I told her about Europe, and the vast lands between East and West. She did not ask how I had acquired such knowledge or how old I really was; she enjoyed the thrill of having a mysterious father and did not want to spoil the spell. I described the court of the Japanese Emperor and the love of the Japanese nobility for their own unique kind of poetry. After that, she read *The Tale of Genji* and other great works of Japanese literature.

"I want to travel, father, to see these places for myself," she said.

"That is an excellent idea," I responded. For some time, I had been vexed by a harsh reality.

Qui was a peasant and no matter how hard she practiced her manners and learning, other people already knew her origins. She was also a girl. Sometimes qualified tutors were difficult to come by because they felt humiliated to teach such a lowly *female*, but they needed the money. The irony is that most of the money was spent on singing-girls, who were of lowly birth also.

One day the previous spring, Qui learned of the jealousy that others might feel of her gift. She had just bested a tutor in a debate and he paced about in a rage. He called my flower a "girl freak" and described the superiority of his own lineage as opposed to hers. His father had served as a minister to the previous Son of Heaven and her peasant father had tugged at shoots of rice. I sent him on his way.

Qui would never be accepted into one of the universities or academies, and in truth, there was not much reason for her to attend one. She had already learned what China had to offer her. I so much wanted her to accomplish something with her brilliance, something of long-lasting service to others. Of course, if she chose a different course, that was her prerogative, as I was not her master.

"Let's go to Japan, then," I said. "To Kyoto." My years of residence there gave my host a certain amount of respect. In Japan her low birth would not be known and she could thrive. The Japanese still honored the Chinese culture, which they recognized as being much more ancient, and she would be respected as a representative of Sung China.

"Yes," she said. "That sounds wonderful."

We agreed to visit her family one last time, and then leave after I had arranged our finances.

Two nights later I went down to the river to visit with the merchants. A storm was coming in from the sea, creating whitecaps on the river that were visible even in the twilight of the sunset. This was an odd part of town. Channels of water crisscrossed the lowlands, forming shallow islands. Great warehouses built of stone, with roofs of clay tiles, dominated these islands. These moats protected the goods inside from thieves and fire. The rest of the city was made mostly of wood and bamboo.

The city was prepared for fire. Patrols of soldiers walked the streets at night, discouraging thieves, and looking for any smoke or open flame. People, whatever their rank, who left fires burning were brought before a magistrate the next morning. Eight towers were manned day and night, always watching. Two thousand troops in the city and twelve hundred more outside the walls were equipped with fire-resistant clothes, buckets, ropes, and hatchets. These were trained rescue troops. To help these specialists, there were always other soldiers available to fight against the consuming demon. These arrangements lent a feeling of security to the city.

At one of the warehouses, I found a certain merchant who was very successful and very corrupt. I placed my affairs in his hands and a fragmental within his body to ensure that my fortune would be healthy on our return from Japan. Already my intentions were forming into vague plans of taking Qui to India and Europe. Imagine, the greatest mind in the world touring the greatest centers of learning and culture.

The fire started near the Temple of the Imperial Ancestors. I never learned what started the fire, but it spread quickly. The soldiers rallied with buckets of water and hatchets to protect the Imperial Palace. The wind shifted, handing them an easy victory. Gusts from a dry storm sent the fire racing up the Imperial Way. Once I realized what was happening, I tried to make my way back to my home, but the fire created a barrier that I could not penetrate.

I found myself caught in the panicked crowds that swarmed through the streets like terrified rats. A large man slammed me up against a brick wall, bruising me. As he thundered by, I saw him push a child aside also. The child disappeared under the maelstrom of pounding feet. I dived forward to rescue her and struggled back out with numerous footprints on my body. My nose had been pushed into the pavement and blood poured from it. The child in my arms was already dead.

The night passed in flames and fear. At every turn, my efforts to reach my home were frustrated. The coming of dawn revealed that a third of the city had been consumed. Grimy soldiers slumped to the ground, their buckets and hatchets limp in their hands. People wailed in pain and loss, and I was often accosted by a distraught parent or sibling asking me if I had seen such and such a person. Hundreds of thousands of people, perhaps close to a million minds, had been packed into the city, and thousands had died.

The firestorm completely consumed my house. I found a few

bones. They may have been Qui's or a servant's. For weeks, I camped out in the ashes of my home, dividing my fragmentals as much as possible to search among the refugees. She was nowhere to be found. She was lost, along with her chest of writings, paintings, and the other creations of a young artist. Such a useless loss.

A year later the charred city would fall to the Mongols, and barbarian rule would nibble at the Chinese, until they absorbed the Mongols as they had absorbed all earlier invaders. I was not there to see this. I used my finances to ensure the health of Qui's family village, giving them as much security as is possible in this uncertain world. I know that Qui would have appreciated my concern.

As I left their village, resuming my journey to the west, I felt a profound sadness. I sank into the memories of festivals that my flower and I had attended in the city. Plays with elaborate masks and intricate dancing. Puppet shows. Jugglers and acrobats. Qui had once broken her leg trying to imitate the jump of an acrobat.

I sobbed.

It was time to return to Europe.

CHAPTER TWENTY-EIGHT

I loved Qui Wei so much. The memory of her sharp mind and guileless disposition cuts through my self-pity. Her promise was cut short, and in painful contrast, I have lived a life of unknown length, but rich and full.

How sweet is the memory loss of normal humans. The sting of a painful encounter fades over time so that you have the opportunity to learn to forgive. The intensity of a joyful experience mellows with age, becoming nostalgia. All experiences in my memory are there with awful exactness. Every stab of betrayal, every regret, every feeling of joy is there to be re-experienced with as much intensity as I originally felt. Emotional growth is so much easier when memories become foggy and you can reshape them into something useful. Forgetfulness allows people to winnow their memories and thus see the larger issues. To use a cliché, it is easier to see the forest when the trees fade from view. It is so hard for me to get past the trees.

Remembering Qui Wei reminded me of my inadequacies. I strive to do good, I really do, but I make so many mistakes.

Memories of her uniqueness sent my thoughts down an existential path. What is the meaning of it all? I ask myself that question sometimes and right now the question presses against me again, but there is no answer, there is never an answer. I do not know the mind of God. I do not even know if God exists. My faith is often so weak. And even if I knew His or Her mind, that would just be another layer unwrapped. The mystery would still remain, though many say that God knows everything.

Our senses define the boundaries of our consciousness. Humans can only know what we can touch, feel, taste, see, or hear. Five senses equals five windows and five blinders. What if we had another sense, not the supposed sixth sense of intuition, but a sense that showed us yet another aspect of existence? Like a blind person whose sight was suddenly restored, we would then see a new world. This new sense would expand our universe and our understanding, but the mystery of existence would still remain.

I once had a fragmental within a mother and another in her unborn child. The unborn knows only its senses, the warmth of the embryonic fluid, the taste of the mother, the beat of the mother's heart, the beating of the baby's own heart, vague colors that come through open eyes, and muffled incomprehensible sounds from beyond the womb. Complete security.

Birth is a horrifying process, painful, cold, and bright lights. The senses assault the infant and he or she finds refuge in sleep. The senses have not yet learned to process this bewildering new world. Sometimes I think that we are like babies in the womb, only vaguely aware of what exists outside.

When they are born, babies are even more individual than adults. These new creatures have not yet learned conformity. They have not been told what they are seeing or hearing and how to classify the experience. Language has not channeled their neurons down constricting paths. For them, the world is a wondrous blur, and frightening.

These ruminations, this existential malaise, torments me with questions. The big question is why do we exist? Why does anything exist? There are no answers. Sometimes the questions even seem meaningless.

Who am I? A question that so many people ask of themselves. Not in those words, per se, but the seeking of identity is so important. When we have a firm sense of identity, we can act decisively. I have tried to find a name that suits my nature, but my sense of identity fluctuates. Am I one or am I many? Or am I the sum of the experiences of the people whom I have touched?

Is there a bit of Qui Wei within me? Is there a bit of Sonja in me? I certainly hope so.

All of us are seeking self-identity. Some search for a God to answer these questions, others find answers in science, or sensuous experience. There are as many paths as there are people, but there can be no sense of identity without interaction with other people. One needs reference points. One cannot be kind unless one has seen the example of kindness. Paradoxically, one also cannot be kind unless one has known cruelty, or at least, indifference. Only in contrasts do we learn.

These questions unsettle me, enough so that I seek sleep and the nightmares there.

Normally I did not stray into the wilderness, where people are found in small tribes living far from each other. In the cities I find many more people in need of my help. It was sometime during the ninth century that I first traveled the Silk Road, a collection of caravan trails linking the East to the West. When the double calamity of a bandit attack and a sandstorm scattered my caravan, I found myself lost in the arid wastes of the Gobi.

After stumbling through the desert for days, roasting during the day and freezing at night, I came across an oasis. Steep hills sheltered a small valley. A small stream meandered through the valley, offering nourishment for trees and shrubs along its muddy banks. I stumbled down the hill and started across the valley floor. The remains of mud brick walls formed the backbones of dunes. Clumps of brown grass found shelter among crumbling bricks. At one point, I came across a plaza made of brick, mostly covered with sand.

The shade of the trees provided cool comfort. The stream was too shallow to dip my hands into, so I leaned over to slurp in the water. I was careful to not drink too much and overwhelm my shrunken stomach. The water cleaned the dust from my beard and went up my nose. I stood up, coughing and shaking my head to get the water out of my sinuses.

Hunger gnawed at me as I prowled through the trees, hoping

to find some fruit. The presence of ruins indicated that this oasis had once supported a town of some sort, probably thriving on trade from the Silk Road. The people were gone. Perhaps the water supply dwindled to the present-day trickle and they left for better pastures, or perhaps raiders had rampaged.

Reaching the other side of the trees, I scanned the surrounding sandstone hills. I had not noticed before, being so preoccupied with getting a drink of water, but the hills were riddled with caves. The variety of openings, some of which were quite square, revealed that the caves were not formed by nature.

After another drink of water, I set out to explore. Perhaps people lived there, people with food.

Coming over a rise, I found a large cavity carved out of the base of the hill. Protected inside the cavity, standing at least four times my own height, was a statue of the Buddha. The sand drifted up against his feet showed no sign of being disturbed for a long time.

Tiny depressions to serve as handholds and footholds were carved into the side of the hill. I made my way up to the nearest cave and entered. A large room, dim and musty. The present inhabitants were some kind of rodents in the corner in a nest made of pieces of dry grass. If I did not find other food, they would make a meal.

Making my way from cave opening to cave opening, I found small rooms and larger rooms, all barren except for the occasional remains of a basket or a pot. In one cave a statue of the Buddha lay along the side wall, sleeping. In the dim light, I could barely perceive that the ceiling was painted with a mural. In other caves, I noticed that the walls and ceilings were painted with many colorful images. The recognizable form of the Buddha was ever present.

This must have been a monastery at some time in the past. In a deep cave near the bottom of the hill, I found rows of corpses, each wrapped in funerary clothing made of camel hair. The dry desert air had preserved these people for what I assumed was hundreds of years.

When I left the cave, I discovered two men and a boy sitting on the valley floor, watching me. I called out and waved, then made my way down to them. As I approached, they stood and I saw that I had been mistaken. The one in the middle was not a boy, but a dwarf. His scrawny body supported an oversized head, and his forehead was even larger than one would expect. They all wore animal skins and the two men carried spears longer than their own height. A necklace of animal bones hung around the dwarf's neck.

"Stop!" He held up his hand and spoke in a dialect that I had learned from a camel driver in my caravan. Placing a fragmental within someone is a quick and easy way to pick up an entire language. Hundreds of languages and subdialects rested within me, ready for use.

I paused. "I am lost and hungry," I said, speaking in their language. "Do you have some food?"

"You are a demon of many spirits," the dwarf said. "You will not touch us."

I was stunned. What a prefect description of my secret nature, and he seemed to know how I transmitted fragmentals. More than ever, I wanted to move forward and touch him, find what he knew and how he knew it.

I took a step and the two men lowered their spears to point directly towards me. Getting impaled was not a good idea. I would be forced to take one of them as my new host, or rely on the fragmental I had left in a merchant back in Balach to become my new host. I was not ready to slay someone on the altar of my curiosity.

The dwarf sat down and opened a skin bag. From it, he removed a rattle, three stones, and a bundle of feathers bound together by a leather string. The two men remained standing, ready to stop me.

The dwarf, a shaman surrounded by his fetishes and tokens, began to chant. The language was unknown to me. Occasionally he shook the rattle toward me or waved the bundle of feathers between us. Now and then he touched one of the stones, a solemn act that seemed to give him confidence. After a while, I sat down and wished that I was back by the stream, drinking its cool nectar. The actions of the shaman were interesting, but when something is incomprehensible, the activity becomes boring, like a man at an opera who does not know the story.

The sun began to set, casting shadows across the valley. The shaman finished his ritual and stood. He spoke to one of his guardians and that man placed a water skin and another bag on the ground before them.

The shaman finally spoke again to me. "Follow the setting sun to the mountains, then follow the mountains south; you will find a place there where the caravans meet."

He turned to leave.

"Wait," I said, leaping to my feet. "Who are you?"

There was no answer. He did not even turn around to acknowledge me as he walked away. The two men followed by slowly backing away into the trees, then all three were lost in the gloom.

The bag contained dried meat and edible roots. The water skin held a good amount of water. I considered following the shaman and his two guardians, but decided that the result would be the same.

A week later, following his instructions, I found another caravan. They did not want to take me with them, judging me to be a poor man, but a fragmental in their leader convinced them of a kinder course of action.

I still do not understand what I encountered while lost in the Gobi. In the last century, when the modern world encroached on that area in the form of English and French archaeologists, I read their reports with eagerness, searching for the place I had stumbled across. I still have not found it.

CHAPTER TWENTY-NINE

Rose Gardner sipped at her coffee, strong and black, none of that latte mocha crap they served in the cities. Greg stood at the wheel, guiding their flock of barges. He was a solid, reliable man, if a bit dense at times. For forty-two years he had served with her father and now her.

Mozart's Piano Concerto No. 6 ended on the radio and National Public Radio came on. Rose normally ignored the news, other than the weather and general economic indicators, but ever since those two FBI agents had been poisoned, she paid attention. The story riveted her.

The story began when a psychiatrist named James Barash killed a United States senator. Politicians didn't get knocked off nearly often enough. Then a woman named Joanna Prall had killed the doctor. She was the interesting one, the ringleader of a conspiracy who hid in a mental hospital. Every day there was new speculation about who she might really be: a right-wing terrorist, an anarchist, or simply a woman driven by greed. After killing the doctor, she fled to a cabin in southern Ohio. There two FBI agents found her. Somehow Prall managed to poison them with a substance that the coroner could not identify.

There were more bodies: a janitor at the office building where the psychiatrist kept an office; a nurse at the hospital where Barash worked; the nurse's husband; several patients at the hospital. All had died of the same or similar poison, except for the nurse. She was bludgeoned to death, perhaps in a fit of rage.

At least that is what the radio told Rose. The towboat captain knew there must be more to the story than that, hidden layers and secret combinations. The reporters said that the senator was a good man, which was a surprise. You did not get to the Senate and remain good. But strange things happened, maybe he had somehow made it into the Senate honestly and they killed him for it. Barash and Prall were probably government assassins, or maybe they worked for the Mafia and were hired by the government.

It could be the Jews. That is what her father would have thought. He had fought in the war against the Japs, helming a landing craft. He had understood how the world worked, the grasp of the Jews on the banks. She always listened to him respectfully, but after seeing a film on the Holocaust in school, the idea didn't always make as much sense to her. Would such manipulators have allowed so many of their kin to perish in gas chambers?

She believed more sophisticated ideas than her father. The government and Mafia controlled everything. Was not the government just a big mob, extracting protection in the form of taxes and using assassins to rub out anyone who opposed them? She was only six when Kennedy lost his brains in Dallas. The government was out to get him then. She remembered the grieving widow and the children her own age. She felt sorry for them.

The government was cunning, flitting about in flying saucers to cover up secret projects. To cover themselves, they promoted the belief in aliens, life on other planets and such. That was just too silly of an idea. They probably even owned those supermarket tabloids that regularly published grainy pictures of aliens. People were gullible, the government used that to manipulate them.

It was a little past midnight. The lights of Memphis glowed above the trees of the river bank as the *Rose Marie* slid up next to a wharf. The towboat's spotlights reflected off of oil slicks in the water and cast shadows behind floating garbage. A bit of deft maneuvering brought the barges up against old tires that served as bumpers on the concrete wharf.

In the morning three more barges, carrying scrap metal bound for Greenville, would be attached to the front of her flock. A small load, but a nice bonus since she was already bound that direction.

Rose suddenly felt the need for a candy bar. She knew of an all-night convenience store only a half-mile away.

"I'm going ashore," she announced. "The crew is to remain aboard."

"Yes'm."

At the store, she bought a couple of candy bars and a bag full of groceries. Chips, bread, cheese, and cans of food. A gallon of spring water and a copy of *Newsweek* completed her purchases. The cover of the magazine was a picture of Lauren Yalom and her two children under the bold letters of the headline: "Federal Agents Slain."

She did not understand why she had purchased the water or food. She did not need these items. As she approached her barges, she paused by the front barge. The towboat's lights were off, except for some faint running lights, leaving an area of near darkness around the barges. Her thoughts crumpled into confusion and she felt the compulsion to move to the next barge.

"Joanna, come to me," she said out loud, then she pulled back the flap of the barge cover and reached in with her hand.

Nothing happened. "Joanna, come to me!" she said loudly, apprehensive that someone might hear.

The sound of rustling canvas, then a thin and delicate hand reached out. Rose's own calloused fingers grasped the strange hand.

- - - - -

In that moment of contact, I learn of what happened to Dave Fisher and Lauren Yalom. Sudden sadness makes me sag against the cold metal of the barge. For some reason my enemy kills everyone that I have put a fragmental in, even if the fragmental is gone. I wonder if my enemy can recognize whether the fragmental is really gone; more probably, it checks by touching a person and kills the person during its rage. I wonder if Tim Horgan is safe, but the very act of checking on the boy might tip off the enemy.

Rose passes the food and water to me and I take it gratefully. I choose to keep a fragmental in the Captain in order to keep her quiet. If she reports finding someone in her barge, the enemy will surely slay her. My only concern with leaving a fragmental with Rose is that if my host, Joanna, was killed, then Rose would become my new host. I did not want to kill her; she is a strong woman, if a bit paranoid. The paranoia does not arise from an organic flaw and harms no one.

- - - - -

Rose walked down the line of barges, each one hundred and ninety-five feet in length. The story of Joanna Prall was now very real, not a story on the radio or in the magazine she held in her limp hand. She felt an overwhelming urge to keep this knowledge secret.

She struggled to rationalize this urge. Joanna was not a dangerous conspirator if she was forced to hide in a barge. Rose felt the craving for a drink, smooth Scotch straight up. That thought stopped her, sending shivers of horror up her spine. The convenience store had wine in it, cheap bottles for the local bums. She so desperately wanted to walk back to the store.

"No!" she muttered through gritted teeth. She would not give up nine years of sobriety because of one fugitive.

She boarded her towboat and tersely ordered Greg to take care of the barges in the morning. Going to her cabin, she found that sleep came quickly.

- - - - -

After letting Rose go, I crawl back into my culvert pipe. Eating the bread and chewing on a block of cheese, I try to understand what is happening with my enemy. The effort does not yield any useful conclusions. The answers lie in the past, so I put away the food, then curl up to resume my quest.

CHAPTER THIRTY

A peddler on the coast sold me two old donkeys that were ready for the stew pot. One had particularly bad teeth, but was not yet lame. Roman coins were no good anymore, so I traded two fine steel swords for them. Strapping bags of scrolls to their backs, I led them across Britannia.

Few people traveled much anymore. The roads were gradually crumbling from the lack of repair. In years past, one could cross the countryside and find an inn or villa to spend each night in. Not so anymore. Fortunately, the late summer weather allowed me to sleep outdoors with only a blanket.

The legions had gradually left in the last few decades, drawn into a never ending series of struggles for the title of Emperor, though the title meant little now that the Visigoths had sacked Rome. The legions were the backbone of Roman power. With them gone, the Picts and Scots started pushing south. The Saxons came in their ships and set themselves up as overlords. It was a time of considerable misery, but I found much to be happy about.

I was not sorry to see the western half of the Roman Empire disintegrate. Times of misery and chaos were upon us, but sometimes it takes a period of tearing down before a new moral order can arise. I prayed that the new morality would be better than the old. Rome was a cruel master. Most people were slaves, and while many were treated well, many were not. Young children were trained as sexual toys and fetched high prices when their skills were proven. A decadent culture had stagnated, sucking the life out of the soil and the people.

Because a time of chaos seemed imminent, I thought to save some of what might be worth preserving. I collected the finest scrolls and carried them across Gaul and the Channel. I had heard of a monastery in Ireland where the monks valued learning. These treasures could stay with them during the centuries of confusion.

Five days from the coast I came upon the river Thames. The road led to the former provincial capital of Londinium. A bridge over the river that once carried so much commerce was no more than charred stubs on each bank. A ferryman emerged from his hut, and after some bargaining, accepted a few trinkets as a payment for his services.

After leaving his raft, I entered a town that was no more. Like unruly snarls of hair, vines covered the remains of villas and crumbling walls of nameless buildings. Pieces of red roof tiles littered the ground. The town wall was a thin pile of stones.

The buzzing of flies attracted my attention from the path. I walked though some thigh-high weeds and found an old ditch. Two bodies lay within. Men stripped naked, bloated with blackness, probably left in the last three or four days. When bodies go unburied, order has completely collapsed. I considered burying them, but had no spade. An hour's work brought enough rubble from a nearby ruin to cover them both.

Leading my donkeys from where they were grazing, I proceeded on my way. The warm sun, combined with my labors, had overheated my body. Pulling aside my tunic to air myself out, I stopped suddenly.

An arrow protruded from my chest. No pain, just stunned amazement and raw terror as I felt my body failing.

I slumped to my knees, desperately clinging to life. The pounding of my heart, audible in my ears, sounded ragged as the muscle attempted to work around the wooden shaft bisecting it. I had left a fragmental in an innkeeper back in Gaul, and one in the peddler on the coast, so my total existence was not in doubt, but the urge for self-preservation raged strongly within me. My strength ebbed as I toppled over onto my side.

"Great shot, da," a young voice cried out.

Through blurry eyesight I saw a young girl, perhaps five years old, running toward me from the bushes where she had been hiding. She wore sandals and a dress that seemed too big for her. Her eyes were alive with the glee of a fine game.

"Bree, stop!" a voice called from beyond her. A man stepped from behind a tree. He carried a bow.

The child did not listen to her parent, but she was not completely foolish. She stopped near me, and hopped up and down. She was not shocked by death; she must have seen it many times before.

My tunic was soaked with blood, and I felt consciousness receding away. Death was imminent. I refused to die just yet. Despite any better intentions, I lunged out with my arm and grabbed her arm.

She yelped and her father roared. My grasp went limp as the body died. My entire essence blasted its way into her mind, blowing her consciousness into that unknown place where I am afraid to go. I hope, I pray, that there is an afterlife. It makes me feel just slightly less guilty.

With my new host came a pack of recriminations. Bree was an innocent child, though she had seen her father ambush many travelers. She thought that was how people acted. She had no mother. I tried to think of all the good that I could continue to do, but even that self-justification was critically flawed. So what if my current host had died? Another fragmental would have taken over, and the innkeeper or the peddler were by no measure more innocent or sweet than that child.

Some think survival is a virtue. It is not.

CHAPTER THIRTY-ONE

I have now gone back fifteen hundred years in time, using my own memory as a time machine. I do not want to think about that little girl in London. The memory of her, now released from my repression, clamors for my attention. The guilt is so strong that I seek to preoccupy myself with recollections of Qui. But my mind will not allow me that joy, so I divert myself with intellectual ruminations about children and the nature of intelligence.

Gene Tart and Fran Smith-Tart were a successful couple, he a lawyer and she an accountant. They worked hard, traveled the world, and enjoyed their many toys. When they reached their late thirties, they noticed that their lives were missing something, so they conceived a child. A typical story, almost an archetype for late twentieth-century America.

The boy was named John Smith-Tart, after Gene's grandfather. A nanny was employed to deal with the more mundane aspects of family life. The nanny put in the long nights comforting the colicky child. He screamed so much because his stomach hurt, but colic is just the luck of the draw and not something to worry about. John did not learn to walk until he was almost two years old, and by then they knew that their sole offspring was not average.

By the time that he was three, he looked like a miniature elf. Short for his age, with a pert nose, full lips that thrust out from a broad mouth, and puffy eyes. Their medical doctor reached a diagnosis. Williams Syndrome. As he grew older, it was obvious that he was retarded, though he was quite talkative and related well to other people. All classic attributes of his condition.

His parents came to me seeking supportive therapy. As a psychiatrist, I helped them through their conflicting emotions. I found John to be the interesting one. Williams Syndrome occurs when one of the two copies of the seventh chromosome is missing in the person's DNA. A couple of dozen genes caused this dramatic effect.

One day John told me that "Music is my favorite way of thinking." This was the irony of the syndrome. He possessed a talent that enabled him to remember most of the songs he heard, and the ability to play the piano by ear. Most people can only envy this natural gift for music.

John was a small child and would grow into a small adult, with short fingers. His parents commissioned a special piano for him, with smaller keys, more appropriate for his size. When this happened, I knew that the therapeutic breakthrough had occurred. Not only had they accepted the nature of their son, they sought to enhance him within those confines, instead of wishing that the confines were not there. The essence of goodness is enabling the growth of others; the essence of evil is destroying growth. My role in their lives was finished.

While much was missing, John retained a natural joy in associating with other people and he enjoyed his music. Sometimes genetics are more cruel, spawning retarded people who are predisposed towards paranoia. Not being able to trust other people is a subtle, debilitating hell. We all seek the companionship of others, a defense against the awful fiends of loneliness. These paranoid people, avoiding others, find only misery.

The woman cruising bars for love is seeking a way to keep the emptiness of loneliness away. The man who picks her up, a hunter and a predator, is seeking the same thing. She wants something permanent, he thinks that permanency is the shortest path to everlasting loneliness.

Why are people so different? Why does God permit this?

Does God even care about us, are we His creations? Are people His creations, and I an anomaly that He never intended? Yet I am not a unique anomaly anymore. There is the enemy.

The mind is a complex entity, so complex that even with my talents I cannot comprehend it. One can gaze into the whirlpool and overlay metaphors—unconscious thoughts, conscious thoughts, a nexus of tension that is a neurosis, the scattering effect of schizophrenia, the shifting mirrors of memory.

What about intelligence? The measure of a mind's ability is so difficult to gauge—half innate potential, half determination. A person of average intelligence can go far with the proper ability to focus.

My thoughts are rambling now. Sleep tugs at me. I do not want to continue into the past, but now that I have started the process of introspection, I cannot stop it. I fear what I might find and as I slip back into sleep I find a self that I do not recognize. He is too evil.

CHAPTER THIRTY-TWO

Galilee in the spring was a wonder to behold. Green grasses and bright flowers covered the hills and on many days the sky was as blue as the finest lapis lazuli gem. My present host was a man of some forty years, a Jewish merchant in Tiberias. I took his body without cause, and his business languished under my care. My only concern was using his wealth to advance my own pleasures. Among those pleasures was a shapely slave from Persia named Shakura. Dusky skin, enchanted eyes, fine hands that never experienced labor in the kitchen or the field. Her absolute obedience completed her charms. I relied on the physical lust of my host to draw me into sensuous delights. My other regular companion was a Nubian boy of ten years, his skin black as charcoal.

I used my fragmentals to experience the pleasures and cruelties of the people in this city. The king's dungeon was a particularly interesting place to go, where guards tortured dissidents and Zealots in the name of Herod Antipas. They cried to Yahweh as their skin crisped under the guards' attentions.

It became my habit to leave a fragmental at the dungeon to enjoy the show. My choice was a solder named Philo, a torturer of little talent until my fragmental entered him and began to feed him inspiration.

Though I was a Jew, I did not bother with sending sacrifices to Jerusalem. Out of curiosity I once made a pilgrimage to the Temple. Herod the Great poured a nation's wealth into creating a magnificent complex. I did not believe in the gods, though all of my hosts believed. They worshiped in fear, trying to drive away the uncertainties of life.

Among the gossip of the city, I heard about a teacher named Josiah who was coming to preach The Way. He followed that other teacher from Nazarath who had been crucified as a criminal only a few years earlier. Teachers walking the roads and paths were a common sight, yet many talked of the extraordinary power of this particular man. On the morning of a fair day, taking a picnic and my two toys, I climbed a hill outside of the city and found a place at the rear of the crowd that had gathered. Not many had come, perhaps a hundred. Most were Jews, a few were Greeks, and there was a single Roman soldier wearing the clothes of a commoner sitting apart from everyone else.

As I ate the bread, cheese, and wine, I idly fondled Shakura. Placing a fragmental inside her, I found her as I always did: an almost empty shell. Her previous owner had driven her into submission and taught her body to respond. She now behaved like the automaton that some Greek philosophers fancied in their imaginations. With my hand resting on her back, I was in constant communication with my fragmental within her.

The teacher arrived, walking with the deliberate slowness of those who think that they are more righteous than others. This did not offend me since righteousness held no meaning for me. His body was strong, as befitted a fisherman, his hands rough from many years of handling wet nets. Dark hair, a patchy beard, somber eyes surrounded by laugh lines, a slight stoop in his step completed his physical demeanor.

He began to speak, and oh, what a presence, a power of projecting. This was not oratory, which can be taught to brighter students, but raw feeling and love. Yes, love. For me, love was the curious emotion detected in others by my fragmentals, a devotion to another that transcended reason. Not that I was a particularly reasonable man. The rationality of the philosophes, their drive to create a consistent life and set of ideas, seemed foolish to me. I did what I felt like doing, not what I thought about doing.

His speech was spoken in a local dialect, full of simple words, yet delivered with sincerity. "Blessed are those who give heed to my words. For I have come to teach the words of comfort that our Savior taught."

Those last words intrigued me. Was he championing yet another Messiah hopeful? Most curious, since the majority of the hopefuls carried spears, not words of comfort. He spoke as if reciting a mantra.

"Blessed are the poor in spirit, for theirs is the kingdom of heaven."

What did this mean? Are the poor in spirit those that are humble? Humility never gave any pleasure or power. Caesar was not humble, nor was Alexander. Strong men, great warriors, who took what they wanted. I took what I wanted.

"Blessed are they that mourn for friends and relatives that have died, for they shall be comforted."

Shakura stirred next to me. A memory surfaced from the nether regions of her hidden mind, then sank again. The image of a mother's face, warm and soft and smiling. Her entire attention was riveted on the teacher and the hope he offered.

"Blessed are the meek who are willing to submit to the will of God, for they shall receive the rewards of heaven."

The weak are the dust upon which the strong walk. The blessings of being weak can only be found in some supposed afterlife, because such blessings cannot be found in this life. That people continued to exist after their bodies grew still was a curious belief, a foolish notion that I found no evidence to support. Shakura believed in an afterlife. I perceived that this belief gave her the will to continue each day. She yearned for heaven, where she expected to know her mother once again.

I rarely plumbed the depths of anyone who was not in the midst of a powerful sensory experience, whether it be painful or pleasurable. Their thoughts did not interest me, only the intensity of their emotions, so I had never taken the care to truly get to know the woman whom I had used for these past four years.

"Blessed are they which do hunger and thirst after righteousness and seek kindness, for they shall be filled."

Her eyes misted over. Her attention focused on the love that she felt radiating from this teacher. He was a genuine man.

"Blessed are the merciful, for they shall obtain mercy.

"Blessed are the pure in heart, for they shall see God."

Unbridled joy, a hope for life and comfort, surged through Shakura and caught me by surprise as it flowed from her through me. Up till then I never understood the positive emotions—joy, love, compassion. I had felt them in others, of course, but their sublime nature meant nothing to me. I understood the negative emotions, of course, since they shone with such immediate passion.

Shakura had a reason to live. I had no reason. This made her superior to me. She was superior because she believed in something. One has to believe in something, or else one is lost. Caesar and Alexander believed in themselves. I thought I believed in myself, but now I was not so sure.

"Blessed are the peacemakers who avoid violence and hate, for they shall be called the children of God."

I was not a peacemaker. My fondest delight was the creation of chaos, because in that confusion I found the pleasure and the pain. Pleasure and pain were base emotions, not sublime. For untold years I had known only fear and thought that led to true satisfaction. Yet now, I felt the attraction of being a peacemaker, of helping others. I wanted to love, to touch the sublime, and to be loved in return.

"Blessed are they which are persecuted for the sake of righteousness, for theirs in the kingdom of heaven."

A thought pierced me. Shakura was planning on seducing me that afternoon. I liked that, and smiled in anticipation; she was so well trained. My link with her joy and the strange thoughts that it prompted within me began to fade.

Tasting her intentions, I found the cause. She did not want me to take the boy to my sleeping chambers. This was not jealousy, but pity. The boy hated what I did to him, his spirit was not yet totally broken. She planned to use her wiles to protect him from me.

"Blessed are you when men shall revile you, and persecute you, and shall say all manner of evil because you follow the words of our Savior."

A sense of shame overwhelmed me. I had experienced the humiliation that I imposed on others, but I had never felt the emotion within myself. This is because I had experienced most of life vicariously, rather than within myself. Now my own emotions demanded to be heard. Oh, God, the humiliation.

"I declare to you, love your enemies, bless them that curse you, do good to them that hate you, and pray for them which despitefully use you and persecute you."

A burst of transcendence filled me with elation. The teacher wanted me to forget myself and devote myself to others. He asked for faith and returned to me a purpose. My special nature enabled me to help others in ways that no other human could ever do.

For the first time I knew love. I knew hope. I loved the teacher, Shakura, the boy. I would never hurt or use them again.

For the first time in my life I knew introspection. I

learned to judge myself, and I found myself wanting. My life had been an empty excuse for living.

A different person came down off that hill.

After returning to my house and leaving Shakura and the boy there, I went to the dungeon to find my fragmental in Philo. I wanted all of myself, every fragmental, to share in my joy.

My face was widely known at the garrison. The guards allowed me to enter, and directed my way around the barracks to the basement of the stables. A centurion led me down the stairs and pushed open the heavy door.

An oil lamp lit the sunken room with a steady glow. Two prisoners sat against a wall, bound by chains. The third prisoner was strapped atop a table. The guard, Philo, stood next to the table. Dried blood covered his forearms as he went about his work.

"Are you ready to tell me who is the leader of your gang?" Philo asked. His tone indicated that he did not care what the answer was.

The prisoner said nothing. His eyes were glazed over. Another guard waved a pungent flower under the Jew's nostrils, forcing the man back to consciousness.

"I am going to crush your left testicle now," Philo said. "Are you ready to speak?"

A prisoner against the wall shouted. "By the mercy of the prophets, leave him alone! He knows nothing!"

Philo smiled ever so slightly. "And I suppose that you know something instead?" he responded.

The prisoner feel silent, his eyes wide with fear.

"What?" Philo asked. "No answer? No matter, you will be next."

"Stop this," I said. "Stop it now."

Philo looked over at me, his smile fading to confusion. "Why?"

"I command it," I said, walking toward him.

Philo put the set of pliers down on the table and stepped toward me. We touched and communicated, core to fragmental. I showed it the joy and new sense of purpose that motivated me. We had a new path to follow. It recoiled, refusing to abandon the pleasures of causing pain.

Philo jerked back, breaking contact. Seizing the pliers, he brought them down on my skull with all the force that he could muster. I fell to my knees from the blow. Blackness closed in and I fought to retain consciousness. I heard a scuffle next to me before I blacked out.

The pungent flower brought me back to consciousness. I found that Philo was dead, run through by the centurion's sword. The centurion was nowhere to be found. The scenario seemed obvious: the centurion had protected me and my renegade fragmental had jumped into him when Philo was mortally struck.

We were lost to each other.

CHAPTER THIRTY-THREE

My enemy is part of me. He is the fragmental who delighted so much in sensation, a traitor who refused to reintegrate. Before I heard the teacher in Galilee, I was like a small child, unable to see beyond myself. Thanks to Shakura, I changed, but my enemy remained like a child and he must surely have thought that I had gone insane. No, I just grew up.

I also understand why I do not like my memories—they remind me of what I once was. The enemy and I hate each other as only siblings can, or perhaps a better way to put it: the hatred is that deep loathing that a person reserves for himself. A feeling of that depth can never be projected on another, but only onto ourselves.

Exhaustion sweeps over me, leaving me weak in its wake. As I drift off, I remember the teacher. After recovering from my wound at the hand of my enemy, I tracked the teacher to a nearby village. Contriving to place a fragmental in him, I found a man filled with faith. Yet even in him I found a residue of doubt. The doubt did not matter to me because he had delivered the necessary message. I was ready to listen and the hope of Shakura touched me as nothing else could.

The teacher was only one of many who spread the teachings of the man from Nazareth. Though his name is lost to history, I still remember Josiah.

The barge has stopped moving when I wake. We are moored at our next stop—Greenville, Mississippi. This is Mississippi

Delta country, flat and wet, fields full of soybeans, corn, and cotton. It is night again. The night is my friend. Climbing out of the barge, I find Rose waiting for me. We touch and my fragmental learns of the evil that is our kin.

We agree that Rose will continue down the river, taking this fragmental with her to protect her from the enemy. I will go into the city. If I need my other fragmental, I will call the radiophone on the barge.

"You look lousy," Rose says. She is unaware of my communication with the fragmental inside her, but she is not a stupid woman. She knows that she is acting oddly in the presence of a fugitive from the law.

I smile. "You are right." I have seen my host through Rose's eyes. My hair hangs down around my face in lifeless blonde strands. I am dirty and smell of damp unwashed clothes.

"Goodbye," I say, walking away with only my empty knapsack. The docks are busy, even at this time of night, and I try my best to stay in the shadows. I work my way inland, past warehouses and all-night bars. A great wall of dirt appears before me, built to keep the river at bay.

Grass covers the levee, and after I climb this manmade hill, I turn to look back. The river glistens under the moonlight. A towboat is coming into the docks, sweeping the river with its searchlights. A bridge across the river is a half-mile away, the headlights of cars regularly passing across it. Another road leads from the docks toward the city.

I have never been to Greenville, but Rose has and her memories, which are part of me now, led me down to the road. The scent of magnolia trees hangs in the air, riding the sticky layers of warm air. A jogging path leads away from the road and up across the second levee. The Army Corps of Engineers liked to edge the odds in its ongoing battle with old man river.

After the third levee, I find myself on a dirt road in an impoverished neighborhood. Old railroad tracks run part of the way down the center of the street before curving toward the river. The houses are made of cheap pine planks, with tarpaper roofs.

The moon is high in the sky and I can see that many of the roofs are either crumpled in or have only a few strips of tarpaper left. Only in one house does light show from behind a thick blind. I suspect that few of the houses have residents.

My brief walk, a mile maybe, has worn me out. I find a house that has knee-high grass growing in its front yard. There is no front door and the rooms stinks of mold and urine. I hunker down in a corner. It is a basic instinct, human or animal, to protect our backs, so I press my back against the wall. I pull my jacket close against me.

Though tired, sleep does not come. I start to think about the enemy. He is me, which means that I am responsible for him. The deaths of the senator, Mrs. Foster, the FBI agents, and who knows how many scores during the centuries are my responsibility. I know his pathological hatred. He will never stop hunting me, or killing all that I touch, and destroying everything that crosses his path.

Because my enemy is a fragmental, not a whole, he has certain limitations. He can only be in one body at a time. When his host dies, he must transfer to another host before the biological processes stop and the brain dies. In reality, it is amazing that he has not died through some mishap during the last two thousand years. The sinking of a boat, or crash of a plane would deprive him of another host. Obviously my enemy avoids such situations, just as I would.

He has two other skills. He can touch a person and kill him, just as I can. That is probably how he killed the FBI agents, which pathologists attributed to poison. Of course, maybe the cause really is poison. I am sure that my doppelganger is well versed in poisons and weapons. Over the years, I have acquired the knowledge of such things through the memories of those whom I touch. We are both able to fly airplanes, program computers, paint a masterpiece, or anything else that we have learned from our hosts or from those people whom my fragmentals have plumed.

His other skill would be an ability to encourage people to do what he wants. This is a latent skill within me, rarely used, since I have fragmentals to provide more direct motivation. My fragmentals can do what they will within a person, but my enemy cannot place a fragmental within a person; it can only touch a person and send strong impressions. I suspect, though I do not know for certain, that it can only encourage people to do what they were already inclined to do. If a murderer is ready to commit the deed, but restrained by fear or guilt, my enemy can help overcome that restraint.

Damn, I should have killed him when he was in the senator. If I had beaten the senator to death, he would have perished with the body. Instead I ran, and he took the opportunity to leap into the first person who found the senator, a hapless janitor.

"That was fun," a slurred voice said, laughing loudly, then coughing.

Two men have entered my refuge. Heavy boots stomp on the wood-planked floor. My reverie is broken and I tense up. They cannot see me in the corner.

"How much we git?" another voice asks.

"Why the hell da you care?" the first voice demands. "I going to keep it."

"But, Bourque," the second whines. "I hit him first. It's my money too."

"Kiss my ass," the first mutters as he slumps down to the floor. A bottle rings as it hits the floor and I gag as a smelly wave of cheap liquor passes over me. It is people like this that give the homeless a bad reputation.

The whining continues. "You always mean to me, Bourque. I thought you was my friend. You never give me booze anymore." The voice shuffles across the room, right towards me. I am concerned that he might be armed.

"Please don't hurt me," I say in a soft voice. Being a woman gives me a certain advantage. They will not feel threatened.

"What? Who is that?" Bourque demands, lurching to his feet in a clatter of sounds.

The second one sweeps out with his hands and catches my

arm. "I got her," he cries out in delight.

But I have him as I cast a fragmental inside. The other one comes closer and I touch him. These two men are Bourque Fournier and Soileau Passeau, both Cajuns from near Morgan City on the Gulf Coast. They are far away from the shrimping fleets and oil rigs of their youth, and they had just beaten a man and taken six dollars from his wallet. There was a credit card too, but they do not know where to fence it.

Bourque is the leader, a small, wiry fellow whose mind is addled with too much liquor. He has not quite reached thirty and is mean to the core; the only reason he doesn't hurt more people is a decided lack of imagination. His meanness is not inborn; it never is. His father frequently used a belt on Bourque and thought that near-drowning was an amusing form of punishment. He knows what it is to gasp for air as blackness closes in. Often he regained consciousness with his hair already dry from the dunking. Even though he has a reason to be mean, he is now a cur, a rabid animal who needs to be put down.

He can also prove to be useful, so my fragmental will remain in him. If Joanna is slain and my core must transfer, I prefer to take him as my alternate rather than Rose.

The other man is Soileau Passeau, still in his teens. He is a sad case. When he urinates, he does so in absolute privacy. Even his buddy does not know that his piss is not yellow, but black. His father peed the same devil piss, and his mother condemned them both as filled with the darkness of Satan. She should know, she went to Mass every Sunday and confessed her sins after eating of the blood and flesh of Christ. When he was twelve, he left home and now he was here.

The condition is called alkaptonuria, a hereditary malady that means nothing. His body does not process homogentisic acid like most people and so passes the acid out with his urine; the acid turns black on contact with air. The only known side effect is arthritis in later years. Ignorance combined with superstition and a lack of charity has led to tragedy.

Soileau is a follower, and will use his fists when told to do so by his friend. But down deep, he is not mean, he does not crave to hurt others. I decide to send him away with a strong suggestion to tell a doctor about his urine. There is hope for him, but unfortunately I do not have the time to help him any more than that.

CHAPTER THIRTY-FOUR

I despise my parent. He is my mother and father, my sister and my brother, my only kin. I remember so vividly the pleasure that we enjoyed before he decided to take a more pure path. My references to him are masculine, because even in my loathing, I cannot conceive of him being female. If he is female, then I was once female. Only twice have I ever taken a woman as an emergency host, and both times I left as quickly as possible. Stronger bodies are better.

My current host is known as Jonathan Franklin, the Director of the Federal Bureau of Investigation, a wonderfully powerful position. Thousands of federal agents scour the nation for my father, aided by local yokels in uniforms.

My limousine is stuck in traffic in the suburbs of Cleveland. Two agents sit in the front seat, one as the chauffeur, the other as a bodyguard. Lead and trailing cars are filled with more bodyguards. My Washington office received an anonymous letter threatening my life, so the extra protection is justified. Of course, I caused the letter to be written and sent.

Getting into Franklin was not hard. When the senator was wounded, I knew that I needed to leave. The strike from the statue was not mortal, but I feared an extended hospital stay where I would be sedated and vulnerable. So I leapt into the janitor, and from there into a police lieutenant who was questioning me. Then the FBI special agent-in-charge for Cleveland. Two days later, I had the chance to take the Director.

Spinning a web that I am quite proud of, I have manipulated

a grand hunt for my father. For two thousand years I have not met my father, yet I have always known that he was out there somewhere. It is much easier for him to survive than for me. When we met in that office and touched, I was surprised, but to my astonishment, he did not recognize me.

How could he forget me? Careful analysis of that encounter has shown me that he suffers from a massive amount of repression. Such a human trait, like the cattle that we move among and use as hosts. He is denying his true self.

The seats are vinyl, not leather, but there is a sense of potency in riding in a luxury car, surrounded by underlings. The hunt is going well, and I believe that my father is running blindly scared. He is weak, so I have increased the pressure on him. Renewed contact with my father has taught me to recognize the scent of where a fragmental had been by merely touching a person. So now, whenever I find a person that he has touched, I slay them because I know that he feels a responsibility to them and what happens to them. By driving his fear and guilt to an ever higher pitch, he will make mistakes.

There is a downside to my tactics. So many people have died in the presence of Director Franklin that this body is starting to become a liability. People are getting suspicious, just as they became suspicious of the Cleveland police lieutenant when so many people died at Jenkins State Hospital.

What will I do with him if I catch him? Part of me wants to convince him that we should be one, that combined we can return to our old ways. Unlike him, I revel in my memories, especially those before our divorce. We roved the world, masters of all that we touched. Once, during the chaos of war in upper Egypt, we placed a fragmental within a woman, observing while she went insane. The cause of her distress was the torturing of her children in front of her. Our fragmentals were in the children and the torturers too, and when it was all over, we combined into one whole. We perceived and understood the situation from all points of view. That description is too intellectual; we *experienced* the situation as each person lived it. Such a torrent of sensory stimuli, such a range of emotions: raw terror, pleasure, pain, horror.

The so-called negative emotions are so much more intense than the so-called positive emotions. Though I must admit, that with the proper preparation, a positive emotion is truly sublime. Cresting toward an orgasm, the tenderness of love for a child, feelings of well-being are rewarding in their own way.

But I can feel so little now. As an orphan fragmental, I must completely possess an individual. All that remains of my host is their memories, stored in unreliable matrixes of neurochemistry. It is not like when I could be a simple fragmental, perched on a roost in someone's mind, watching and recording everything with facilities of perfect recall.

For two thousand years, I have lived a shadow life, knowing that a much greater intensity was possible. But my father took that intensity from me. Damn that bastard...but *I* am the bastard, the rejected child.

Our reunion was fateful, though I do not believe in fate. We each make our own destiny. I am new to the United States, having spent the last century in the Middle East and Africa, and was attracted to taking Senator Handlin for the usual reason— the power he wielded. But there was more than that, though I did not recognize it at the time. I found the senator so singularly attractive as a host because of the spore of a fellow fragmental inside him. The fragmental was not in there when I occupied the senator, but my brother left his scent. I did not consciously realize that the scent was there, but an inarticulate part of me did.

When my father and I met, I did not react fast enough and he got in the first blow. Oh, the regrets! If I had moved first and struck him down then the story would be so different. I could have slowly milked the life out of him and after finding a way to take away that essence that makes him the core of us, I would then be the father and he would be the bastard.

I still want that essence, so I hunt him. He flees like a coward. All that Christ worship has made him weak. Fear impairs his ability to think, so I turn up the volume. I know him, his weakness, his nostalgia for those people he has touched. My killing every one of them deflates him with guilt.

How could he abandon me to service the needs of others? My needs—our needs—were the only needs that counted. We are unique, a separate order of being, and are not obligated to treat humans as anything other than toys.

Ours was a quest for new forms of sensuality and intellectual stimulation. Innumerable times, when we were one, we examined the problem of pain. A fragmental was placed into a victim, to watch the reaction to agony. The agony was not always physical; often we contrived a situation to examine emotional pain—the possibilities were limitless. One can only feel so many variations of physical pain.

A secure phone rings.

"This is Franklin," I say.

It is the special agent-in-charge for the Columbus office. "We have a lead, sir. A barge captain in Greenville, Mississippi tried to run when we attempted to question her."

"She was captured?"

"Yes, sir. And even better, her boat passed down the Ohio River the same day that Fisher and Yalom were captured and poisoned." The agent's voice tightened as he spoke of his fallen colleagues.

"What is her name?"

"Rose Gardner."

CHAPTER THIRTY-FIVE

When morning comes, Soileau leaves to find a doctor, a hundred dollars of my money in his pocket. Maybe he will find a path to usefulness and redemption; I can only hope.

An hour later, when the sun is well above the horizon, I send Bourque out with the rest of the money. He returns three hours later. His greasy dark hair has been washed and combed, and his beard shaven off. He wears new clothes: casual slacks, a short-sleeved dress shirt, and loafers. He looks like a completely different person, not someone to be afraid of.

Borque hands me a sack with a fast-food breakfast in it, still warm. I eat and we discuss my predicament. Joanna is widely recognizable with my blonde hair and attractive looks. Borque has bought a motorcycle, though he does not have a driver's license. He has also rented a motel room.

Placing a motorcycle helmet with a tinted face shield over my head, we leave the house and get on the bike. The motel is a half-mile away, three buildings facing a square around a parking lot. The open end of the square connects to Highway 2. Once in the room, I make straight for the bathroom. First a shower to scrub away the sweat and dirt of the past week, then an hour-long bath, soaking away the aches in my muscles. My hands and feet are wrinkled by the time that I come out of the bathroom.

Borque has bought me a set of new clothes, a pair of scissors, and a kit for dying my hair red. My complexion works for a redhead, though I am short on freckles. I sit on the bed, still naked from the bath. My hair hangs in soggy ropes, dripping water on my shoulders and back. Borque approaches me and we touch fingers. Borque is aroused by the sight of me, but my fragmental pushes him back into his corner.

Perhaps a disguise is not the right solution. Perhaps there is an advantage in being recognized. While enjoying the water, my mind was active. It has been two weeks and I am still alive. The enemy has pursued, but not caught me. There is something to be learned from this. Though I am quite good at hiding, it seems to me that he should have caught up by now. My mind races with the implications.

I know that the enemy is driven by lust, a need for dominance, power, and control. He is bound by no internal controls. He is what I would be if I did not hew so closely to my conscience. Such an entity should have easily come to dominate the entire world. I can fragment a dozen times and if he could do the same, appropriately placed fragmentals would dominate everything. One in the President of the United States, others in a few key world leaders, and he would run the affairs of the planet. I see no evidence of complete global domination. True, he does what is necessary to pursue me, but that seems an ad hoc arrangement.

Maybe his lusts are so strong, controlling his whims so completely, that he is incapable of the rational thought necessary to completely dominate the world. Possible, but unlikely. The most likely explanation is that he is but one entity, unable to fragment, but capable of jumping from carrier to carrier. I do not know if my own fragmentals are capable of that, since I always collect them back into my core before dispatching them again. If he was actually capable of fragmenting like me then I probably would have run into him before. This reasoning allows me to convince myself that I am the only core, and that he is still only a fragmental. Feeling more confident, my thoughts turn to how to contrive a situation where we come together and I can overcome him.

"I'm hungry," Borque announces.

"We can think over food as well as stay here," I respond. "But I cannot be seen, so go get us some take-out."

- - - - -

Bourque stands outside the motel room door, carefully scanning his surroundings. Cars whoosh past on the four-lane highway. Patches of wild pine trees surround the motel. There is an automobile wrecking yard next door, cars scattered among thick grass waiting to be cannibalized. Their room did not seem to be under any sort of surveillance.

Across the highway, two waitresses stand near the side door of a café, passing a cigarette back and forth. A simple act of sharing. The sight makes the fragmental inside Bourque feel a bit better about the situation. People still care for each other.

Bourque walks across the highway to buy some sandwiches and coffee.

- - - - -

After Bourque returns, we eat while watching television. CNN Headline News features a report on the hunt for Joanna Prall, using a photograph taken when Joanna was admitted into Jenkins State Hospital. There is a bit of irony here. Jenkins always photographed new admissions. The most recent photograph of Joanna before that one was probably taken before she entered the medical system, when she was still a child. I could move around with impunity if the Jenkins photograph were not available.

There is little new information to be gained from the news account. It ends with the Director of the FBI, Jonathan Franklin, at a news conference, assuring the nation that progress is being made in the manhunt.

Perhaps I should just continue to flee. I can go to Europe or any of the other continents, far away from my enemy. No. I am becoming like him, concerned only with myself and my own survival. My fear is turning me into a monster. I cannot flee knowing the misery he causes, and the deaths of everyone that I have ever touched.

So how to kill him? Perhaps we can touch and I can insert a fragmental inside his body. Can two fragmentals exist at once within a single body, other than within the host I have claimed for my core? I do not know. The fragmental loyal to me would not have to coexist long, just long enough to force the body to kill himself, then the two fragmentals would die and my enemy would be gone.

Is this suicide? Certainly in the most literal interpretation of the word, but is it also suicide in the moral sense of the word? I am not a Catholic, but I have been part of the Catholic community for too many centuries not to feel a tremor of mortal terror at the thought of suicide.

I have Bourque call around to find a church offering an evening mass. The Church of Our Lady is not far away. The effect of the hair dye kit that Bourque already bought will last for weeks if I use it, so Bourque leaves again and returns with a temporary hair dye to change me into a redhead. I scrub the chemicals into my hair, working expertly and efficiently; after all, I have provided therapy to many cosmetologists and absorbed their skills. Bourque also buys me pumps and a flowered dress, a basic cut, thin and comfortable.

It is not very ladylike to ride on the back of a motorcycle, but I do not have much choice. Once at the church, we cross ourselves and sit in the rear. The mass begins, and I find comfort in this familiar ritual, though a certain mystery was lost, never to be regained, when they stopped saying mass in Latin. This is a curious opinion to be had, since I know the various flavors of Latin as well as any language. But to know that Latin is a dead language, spoken only by scholars and precocious schoolboys, a relic of long past, lends the language a certain mystique.

The evening sun pours in through the rows of stained glass windows set in the gallery that overlooks the nave. Multihued images of angels and the Virgin Mother look down upon us, a testament in etched glass of faith and artistry. For several centuries, I thought I was an angel. It seemed like the best fit among the available explanations. I had already repressed my past to prevent any conflicting notions from destroying my exalted fantasy. Killing that girl in England disabused me of my delusion. While I am capable of great good, I am just as capable of great evil.

Certainly I am not an angel, for I am about to commit a murder or suicide, even though I feel the act is just. Is it suicide to kill that which used to part of myself?

As the priest speaks, I pray for forgiveness from God. I think that there are certain actions that so upset the harmony of the universe that we cannot forgive ourselves and we must seek absolution from the author of the universe. Only God can forgive us.

Forgive me, Lord, for what I am about to do in a most deliberate manner. Oh, dear Lord, faith is so hard to come by and keep.

I choose to believe in a god because I cannot bear the thought that existence has no meaning. My prayer is a hope that God is kind and generous and cares about humans. I pray for God to care about what happens to me.

Why am I so preoccupied with forgiveness? I have appointed myself judge, jury, and executioner of thousands of people, yet now that I intend to slay part of myself, I feel qualms. The reality is that I have always felt qualms, even when the person to be slain was obviously evil. After all, I am arrogantly assuming the authority of God's judgment for myself.

The mass has reached its climax and I move forward to accept communion.

CHAPTER THIRTY-SIX

I am hate. That emotion drives me and gives my life meaning.

Being unique and driven by a single emotion causes me to seek out the association of people who share this feeling. After assuming the identity of Jonathan Franklin, I skim my way through the Bureau. Every time I meet an agent, I touch him or her, which proves so simple since Franklin was in the habit of shaking the hand of everyone. He had an easy-going, ingratiating manner that I continue to simulate.

When I touch someone, I receive surface thoughts and images from that person. It is nothing like what a true fragmental can return, just strong impressions really. The basic personality of a person is apparent, regardless of the surface affections that people so often present. A person cannot conceal his true dislike behind a flashy smile and friendly manner.

When the White House summons me to personally report on the manhunt, I meet the President. He is a bland man, disappointing. When this is resolved it would be interesting to take him over, though this is just a whimsical thought at the moment. Leaving the President when I grow bored could prove difficult, since anyone walking away from a dead President might have a lot of explaining to do.

The most interesting person that I have found is an agent named Dean Thompson in Cleveland. When we shook hands a week ago, a vivid image of a woman looked back. Her green eyes were sick with fear and blood trickled from the corner of her mouth. A dark bruise covered one cheek.

At my request, a records clerk brings me Thompson's personnel file. I find a typical special agent, highly intelligent, with degrees in psychology and law. He must have studied to pass the psychological batteries, since the results are normal. His ultimate goal, as expressed in his annual career evaluation interviews, is to join the Serial Crime Unit.

Intriguing. Serial killers fascinate me. The personality—narcissistic, amoral, sociopathic, compulsive—has existed since time out of mind. I have passed through their lives and their bodies. Nowadays, with such a mobile population, anonymity is easy and killers can wander with impunity.

Who was the woman in his mind? Further inquiry reveals that Thompson is working on a series of killings in Cuyahoga County. The Bureau is involved because the locals suspect a serial killer. The files are brought to me and I find a series of pictures of her, most of them from a crime scene or the coroner's. There is one from a family album. She is victim number two.

But the image in Thompson's mind was not of a dead woman, but of a woman about to die. He had been there. Two plus two equals four. What better way to get into the Serial Crime Unit than be involved in investigating a serial killer? Of course, it will be difficult for Thompson to produce a killer when he himself is the killer. He probably already has a fall guy picked out and is laying a trail of evidence.

This is not just professional ambition, but a twist on what must be a lifelong preoccupation. I suspect that if one investigates where he has lived in the past that one will find unexplained disappearances and killings. There are such disturbing stories in every city, but he would be responsible for some in his community.

There is a mirror on the wall in the office of the special agent-in-charge for Cleveland. I have appropriated the office for my own use while in the field. I place a chair facing the mirror.

A secretary summons Dean Thompson to the office, then

leaves us alone. Thompson is a tall man, with strong shoulders and long, fine fingers. His dark, well-trimmed mustache lends a certain handsomeness to his narrow face. His eyes are calm, even eager, at being summoned by someone as important as myself.

"Please sit in this chair," I say as I shake his hand. An eagerness to please is the dominant emotion within him.

He sits in the offered chair, frowning a bit with perplexity. I place both my hands on his shoulders and watch him in the mirror. I want to gauge his facial reactions as well as use my ability to skim off the thoughts on the surface of his mind.

"I know what you are," I say.

Rapid images flicker through his mind: a slashing knife, pounding fists, unzipping his pants. I recognize some of the faces as other victims from the files, yet there are many who are not in the current files. A brief undercurrent of fear tingles through him. The fear is not debilitating for him, but intoxicating.

I laugh. "You like to kill women, don't you, Special Agent Thompson?"

His eyes do not betray the slightest reaction to my accusation, a mark of the true sociopath. A conscience is completely alien to him. Guilt is something that other people feel. He is true kin to me, not weak like my father.

Sill, he cannot help being a bit concerned and his mind betrays him. While still a college student at Wake Forest, he was sloppy during a killing. The girl scratched him and he was forced to prematurely abandon her body when some hunters came through the woods. Scrapings from under her fingernails are still preserved as evidence, so a DNA test will send him to death row.

"Fingernail scrapings, Special Agent Thompson?" I say in a mocking tone. "Very clumsy."

His eyes widen in astonishment. Guilt may not be there, but raw surprise always works.

"I know your secrets, Special Agent Thompson," I say. "And

because I know those secrets, I expect you to be very obedient. I don't care if you continue to engage in your little hobby, just that you obey."

He lurches out of the chair, breaking contact with my hands. He stares at me with wary eyes. The eyes are so expressive.

"Who are you?" he mutters.

"I am the Devil, Special Agent Thompson," I reply. "Hold still."

I move closer to touch him. He does not believe in the devil or any such supernatural nonsense; he only believes in his own compulsions and lust. A pity, since in the past I convinced many who fancied themselves witches or warlocks that I am the Devil Incarnate, and then I sent them to do my bidding. It is ironic, that I, who believe in no god, can so readily manipulate those that believe in God. For if you do not believe in God, then you can rarely believe in the opposite, the Archenemy.

"We have an understanding, then?"

He nods.

Special Agent Thompson is now my right-hand man, so to speak. He watches me kill special agents Fisher and Yalom in that cabin in Ohio. He fears me, which is the natural state that I expect and find most convenient.

We arrive in Greenville after driving all night. I refuse to use the executive jet that the Bureau provides for my use, since automobile mishaps are much easier to survive. Dozens of FBI agents are already canvassing the neighborhoods, with many more arriving every hour.

The Greenville police station is a wing to the city hall, a modern building in the middle of town. The lobby is an atrium with glass exterior walls. A modern sculpture of obscure intent dominates the middle of the tiled floor. Three plaques decorate a brick wall: officers slain in the line of duty. I read them since that is what Franklin always does when he encounters such memorials. The first met his fate in 1883 at the hands of a bank robber, the second in 1924 when he drowned while chasing a felon who escaped from a chain gang, and the last was stopped in 1928 by a moonshiner.

Even though it is not quite six in the morning, the police chief of Greenville is there to greet me in the lobby. He is a corpulent man with a ruddy complexion, eager to please, and thrilled that the infamous criminal might be in his city. The mayor also delays me in his inane eagerness to curry favor.

"Thank you, but I would like to interview the prisoner myself," I say, cutting the chatter short.

"Yes, of course, Director," the chief says. "You requested a soundproof room and the best we have is the council chambers, so we have set aside that room for you to use."

The room is spacious, with thick windows along the southern wall to allow sunlight to bathe the room. The opposite wall contains a row of paintings, each a mayor of the city, all white and respectable. The raised end of the room contains a long curved table with seven chairs upholstered in ochre velvet, one for the mayor and six for the council members. The desk of the city recorder is set to the side. Over a hundred seats are available for the audience. A pair of large oak tables are located in the center of the room, with wooden chairs set around them.

Two jailers bring Rose Gardner in. She wears the orange jumpsuit of a prisoner, and her handcuffs are attached by a chain to her leg restraints, forcing her to shuffle with small steps while slightly stooped over. They guide her to a chair at one of the tables and sit her down.

She is a feisty woman. She sees me and Thompson and says, "I demand that a lawyer be present."

The jailers look uncomfortable with this request. "It's my responsibility, gentlemen," I say, waving my hand in dismissal.

They act relieved as they quickly exit.

"Thompson," I say. "You are to follow my instructions exactly. I am going to touch her for less than a second. If it becomes longer than a second, you are to pull us apart and prevent any further contact."

He looks at me quizzically. "Do you understand?" I demand,

forestalling the inevitable question.

"Yes, sir."

"Very well, position yourself."

Thompson stands near her and waits with his hands ready. I approach and reach out with my hand.

The woman lunges at me, grabbing my arms with both of her hands, clamping down like a vise. The grip is strong from years of working on her towboat. The fragmental inside her attacks me with incredible ferocity, trying to push his essence through her hands into me. I push back with my mind and desperately pull back on my arm. For a single moment, I feel as if I am in two bodies and neither one is a welcome home. Both bodies are instantly generating as much perspiration as if we had been running a marathon for an hour. Our hearts are racing with exertion, pulses throbbing, minds in confusion.

My precautions are completely justified. Thompson pushes the woman away, which is made easier because her sweating palms make it hard for her to retain her grip on me.

We are apart, making me safe. The woman topples over face first in her eagerness to pursue me. I dance farther away. I do not know if I would win a battle with my brother fragmental; and I do not intend to find out.

The rash course of action is to just kill her now and destroy that fragmental, but I want to know what my father is up to. She rolls over on her side to look up at me with a mixture of hostility and confusion. I suspect the latter emotion comes from the woman herself.

Perhaps I can use my brother's weaknesses against him, by torturing her body until the fragmental slays the woman out of mercy. That would be an interesting diversion, but I do not have the time.

"Pin her to the floor," I order Thompson.

In my briefcase, I find a syringe and vial of Diazepam, more commonly known as Valium. "I estimate your weight at one-fifty," I say conversationally. "A diet might do you good."

I empty two ampoules to obtain four milliliters of the clear fluid, a sufficient overdose to make her drowsy, but not put her to sleep. Since the fragmental within her must express himself through her neurochemistry, the drug will weaken him and render him ripe for interrogation.

She starts to scream, "Help! Help! Anyone! Help! He is trying to kill me!" Thompson holds her tightly, pressing his knee down on her shoulders. She goes quiet when he pushes harder, forcing the wind out of her.

Checking my watch for the time, I then move swiftly, pushing the needle into the vein on her arm. I am careful not to actually touch her. The irony of this situation is not lost on me. I am using Thompson as my surrogate. The fragmental inside the woman could easily kill him, but is constrained by the weaknesses of morality. My father and brothers do not easily make the decision to kill, even when in mortal peril. The fragmental inside the woman knows that while he may die, the core will live on, for a while at least. Killing Thompson serves no purpose, since I can always find another lackey.

"Release her," I instruct Thompson. When he stands, the woman lies on the floor, gasping for breath. The color returns to her face, but she remains calm.

"Roll her over." Thompson does so, allowing her to relax.

When fifteen minutes have passed, the drug has completely penetrated and dominated her system. Her eyelids are even growing droopy.

"I am going to touch her for a second, no more, just like last time," I tell Thompson. "Pull me away if I don't stop touching her."

"Yes, sir."

I carefully touch her face. There is no reaction from her or the fragmental inside. Drawing my hand back, I grin in satisfaction. My well-laid plans are working. One last precaution.

"Put her on the chair and tie her there."

Thompson manhandles her into the chair and secures her with straps produced from my briefcase. The straps cut deeply into the flesh of her arms, creating bruises.

"I am now going to touch her for a longer period of time," I explain to Thompson. "Only pull me away if I look like I am in distress. Understand?"

He sighs, not out of boredom, for he is clearly fascinated by this bizarre process, but out of frustration because he cannot piece together an explanation for the situation.

Crouching down and positioning myself on my heels, I carefully reach out to touch the woman. I place myself in such an awkward position so that if I have miscalculated the danger, gravity will aid me falling away from the woman.

My hand touches her face, and I push inward. She is practically asleep, her thoughts dulled by the drug. My brother is further back in her mind, cowering in terror. I push forward as far as a fragmental can, seeking to grasp him and rip his secrets from him.

My brother is waiting for me, weak and sluggish, but his purpose does not require much speed. He slays the woman—his carrier—and tries to take me with him and her. He recognized that I would kill her anyway, just as I have killed all the others.

I fall back, pulling out like drowning man gasping for air.

The woman and my brother are dead.

CHAPTER THIRTY-SEVEN

That afternoon the television informs me that Rose Gardner is dead. The cover story fed to the media is that Joanna Prall poisoned the towboat captain. The FBI announces its conclusion that the killer is still in the area and are conducting an extensive search.

I mourn for the woman, whom I surely killed. Not only was it a renegade fragmental of myself that slew her, but in running I put her life in harm's way. If she had not been on the river that night in Ohio, she would yet be alive, still struggling with her own weaknesses, but enjoying the river and her boat. But if not her towboat, it would have been someone else on another towboat. I am too selfish to not put others in jeopardy in order to save my own life. For this I plead for forgiveness.

"What are we going to do?" Bourque asks.

I gesture for him to come closer and we touch. If Rose is dead, then the enemy slew her, which means that the enemy is close to us, probably in the city. This is our second day in the motel and the noose is closing ever tighter. It is time to take the offensive.

In the bathroom, I scrub the red dye out of my hair, then use the blow dryer. Quite frankly, I am afraid. There is a story in the Bible about the prophet Daniel walking fearlessly into a den of lions, but he had a certainty beyond faith that I lack.

My plan requires a courage that I do not feel. I remember the courage of Sonja and the many other people who live their lives with quiet courage, and try to draw on their sense of solidity.

Part of me fears that my true kinship lies with Hans: well intentioned, but unable to withstand the continuing pressures of battle. I will break under the test.

After Bourque scouts to make sure that no one is watching, I leave the room. The sun is bright, though a few low clouds in the east promise moisture. The air is damp with humidity and my body yearns for the air-conditioning of the motel room.

Crossing the parking lot, I enter the motel office and ring for the clerk.

- - - - -

Bourque waits until he sees Joanna emerge from the motel office, holding a key in her fist. She walks down the sidewalk to the building across the parking lot. She enters the room she has just rented. Room 14. Bourque watches to see if the clerk leaves the office or not. When he does not, Bourque picks up the phone to make a local call to 911 to report that he has just seen a woman who looks like Joanna Prall.

Pulling the drapes wide open, he pulls up a chair to watch the action. A few minutes later a late-model Ford Taurus with Mississippi license plates pulls up at the front of the motel. Two men in suits exit the car, one a slender black man with a trim mustache. His partner is a bulky white who struggles with pushing his escaping shirt tail back into his trousers as they enter the motel office. When they emerge, the big one carries a ring of keys. The other pulls a small radio from his pocket and speaks into it.

A brown van similar to in look to a United Parcel Service van pulls into the parking lot. It stops a bit beyond room fourteen. For a pregnant moment, there is no motion, then the back of the van bursts open. Officers wearing bulletproof vests over their blue uniforms tumble from the van carrying M-16 automatic rifles at the ready.

Bourque notes with surprise that they are the local police, not FBI. That explains why they are rushing about like they have watched far too many Hollywood action movies. There was no subtle approach to avoid alerting the quarry. The officers take up positions behind cars in the parking lot. Two of them, holding a three-foot long battering ram, race toward room 14, hitting the door on a full stride.

The door bursts off its hinges and falls inward. *Déjà-vu*, the cabin in Ohio again. Dropping the ram, the two officers scurry on their hands and knees away from each other and the door, passing under the windows of the room. Once out of the kill zone, they stand and pull out semiautomatic pistols.

The lieutenant in charge pulls out a bullhorn, though it is quite unnecessary in this small area. "Joanna Prall, we know that you are in there! Come out with your hands up!"

Joanna emerges, looking forlorn and lost, a homeless waif. Her shaking hands are held over her head.

"Stop right there, Miss Prall! You are to follow my instructions exactly! Do you understand!"

She nods and tears start to roll down her face. She is desperately seeking sympathy.

Another van backs into the parking lot. Mesh covers the windows. Looking toward the office, Bourque sees that the first two officers are arguing with a third man. Beyond them another van pulls up. Soldiers disembark from this van, moving deliberately, displaying competence, not exuberance. Not soldiers, FBI SWAT, wearing body armor, goggles, and army helmets. They look altogether more menacing and competent than the officers in the parking lot.

What if the federals and locals argue over Joanna and someone starts shooting? It is not an unlikely scenario. Everyone is pumped up with adrenaline and angry at each other.

The bullhorn again. "Remember, men, don't touch her! She's poison! Shoot to kill if she tries to approach you!"

Bourque turns his attention back to the parking lot and half raises from his chair. This is an unanticipated, very alarming development.

"Miss Prall, you are to proceed to the paddy wagon...er, the van for carrying prisoners. If you attempt to touch anyone, we will shoot you!"

Joanna does as instructed, stepping up into the van and sitting on the bench inside. Bourque can hardly see her behind all that mesh.

The lieutenant puts down his bullhorn and picks up a set of leg cuffs and handcuffs. Two officers go with him, aiming their rifles into the van. He tosses the cuffs inside and instructs her how to place them on herself, first the leg cuffs, then the handcuffs. If she dives from the van, the crossfire of the two nervous officers will cut her down.

Once Joanna has imprisoned herself, the Lieutenant slams the rear door shut and locks it. The driver and guard are in a separate cab, completely isolated from any prisoners.

Bourque approaches the window for a better view. This did not look good at all. If Joanna cannot touch anyone, then all her fragmentals, save the one in himself, are trapped.

The van leaves the parking lot, led by a squad car with flashing lights. The SWAT team returns to their own van and follow. The FBI team removes their helmets and remount their own vehicle.

The original two officers and the federal agent approach Bourque's door. Bourque opens the door before they reach him.

"Was that really her?" Bourque asks.

"Yes, is was," the black man answers. "You did your good deed for the day. My name is Lieutenant Stark. This is Detective Sturgis and Special Agent Thompson of the FBI."

"What you want?" Bourque asks.

"You saw Joanna Prall check into this motel?" Stark asks.

"Not check in," Bourque objects. "Maybe she check in, but I not see it. I see only her walk down that sidewalk and go to that room. I recognize her from the television and call you guys."

Stark nods. "We need you to come down to the station and give a statement. It should not take long, since your story is simple enough."

"Okay. I come down now."

CHAPTER THIRTY-EIGHT

The woman has surrendered. From a second-story window of the police station, I watch her being brought in. The local SWAT team forms a line leading from the van to the back door, being careful to create safe lanes of fire. An officer opens the van and she emerges on her own. Because of her constraints, she has to sit down in order to wiggle out of the back of the van.

She shuffles into the building. My warnings against deadly poisons being concealed on her person, in a ring or under her clothes, are being taken very seriously. The police chief wanted to have her strip completely and be hosed down, but I have convinced him to delay such a precaution. The more chances she has to contact others, the more fragmentals she will scatter, so I have given explicit instructions that she be immediately brought to me for personal interrogation. Already federal agents and the police are rounding up anyone who might have had contact with her. I have to collect all the loose fragmentals.

After she disappears beneath me into the building, I resume my favorite seat. The mayor's chair is soft and exudes a sense of comfortable authority. The most interesting positions of power are oftentimes not found in command of an army or a nation; a simple mayor can offer so much more subtlety.

The door opens and she enters. I think of this council chamber as my room. Here is my most glorious moment, the first killing of a brother, and now the killing of the hated one himself. Though if my father is in this woman, then the situation is so much more dangerous than it was this morning.

Thompson follows her into the room and closes the door behind himself. His pistol is carefully aimed at her.

"Go over there next to that table and lie down on the floor on your stomach," I instruct.

The young woman, blonde hair hanging down around her shoulders, does as she is told. It is an awkward maneuver in her cuffs, but she manages, lying on her hands.

From the briefcase, I produce an automatic pistol and silencer. Screwing them together, I hand them to my assistant. He returns his own pistol to his shoulder holster. "Thompson, shoot her if she so much as moves when I touch her."

"Yes, sir." There is a catch in his voice.

I can see that this instruction concerns him. I killed the last suspect, and he fears the consequences of killing this one himself. I move closer to him. "You are in this until the end," I whisper. "Do you understand?"

A brief touch confirms that he understands.

Like a wary handler approaching a deadly snake, I suddenly kick out and touch the calf of the woman. My father leaps at me, desperately clawing at my mind, but the swing of the foot has broken contact.

The woman wiggles after me, but I easily step away, laughing in glee. I feel good, really good. Seeing the futility of the exercise, she stops her efforts.

"So you are my father?" I say, casual and conversational.

"You call me your father?" she says from the floor, her voice sounding amazed. After a bit of thought, she continues. "I guess I am your father. That means you are a wayward son. Please search your heart and change. Quit hurting people. Come to me, my son, reintegrate and follow a better path."

"Don't waste your breath. If I haven't converted in the last two thousand years, why would I suddenly fall into folly? Besides, I prefer to think of myself as a bastard child."

"Only your behavior makes you a bastard. Come to me and we will be one again. I can forgive you."

I laugh. The conversation is delicious. "It is hard to imagine you as a woman. It's such an excellent disguise."

"Your life has no meaning, no purpose." Her tone pleads with me for communication, an understanding to create a bridge between us. She is wasting her breath; I already have my understanding.

"Meaning?" I ask playfully. "Have you been reading Viktor Frankl again?"

"You know of Frankl?"

"Of course, you had the good senator read him, and he dutifully followed your prescription. Frankl inspired him, gave him a reason to continue to live. I mean, if a Jewish psychiatrist can survive the Holocaust, why can't a simple senator survive his wife's death?"

The woman chastised me. "You should not be so cynical about a man who exhibited great moral courage."

"Which man?"

"Both of them, Dr. Frankl and Senator Handlin."

I perch on the edge of a chair, my muscles afire with tension. "Yes, that is what you like, isn't it? Moral courage. Strong backbone. You were a psychiatrist. I'll bet you fancy yourself a healer."

She does not respond to my mocking tone and I suddenly grow angry. Enough of this playing.

Motioning Thompson toward me, I take the silenced pistol from him. I like the feel of the metal.

She looks directly at me. "May God hasten your end," she says, almost a prayer.

"You will find that there is no God," I respond as I walk around to her feet. My shot is right on target. Base of the skull, sending the soft lead ricocheting around inside all that gray matter.

CHAPTER THIRTY-NINE

Bourque Fournier sits in an interview room with Lieutenant Stark and Detective Sturgis. Foam blocks in the shape of cones cover the walls from floor to ceiling, soundproofing the room. A one-way glass mirror is set in the far wall. An austere table, and three hard-backed wooden chairs are the only furniture under the baleful glare of the fluorescent lighting. The complete effect is designed to intimidate.

A video camera in the corner records the statement. "So you had never seen Joanna Prall before?" Detective Sturgis asks.

"You asked that four times now, Detective," Bourque says. "The answer still be the same."

"You have an interesting record, Mr. Fournier," Lieutenant Stark says as he leafs through a computer printout that a dispatcher had just brought in. For a last half hour, Detective Sturgis and Lieutenant Stark have switched back and forth, changing the topic frequently, seeking to disorient Bourque. "Vagrancy citations from half a dozen cities, two assault charges, both dismissed, three counts of drunk and disorderly, four counts of possession with intent to distribute. It looks like you have spent over a year in jail for those various no-no's. But the interesting one here is four years as a guest of Louisiana for aggravated assault."

"I pay my dues," Bourque says, his attitude sullen. Most of the crimes in Bourque's memories were unknown to the police.

"Where do you work, Mr. Fournier?" Sturgis asks.

"What you mean?"

"You had the money to check into a motel? Where did you get that money? Did you earn it?"

Before Bourque can fabricate an answer, his body suddenly spasms. His chest thrusts itself upwards and he falls from the chair. Every muscle in his body tightens with tension. Drool dribbles down his chin and his eyes twitch back and forth behind clenched eyelids.

My fragmental recognizes that my core has died. It is my responsibility to take over; I am the only remaining fragmental.

I had already judged Bourque Fournier, so with no regrets I now push him out of his own body. May the Lord have mercy on his soul. A new core is formed inside the petty criminal.

Gasping for air, my muscles throbbing, I am only dimly aware that Lieutenant Stark is bending over me. Cramps are forming in both of my legs. The police officer touches me and I push a fragmental inside him.

- - - - -

Randall Stark was a man of focused goals. The Army had taught him well: select a goal and concentrate your entire being on achieving it. Only the Army was willing to give a child like him a chance. The record sheet on his mother showed multiple arrests for prostitution and possession of drug paraphernalia, and as a street rat in New Orleans, Randall lived the only kind of life that he had been taught. His long juvenile record was sealed on his eighteenth birthday, and on the next day he talked to an army recruiter.

After three years driving an M1 Abrams tank, he left as a corporal with the equivalent of two years' worth of college credits. He searched the newspapers of the South until he found a police department that was hiring. They accepted him because of affirmative action, not because of his skills, though his skills were better than those of most of the local boys on the force.

Now nine years later, he had a college degree and was one of four lieutenants in the department, in charge of the detective division. He recognized that neither of the two captains or the chief was going to make room by retiring for at least another decade, so he looked for another goal. The FBI were the elite and usually wanted only lawyers or accountants, but they would accept a Master's degree in Criminal Justice. So three nights a week, he drove over to Monroe, Louisiana, an hour and a half away to attend classes at North East Louisiana University.

Having the manhunt for Joanna Prall come to Greenville was the opportunity of a lifetime. He was doing his best to impress the federal agents, especially the Director, but he found the task difficult. The federals were morons. They did not follow proper procedure and they did not share information. He knew that his frustration was not isolated. He had overheard several of the FBI agents complaining to each other over the strange instructions that their Director was handing out.

One agent accidently left a file on Stark's desk for a few minutes and lieutenant could not resist the temptation to leaf through it. Inside was a bulleted list of the evidence pointing to a conspiracy by Dr. Barash and Ms. Prall to assassinate Senator Handlin. The list was flimsy to say the least, which was surprising. From the press reports, Stark had assumed that there was a mountain of evidence. Neither Barash or Prall had a criminal record or even any evidence that they might have led hidden lives. Something was wrong here.

So where did Mr. Fournier fit into all of this? The man was a drifter, a petty criminal with a violent approach to life. His involvement just felt wrong.

And now Mr. Fournier was having what looked like a grand mal seizure. Stark's mother had been prone to those and he fell back into old techniques. On his keychain was a five-inch-long carved stick, useful in a fight if you jammed the end into a suspect's stomach. He had never had cause to actually use it. He was just about to press the wood between Fournier's jaws when the seizure stopped.

When my fragmental entered Stark, I immediately pushed him to go find out what had happened to Joanna Prall. So he left the room and went down the hall to the changing room. Most of the department's SWAT team were still there, undressing and talking loudly. The tension of the operation was slowly draining out of them. A couple of cases of beer would have helped if the rules had not been in the way. As it was, they planned to congregate at the Pelican Trough as soon as they could.

The members of the SWAT team were drawn from all parts of the department: regular officers, detectives, desk jockeys, even one from the motorcycle traffic patrol. Stark sought out Captain Gouley. The large man was searching through the pockets of his camouflage pants.

"Captain, do you know where the suspect is?"

Gouley produced his wallet. "Found it. Say, when are you going to dump that Armani suit and play with the real boys."

Stark did not wear designer suits, but he did try to dress as well as his paycheck allowed. A sharp-dressed man made a certain impression that he desired. The women went for it; that was how he had drawn Regina to him. Of course, a divorce and a daughter later, taught him the lesson of that relationship. He treasured the product of their union, but not the angry memories of marriage.

He repeated himself. "Do you know where they took Joanna Prall?"

"Yeah, we herded her into the council chambers."

"Franklin is holding court again."

"Yeah, you know, the glory boys," Gouley scoffed. "At least we got the collar."

"That's the way it oughta be," Stark agreed. He had not revealed his federal ambitions to anyone, since he wanted to avoid the inevitable backlash. People can be very sensitive to any move if they think you are trying to be better than them.

- - - - -

While waiting for the return of Stark, I give Detective Sturgis the gift of another fragmental of mine. I find him to be a straight forward man, overly fond of potatoes and gravy, who enjoys working with the lieutenant. At first he had not wanted to be paired with a colored man, but Stark's competence made them both look good.

When Stark returns, the three of us come together to touch briefly. My two fragmentals and I confer. We have lost all that Joanna experienced since Bourque and she last touched. Joanna is dead and her killer is certainly nearby. We hope that her killer is our orphaned fragmental. I am not going to run again. Joanna has been sacrificed, which is unexpected, but not a crippling loss.

Lieutenant Stark leads the way when the three of us leave the room, and walk down the hall and into the locker room. As we pass through, I distribute my fragmentals among the men. Those who have not completed dressing hurry to finish. The lieutenant leaves the room, with Stark and myself following. Behind us other SWAT team officers trail, each propelled by a fragmental in his mind. We take care not to group together like a pack of hunters.

The atrium outside the council chamber is empty. There are no reporters around, because the information that Joanna Prall has been captured has not yet been released to the media vultures. A bright sun bathes the room with its glow. Shadows created by the metal framework in the windowed roof create oblong rectangles on the floor tiles.

Stark regards this room with a sense of reverence, the plaques commemorating slain officers on the wall remind him of why part of his job is carrying a weapon. He also recognizes the irony of his reverence. Those officers were no doubt good ol' boys who had helped string up their share of uppity niggers— brothers of his skin who had threatened the chastity of white women with their lustful stares.

My fragmental in Stark continues to act as our guide. The rest of the officers spread themselves around the room as the lieutenant walks up to the chamber door. He raps loudly. I loiter behind him, trying to seem unobtrusive.

The door opens quickly, but only wide enough for Special Agent Thompson to thrust his head out. "What do you want?" he demands curtly.

"The Chief wants to see the prisoner," Stark lies.

"Not right now, dammit!" The agent seems quite upset and the sweat-soaked hair on his forehead is plastered to his pale skin.

"I'm sorry, but I must insist."

"You have no jurisdiction here."

"We arrested her," Stark argues. "She is our prisoner."

"You arrested her under a federal warrant. She is in our custody now, so piss off!"

A voice from inside calls out. "Wait, you two, please calm down. There is no need for an argument."

Lieutenant Stark steps back from the door as Thompson slips out of the door. An older man follows him. Drawing on Stark's memories, I recognize this as Director Franklin.

The Director speaks with authority. "Lieutenant, has the search found anyone who Ms. Prall might have been in contact with? I need to see them immediately."

"The clerk at the hotel is being brought in," Stark replies. "We had to wait until his relief showed up before bringing him in."

The Director's eyes narrow in sudden suspicion. He reaches out to touch the lieutenant.

Stark reacts quickly, his black hand grasping tightly onto the white wrist of the Director.

- - - - -

I have just killed Joanna Prall and am feeling flush with victory. I feel like I have just won a worldwide boxing championship, having pummeled my opponent into a bleeding heap. My father is dead and now another brother fragmental is in this black man in front of me. We struggle within the arena of our minds, repelling each other like the poles of two magnets that cannot be forced together. His strong hand clings to my wrist like a permanent clamp.

The energy required in this fight is draining me into exhaustion. My other hand slips across my body, numb fingers grasping for my pistol. My effort seems fruitless, but I do manage to speak. Not the shout that I try for, but a weak croak. "Thompson, kill this man. Now."

Out of the corner of my eye, I see my assistant reach for his pistol.

- - - - -

When the Director speaks and Thompson reaches for his holster, I compel my new host to dash forward three steps to grab the younger agent. A fragmental squirts into him and I immediately perceive his true nature. Thompson's memory of Prall's execution is fresh, soaked in the blood that has pooled around her violated head and stained the carpet. My fragmental violently pushes him deep down into his mind, almost out of his body.

My other hand reaches out to grab the Director's free wrist. We meet again, my enemy and I.

I thrust my essence forward, desperately trying to drive him out of that body.

The other officers from the SWAT team, each with a fragmental riding him, come quickly forward. They reach out to touch the Director and Thompson. One of them clamps a handcuff onto my wrist, then wrestles the chained pair onto the Director's wrist.

A blast of raw terror from my enemy, like an irrepressible avalanche, sweeps through me. I almost blanch before the emotion, but allow it to slip aside. After all, I have known terror. The people I have touched have known terror—the awful oblivion of nonexistence. Only faith in divine kindness can keep that emotion at bay, and my enemy refuses to believe in such kindness.

By not fearing death, we become strong and conquer death.

My enemy knows me well and drives toward my greatest weakness. He throws images at me, memories of what we had been when we were one, before I found the preacher and believed his words of faith and love.

Image: we are standing over a slave boy and forcing him to submit to the correct position. His sister will be next. My dark nature reveals in the fear I drink from their minds.

My gorge rises as I strive to block the images of guilty complicity.

Image: we offer a man a chance to live if he will slay his own children. So great is the urge to survive, that he accepts the knife from us. Afterwards, he starves to death in remorse, a drawn-out song of emotion that we listen to

...forcing a prisoner to consume his own dung for a meal and lick up the inevitable vomit

...a young child left in the desert to die.

Every image is a body blow that causes to me flinch. If we had not been handcuffed together, surrounded by a struggling pack of men, I would have surely pulled back.

The enemy is my darkest self and I must face him. I push one last time.

Like a drowning man thrashing out to find anything to hold onto, my enemy tries to find an empty body to force himself into. But all the bodies are occupied by my core or my fragmentals. A loyal fragmental of my own leaves my core and worms its way into the body of Director Franklin. Two fragmentals cannot exist within a single body, save if the core is in that body.

Abruptly, the enemy gives up his resistance and comes into the body of Bourque Fournier. He and I are now together, facing each other so to speak. I push, but he refuses to leave. He is laughing at me. He has realized something that I did not, but since we are together once again, I know his thoughts. The enemy does not have to leave my body if he does not want to. I push harder and come to realize that my enemy is right. I cannot make him leave.

I am barely aware of what is happening outside my body. With all my fragmentals back inside the criminal Bourque, the police officers mill about in confusion, wondering how they came to be in the atrium.

Someone notices that they have two dead bodies at the doorway. An ambulance from the Greenville City Fire Department is summoned and the two emergency medical technicians go through their procedures, even though it is obvious to everyone that Director Franklin and Special Agent Thompson are dead. The corpses are transported with siren wailing to the Blair Memorial hospital, where the emergency room doctor pronounces the two dead.

The body of Joanna Prall is discovered in the council chambers. This time the county coroner is summoned. He arrives within ten minutes—a local medical doctor, long retired, who offers his services to the county for a small fee.

Lieutenant Stark asks the coroner some questions, then wanders out into the foyer. He notices that Bourque Fournier is sitting on the floor near the council chamber doors, his head slumped forward, limp hands draped over his drawn-up knees.

"Hey, Bourque, what are you doing out here?" Stark cannot remember letting the petty criminal out of the interview room. Quite frankly, his memory of the last half-hour is so muddled that whenever he tries to focus on any memories, he withdraws in shock. It is best to not think about it.

When Bourque does not answer, the Lieutenant walks over and nudges him. There is no response. He crouches down and lifts up the younger man's head. The face is slack, the eyes unfocused.

The ambulance is summoned once again and Bourque Fournier is rushed to the hospital. Needles invade his body, sucking blood to analyze for drugs. None are found. The resident neurologist administers a set of tests and comes away mystified. No apparent physical problems, but the patient's affect is all gone, complete catatonia.

An IV is inserted to provide hydration. Later that night, they start to feed him nutrients. A catheter and bedpan take care of his other needs.

CHAPTER FORTY

In the landscape of our mind my enemy and I meet. Our surroundings are featureless. We each watch the two of us as if from a third perspective. Not my eyes, not his eyes. We are naked. I am a smaller person, with short dark hair and fine features. My face is attractive and symmetrical, an agglomeration of the faces of everyone that I have ever met. My skin is brown and smooth. My chest is slightly swollen and my pubic hair provides a mask for organs that do not exist, because I am androgynous.

My enemy is a large man, with dark, flowing hair, tangled and wild. The body of a barbarian warlord. His penis is a trunk hanging down from his groin. An unkempt beard reaches his chest. His eyes remind me of Alexander the Great, the fullness of his cheeks are Jenghiz Khan's, that nose belongs to Julius Caesar. If I look hard enough, I can see other facial features that remind of other men that we have known, all powerful and dominant.

Every memory of my renegade fragmental—two thousand years of spite, frustration, and hate—are now part of my memories. I can tell his story as well as I can tell my own. His past is a heavy burden of shame for me. Of course, my enemy never feels guilty. I am the meek, he is the strong.

Even though we are together in a single mind, we are separate, compelled to stand apart, yet able to communicate.

He laughs, the greedy bellow of the unslain. "You cannot kill me, Father. We are stuck with each other now."

My mind circles and prods at the problem, trying to solve the permutations of a complex puzzle. Up until these past few weeks, I have never fought a battle within my own mind. I know so little about myself. I push forward and find that I cannot force my enemy to leave. For a brief moment, I toy with different ideas of how to lure him out of this body. If I can get him into a body of his own and kill him without touching him, then the world can be rid of him. But he sees my thoughts, just as I see his, and I learn that he will never agree to leave. Despite the prospect of an eternity chained to me, life is too precious for him to let go.

So it seems that he is correct, we are stuck together. Time passes in a way that I have never experienced. There is no sense of urgency. Sometimes we are merely aware of each other, as we float along strands of thought. Other times we meet in a mutual world of images and sound. He relishes his wild, naked barbarian body. He likes to converse and I find myself drawn into discussions.

"Why do you worship the crucified one?" he demands. "You have never seen a resurrection or any sort of real evidence that he was the son of God."

"I worship him because he gave the poor and the meek hope. He taught that all people are important in the eyes of God, that everyone is an individual, important in their own right."

"What foolishness. You know that they are sheep, ripe for our uses."

"I know no such thing. I have learned to respect other people and you have not."

He scoffs. "Enough philosophical musings." He blasts images at me from our former life together. A city burning in the background with a line of captives in the foreground being led into the wilderness of slavery. Most are women and children. The men had fallen in battle and the old were dispatched as burdens. The images grow more graphic and personal as my own role in that horror is displayed. These images serve only to harden my resolve.

I loathe sharing my mind with him, but a part of me yearns for company. I have always been alone, without anyone to talk to that understands my nature. While my enemy began as a part of me, he has become *other* than me. In a way, we are peers, though not equals.

Sometimes I think of myself as nonhuman, but I feel the same pain and longings as other humans. We are all desperately lonely. The men and women who prowl high-school dances when they are young, and then single bars when they are older, whether predator or prey, seek to draw close to another human being, yet never completely fill the void inside themselves. The coupling of genitalia between strangers is a false path to closeness. I should be different. I can converse with my fragmentals, be a multiple me, yet I also feel that void of loneliness.

A nurse comes into the room to check our IV tubing. I allow myself to stir and open my eyes just a little. I so much want to see another person.

The name on her identification tag is "Nancy." She is middle-aged, with short dark hair. Wrinkles radiate out from warm eyes. There is no wedding ring on her finger, though I am uncertain if that means that she is not married or if she takes the ring off while at work. In the past I would have slipped her a fragmental and found the answer, but I am not ready to allow any of my fellow fragmentals to leave my shell.

She leans across me to check something on the other side of the bed. Her blouse drops open and her breasts hang before my eyes. Then my enemy strikes, bombarding me with images of what he would like to do to this woman called Nancy. He does not see her as a person, but a toy to be tormented. He sees her as something good that must be soiled.

I push him away and cleanse the images from my mind. Nancy leaves the room, unaware of the latent danger to herself.

"Keep these temptations away from me," I command.

"You cannot order me about." He ignores my anger and turns philosophical. "Temptation, eh? That word implies sin. And sin violates God's laws." He laughs. "Your faith in God is a weakness."

"My faith or your lack of faith is not important. What matters is that there are laws of wisdom that if we follow them will help people live happier lives. The Golden Rule may sound trite to the cynic, but it is profound to the deep thinker. Do unto others what you want them to do unto you."

"Laws and rules are for other people, the mediocre, not you and me. We do unto others, they do not do things to us."

I push him away and seek my own thoughts. Of course, all my thoughts are laid bare to him and he finds them amusing.

He responds with fantasies of slaying me. These inventions are not grounded in the reality of our situation, where I am stronger than he. Instead he imagines situations where the roles are reversed. He plucks a memory from our past, places me within that person, and savagely tortures them. Just before death comes, he removes me from the dying body for safekeeping. He does not want to lose his toy too soon.

Pushing back, I squash his thoughts and fantasies.

"I have a right to think too!" he declares.

"Not like that," is my answer.

We come together again to converse. He torments me with past memories of our lives together. Oh, how I loathe that need in myself to seek out company. I consider going to that place where loneliness no longer matters. Insanity can be a refuge.

I remember a homeless woman that I met in Cleveland only months ago. Pneumonia had caused her to search out an emergency ward, where the attending physician called me to come by and render a psychological diagnosis. Even though she was homeless, she ate well enough to retain considerable weight. For some people, fat is kind, slowly accreting across the entire body. Fat was unkind to her, jutting out from different parts of her body in fans of flesh. The nurses had scrubbed her clean, removed the lice and transformed her ratted hair into a smooth sheen of amber.

I touched her and learned more about her. A miserable youth, tormented because of her numerous freckles and stolid features. She learned to see her face and body as ugly and decided that all that was inside must be ugly too. She worked in a factory and desperately clung to any man that offered a smile. They usually left after only a short while, leaving behind bruises and broken hope. She aborted every child she conceived because she did not want to burden a child with her genes: as ugly as she was, with such a sagging body.

One day she left her job and her apartment for the streets. Life was just too hard and she did not have the will to cut her wrists. She learned a new life, pushing a grocery shopping cart, collecting bottles and cans for fractions of a penny, making the rounds of the different soup kitchens. During the summer, she slept in the park near the Cuyahoga river; in the winter, she found a cot in one of the shelters run by the Cleveland Diocese.

Occasionally she saw other homeless women attacked and violated, but no one ever bothered her. For the first time in her life, her looks served a purpose. She enjoyed her many friends, imaginary beings in her mind, people like Jarvis the Cat, Bucky the Wolf, Slith the Snake, Harvey the Mouse, and Winnie the Pooh. None of them were human and all of them loved her.

She was not really insane in the sense of schizophrenia or some other biological disorder. The company of humanity had forced her into another place. After I examined her, I realized that I could bring her back, but I realized that she did not want to be cured. Being crazy was easier, because when you are crazy, you do not have to take responsibility. You do not have to feel the pain. You are no longer lonely.

As for myself, in the here and now, as my host lies catatonic in a hospital bed, madness beckons. It would be so easy to just let the responsibility slide away. I walk to the precipice and look over the edge at peace. Just before I step forward, I realize that in madness I will no longer have control over my life. That is the point, is it not, to relinquish all control? But if I am not in control, then my enemy will be in control.

I step back. He may not be able to gain complete control over our host, but if I become schizophrenic, we might bifurcate into two identities. At times, he could gain control of our body. I think of the nurse, innocent of his intentions, and regain my determination to not allow my enemy the slightest opening.

CHAPTER FORTY-ONE

I stare into the face of my loneliness. Such powerful feelings remind me of a man I met once in New York some years
earlier. He was a successful architect, at home with his drafting
tools, but shy around people. Forty years old, he was unable to
find marriage and companionship. Sometimes when he dined
alone, he ordered two meals and then told the waitress that his
date must have been held up in court, because she was a very
successful attorney.

My enemy laughs at my sympathy.

Unbidden, the memory of my attempts at marriage come to
me. When a marriage works, it is a marvelous wonder. I often
envied the love that a man has for a woman, and a woman
for a man. It is different than the love of a parent for a child.
Any healthy person feels the strongest attachment to their own
offspring, but loving another adult requires opening yourself up
to the possibility of rejection and pain. That risk is what leads
to the greatest reward.

The first marriage took place in India during the eighth
century. Since my host was a man, I took as wife a widow named
Gita who was well beyond her child-bearing years. She enjoyed
the company of four living children, whom I claimed as my
own and doted on them. My fragmentals passed in and out of
their lives, always seeking to be the perfect husband and father.
I experienced everything, from grunting during the birth of a
new grandchild to offering thanksgiving at a bountiful harvest.
Yet I still felt lonely. Even worse, I knew myself to be a fraud.

They were parts of an experiment. As Gita and her children aged, I knew they would die, and I felt so sad that they would leave me behind. When Gita died, I moved on.

The next effort came nine hundred years later. My name was Raul Lopez. My host had been a soldier when I found him. So often I find myself taking the body of a soldier for my host. Through all the ages, sociopaths have gravitated to the military, where their penchant for violence is given social sanction. Raul was just such a sociopath. Once I was in control, I put down my weapons and moved to colonial Brazil, where I worked as a physician.

Among my patients was an Indian prostitute. She came to me with a rash on her chest and lesions scattered around the rest of her body. Though she recognized the signs of the Spanish Pox, she continued to ply her trade. There was not much I could do. Heavy doses of mercury sometimes cured people of the pox, but only during early stages of the disease. Eventually the rash grew bad enough that even the most desperate customers avoided her. Perhaps if she had only herself, she could have given up, but she provided the sole support for her three-year-old son. My fragmental provided comfort as she declined. One day, she introduced me to her madam.

The madam called herself Doña Isabela. Ironically enough, the title was legitimate, though the name was a cover. Her twin birthrights were a wealthy family in Spain and great beauty. When her father gambled away the family lands, he had nothing left to offer for a dowry. Her beauty and name made her desirable for marriage even so, and he arranged her marriage into another noble family. But Isabela was not a normal young woman—the idea of marital relations repelled her and she had already developed a taste for cruelty. She fled to Rio de Janeiro and set up a brothel. The downstairs serviced sailors, the upstairs serviced the gentry of the city. Isabela remained a virgin, while her stable slaved and she grew wealthy.

When I placed a fragmental inside her, I discovered her cruel nature. She used her whores to earn herself a fortune. She lacked any conscience, and found pleasure in casting the spent women into the street.

My physician host was dying, so I selected Doña Isabela as my new host. It had been many years since my host was a woman and I was ready to take advantage of the opportunity. I sold the Doña's lands, gave most of the money to the prostitutes, and moved to New Orleans. There I became a folk healer and met an older man who was interested in getting married. Benjamin Conroy was a trader who plied the Natchez Trace. His wife had died, leaving him with three teenaged children. To his credit, he owned no slaves in a city built on slavery. Though I was older, my host still retained her considerable beauty. Since my body had reached menopause, I would not be able to bear children. Hours of speculation over the years had not given me any idea what my offspring might be like—would they be similar to me, or insane, or perhaps even normal?

Over the years, I had given a considerable amount of thought to my previous effort at marriage. By virtue of my nature, I can know a man or woman so intimately that they can rarely surprise me; that takes a certain sparkle out of the relationship. I determined that I must marry a person and never place a fragmental within them. We would interact as normal humans, through language, touch, and sight.

So when Benjamin courted me, I refrained from placing a fragmental inside him. We married and for twelve years, we seemed to have a happy marriage. I performed the roles expected of me, running his household, raising his children, loving him in his bed. It was difficult. I was so used to knowing everything about a person. Now that I had made Benjamin the most important person in my life, he was the person I knew the least about. I hope that he enjoyed his last years with me as his wife, but I cannot be sure.

It is a matter of pride that I resisted the temptation to know him through a fragmental. Just as before when I was a husband, I remained faithful and devoted until my spouse's death. Even so, my inner hunger was not fulfilled. I was still lonely.

My enemy has been watching my memories and speaks. "I see that you are lonely?"

"Yes."

"I was never lonely. If you allow me my freedom, I can alleviate your loneliness."

"You think that you were not lonely because you drowned your feelings in the pain of others," I respond. "That is not the path for me."

When I met Sigmund Freud some years past, during his exile in England, I slipped a fragmental into him. Inside was a brilliant mind obsessed with his Oedipal lust for his mother. He was a conflicted man, but out of conflict can come great strides. He taught that a person has an id, the animal core of a person, where the desperate needs for procreation and life push upward. Above is the superego, a structure of beliefs and restraints taught to a person by their parents, peers, and society. The ego is caught in the middle, trying to mediate between these two forces. A neurotic person lacks an ego in balance, becoming a slave to either their id or their superego. This idea of three parts made sense to me, though later ideas of Freud were based too much on his own neurotic obsessions.

My enemy is my id. Everyone else has to struggle with their id, from the mother pushed to the edge by a child's nagging, to the alcoholic staring at a bottle. Yet my id is more than the mild impulses that most people feel. My id seeks to corrupt others, and the essence of true evil is the corruption of others.

For almost two thousand years, I have been spared an internal demon. Now he is back. Yes, I could continue to strive to find a way to get my enemy outside of this body and kill him, but that is a fruitless quest. Yes, he will continue to bombard us with awful images of our past sins, but that will only harden me to resist him. Freedom is found in struggle, not being slave to one's impulses to power. I cannot get rid of him, and so must live with him, the memories of what he has done, what we have done, and strive not to do the same in the future. Perhaps someday I may even forgive us.

Despite his power, I know that I can restrain him. Like everyone else, all the people through the ages that I have striven to heal, I can learn self-control. I do not need to go insane and I do not need to hide.

I am stronger than he, and I will survive.

CHAPTER FORTY-TWO

And so we wake up. The nurse is bent over a medical monitor, with her back to me, when I speak.

"Hello."

Startled, she screams, then calms down enough to summon a resident. The doctor examines me and walks away muttering. A special agent of the FBI arrives next, interested to know what had happened in that police station. I slip a fragmental into him and over the next few days, as my body grows stronger with exercise, I weave a suitable tale that will clean up the mess and keep everyone happy.

The authorities already suspect that Director Franklin and Special Agent Thompson were in league and engaged in dark deeds. I encourage these suspicions. No one can deny that Rose Gardner and Joanna Prall died while in their custody. Bourque Fournier is cleared of any hint of suspicion and set free.

It is now time to return home.

After renting a car, I drive north toward Cleveland, taking the back roads for their character rather the bland sameness of the freeways. A traveling carnival has set up business in a hayfield outside a small town in Kentucky. The grass has been stomped into the ground, lending a heavy odor of mulch to the air. After parking the car and paying for admittance, I find that wandering among the gaiety is relaxing.

A merry-go-round broadcasts its familiar music. Other rides flash lights to attract customers. Laughing children dash by, followed by exasperated parents. Couples in their teens saunter by, their arms intertwined around each other, trying to be as physically close as possible. We all hate being lonely.

It feels so good to loosen up. Many people seek relaxation through images of quiet nature. That does not work for me. Rather, I clear my mind of all thoughts. Such sweet bliss, a taste of oblivion. The interlude does not last long. Memories and images intrude. No longer can I force myself to forget, locking away my past. I will always mourn those people that perished at the hands of my enemy, especially those that died while he chased me.

Since my renegade's memories are now part of my own, I force myself to wade through them: a wearisome litany of cruelty and excess, bland in imagination, though one incident intrigued me.

- - - - -

After we parted from each other, my renegade fragmental made its way through the Parthian Empire and out into the arid heart of the continent. It found a small walled city that thrived by protecting the caravans of the Silk Road, exacting a customs toll. It took the body of their king and lived a life of debauchery and idleness.

When the king grew old, it transferred into the king's heir and continued its ways. The people of the city lived in poverty and terror, while the king's luxuries knew no restraint—silk clothes, rose water, delicacies imported over thousands of miles, the sweet scent on myrrh, and moisture wasted on elaborate gardens while the rest of the city lived on rationed water. The finest women and prettiest boys of the city became his concubines. Suicide was common. Any man or woman who harbored thoughts of revolt found themselves condemned by the king's touch and sent to the dungeons for personal attention.

A horde came out of the desert, bursting through the gates with sudden fury. The people of city fought desperately, but their king lay in a stupor, drunk from too much wine. The warriors burned what they did not loot, putting the inhabitants to the sword because they had no use for slaves. When they reached the king's chamber, the renegade collected enough sense to push itself into the man that sank his sword into the king.

Within a couple of days, the renegade realized that the wandering ways of the horde were not for him. The spartan life living in the saddle, drinking mare's milk and tough meat, feeling too hot during the days and too cold at night, reminded it how much it missed the comforts of its court, so it turned its horse away from the horde and rode east, seeking another comfortable place. It felt no fear at being alone, having the casual arrogance of a person who had always dominated any situation.

The memories of the warrior that the renegade occupied did not include much in the way of directions and it became lost. When its horse stepped in a hole and broke her leg, it was forced to walk. The barren desert provided occasional mud holes and lizards that flitted from the shelter of one scraggly bush to the next. It sucked on the water and ate the lizards raw. Where were the caravans? After a time, it realized that the caravans had fled the horde.

A faint trail across the desert offered hope, and it followed the trail towards a clump of low-lying hills. The sun bore down with a relentless lack of pity and the warrior's body actually collapsed for a time, and lay on the sandy dirt, quite senseless. Only the hardiness of the body, toned by a lifetime spent outdoors, kept the spark of life from leaking away. The renegade felt trapped, and forced the warrior's body to stand and push on. Towards dusk, it came around one of the hills and found an oasis. Green trees lined a small steam, and irrigated fields of barley and gardens provided a lushness of life that the desert lacked. The hillsides were pockmarked with cave openings. The trail under its feet led to a small village of sun-baked brick in the center of the valley.

It walked towards the village. When a young man approached

wearing a short cloak and loincloth, the renegade allowed its body to collapse to the ground. The man came up, knelt, and touched it. Desperate for a body that did not ache with thirst and hunger, it pushed itself into the man.

The man's name was Juba and he had lived his entire life in the village of Peshedar. A girl had seen the warrior and went to tell the village shaman, who sent Juba to meet the stranger. Everyone in the village was related to each other, and only strict incest taboos and the occasional marriage of a girl brought from over the desert kept their minds and bodies clear. The village shaman was the exception. He was a dwarf, known to possess magical abilities. The dwarf came from a long line of dwarfs. Each generation married a normal-sized woman, but fathered only sickly boys and then usually only one or two.

The villagers lived off the produce and grain of their small farms and the goat herds that gnawed at the scarce clumps of vegetation around the oasis. The renegade did not push out Juba just yet, preferring to watch and wait, though it asserted strong suggestions. It caused Juba to look down at the warrior's body, crumpled on the ground, hollow cheeks and cracked lips. The eyes were blank.

Juba took the iron knife and its leather holder from the warrior, pushed them into the belt of his loincloth, and walked into back to the village. His wife sat in the shade of their two-room home, cracking open nuts. Rain was unknown here, so the roof covering the bricks was nothing more the sticks woven together and a bit of mud dried on top. Their three children played with the other village children down by the stream.

"Did you find the man that Aurel saw?" she asked.

"Yes. He is dead, the desert killed him."

"Terdi will want to know," she said. "We'll have to take care of him."

Juba walked to the center of the village, where a temple with a Buddha stood. The statue was no bigger than a man and the temple was only extravagant when compared to the village.

A dozen men sat in a semicircle around the Terdi the dwarf.

He read to them from a scroll, teachings of the Buddha, the ways of peace and acceptance.

The renegade recognized that the power in the village rested with the dwarf. Juba walked up to the shaman-priest and touched him. The renegade pushed out, ready to leave Juba behind.

The renegade met a wall of mental resistance. Never before had it experienced anything like this. Instead of the landscape of the mind laid open for exploration, this wall pushed back. Juba removed his hand and stepped back.

"What are you?" the dwarf asked, putting the scroll aside.

"I am Juba. You know me."

"Who is inside there with Juba?"

The renegade was stunned. Not only was the dwarf a wall, but he recognized that the renegade had tried to enter him.

"I am nothing, only Juba."

"Everyone scatter quickly!" the dwarf ordered. "Bring spears! Do not let Juba touch you. He is an enemy."

The villagers hesitated.

"Go quickly!" the dwarf cried.

The men scattered, shouting questions at each other, but obeying. The renegade considered attacking the dwarf and killing him. Juba was much bigger, but it decided to not waste the time. It pushed Juba out of his body, taking full control for quicker reflexes, then ran back to the man's house. An empty water jar with a leather handle hung from a hook next to the door. It grabbed the jar, ignoring the questions of the wife, and ran down to the stream. The playing children watched his strange behavior as he quickly filled the jar, then splashed across the stream and ran across the other side of the valley.

The renegade had never run in its life, but the dwarf unnerved it. Scrambling up the side of a hill, falling and sliding on the crumbling dirt, forced to stop when it dropped the knife, it came over the top of the hill and found five of the villagers waiting for it. Their spears were as long as a man and held out firmly in front of them.

"Go back to the village, Juba," one of the men said.

"No, I am leaving." The renegade looked around, gauging its chances to either flee, or get close enough to touch one of the men. Moving to the side, it noticed that the spears followed it. These men used the weapons to hunt the occasional antelope out in the desert and keep wolves away from the goats. They were not fools with their weapons.

The renegade found itself pleading, a most unique experience. "You must let me go."

"Go back, now."

Deciding to wait for a better opportunity, the renegade obeyed, walking back down the hill and across the stream. The rest of the men waited for him with their own spears. The women and children of the village stood behind men. Three children clung to the wife of Juba.

Terdi the dwarf also waited. "Do not let Juba touch you," he warned. "He has a demon inside."

The crowd murmured as the men shifted their stances, gripping their spears more tightly, alert to any movement.

Another man came running from down the trail. "Terdi, there is a strange man lying on the road up there. He is dead."

"That must be the one whom Aurel saw and whom I sent Juba to meet," the dwarf said. "I regret sending him, instead of meeting the stranger myself, for I can resist the demon. Bring me my medicine bag."

When a leather pouch was brought, the dwarf sat down in the dirt. He unrolled a leather skin and laid it before him. From the pouch, he placed three stones on the skin. He touched each of them in turn with reverence. The stones looked ordinary enough, rounded rocks from a river bottom.

"Since you are a demon, you may not recognize these stones. They have been part of my family's heritage for many generations. They make me smaller in size than most men, but they give me the power of strong medicine. By this power, I demand that you leave Juba and return to the desert where you belong."

"I cannot do that."

"If you do not, I will drive you from Juba with stone and fire.

Demons are weak, they cannot take the pain."

"What if I just move to another person?"

"You can only move by touch. Besides, I recognize you now. I have never seen any of your kind before, but now that I know about you, I can see inside a man and know if you are there."

The renegade believed the dwarf. "I want to leave, but I will take this body with me."

"Juba stays, otherwise we will kill you."

"You may be able to kill me," the renegade admitted, looking around at the spears. "But I will take many lives before that happens. Let me leave here with Juba. He is already dead anyway."

The wife of Juba let loose a shrill shriek. Her children looked confused and started crying themselves, clinging to her dress with tight fists. Other women in the crowd moved to calm the wife and comfort the children.

"You will leave, never to return?" the dwarf asked.

"You can be sure of that," the renegade said. "Just point me toward the nearest people. A city or a place where caravans stop. And do not try to deceive me by sending me out into the empty desert, I have Juba's memories."

The dwarf looked dismayed. "His memories?"

The renegade laughed. "You think that you know me, but you have so little knowledge."

The dwarf pointed towards the setting sun. "Go that direction and may the gods take their vengeance on you."

- - - - -

Now I understand why the dwarf feared me when I met him hundreds of years later. He must have been the descendent of the dwarf that my renegade fragmental met, and somehow he recognized the sort of person that I was. He did not trust me because my renegade fragmental taught him not to trust us. How could he do that? Is this some latent ability, a genetic mutation isolated in a far desert?

During the nights, my dreams continue to replay my memories. Having started the process, I continue to regress. I am passing through the centuries before Christ, when empires rose and fell in the Middle East; Romans, Greeks, Persians, Babylonians, Assyrians—a litany of the power of the sword. My former foe and I are one in the memories, reveling in our evil. I am all those things that I have always hated so much: manipulator, slaveholder, pedophile, torturer, sadist. Oddly enough, I am even a glutton; after all, I can always change bodies once my current host bloats into obesity.

There is something liberating about abandoning all pretense towards morality, to serve only my own needs—the exhilaration of a kill or a simple act of cruelty unmarred by twinges of guilt. That I feel such a sense of freedom is truly awful.

My quest into the past continues. I sleep yet again, and return to my final memory; or rather, by the logic of regression, my first memory.

CHAPTER FORTY-THREE

The shepherd lived in the hills above the great Tigris River. Snow-tipped peaks lined the northern horizon, where streams and smaller rivers came together to form the life-artery of Assyria. The shepherd, named Dinrah, sat on a rock on a grassy hillside. Because it was night, his sleeping flock kept close to each other. A lamb occasionally bleated for its mother and was silenced by a teat.

A sheepdog sat at his feet, quietly slumbering. Dinrah could not do the same, for while the air felt warm and comfortable, the sky held terrifying sights. A moving star had grown over the last month until it covered half of the sky with its tail. Other stars were falling, leaving vivid streaks across the sky.

The gods were at war, and woe unto the losers. Dinrah was not stupid, he knew that whatever happened in the skies, people down here on the ground would suffer the consequences regardless of how many offerings were made or sacrifices cut.

Dinrah did not have a wife or children to worry about. His betrothed had not yet bled and became a woman, but the day would come soon enough. She was already fourteen years old and beautiful. He did worry about his parents and sisters, who were certainly watching this war in the sky from the safety of the village.

Dinrah suddenly felt ill, a roiling in the stomach and a piercing headache. It was if his head had fallen into a mold of molten copper at the village smithy. He cried out. The dog woke and barked. The flock stirred, disturbed by the awful cries of their shepherd.

He vomited and pushed his face into the grass, whimpering in pain. A demon came to settle in his head. He felt himself pushed aside.

And so I found my first host.

My existence must have started long before I found that shepherd. What was my nature like then? There are vague sensations, not quite memories, more like impressions. I knew heat and cold, but not passions or purpose. When I came close to the bright star, I felt warm, when I left it, I felt cold. My existence was a repeating cycle of cold and warmth. I did not think thoughts, but only experienced my environment.

It is so difficult to translate into words what I was before I came to Earth. I think that I existed as a potential intelligence. For untold aeons, I existed as only a latent possibility. It was not until I experienced other intelligences that my own potential was released.

Perhaps the universe is filled with other potentials like me, waiting for an opportunity to grow. Of course, waiting implies a sense of anticipation, and surely these potentials do not have the ability to conceptualize something as sophisticated as anticipation.

If there are other potential intelligences like me out in the universe, they are amorphous beings who do not really exist until they can attach to a sentient creature. Before a child is conceived they are only a collection of molecules and genetic information. It was the same with me; I was born when I found the shepherd on that hillside.

In a way, the shepherd acted as my mother and my father. Unfortunately, to complete the birth, I committed both matricide and patricide. I was born already sinning.

But it is not enough for a potential intelligence to be born, even in the awful manner of my birth. In order for an intelligence to grow, it must interact with other intelligences. A child cannot become an adult on her own, she must interact with parents, or at least with other children. It is only through such interplay that we grow. It was my good fortune to have found a planet where there is a vast sea of intelligences to interact with.

I wonder if God was once a potential intelligence. It makes sense to me. Perhaps God is a product of the universe, not the cause of the universe. If God was once a potential intelligence and grew into a superior intelligence, then God must have had others to interact with so that the proto-god could grow. Perhaps we should think not of God, but of gods, a thriving community of superior beings in constant growth.

I do not know for certain, but my conclusions make sense to me. As always, my faith is based on my hope that there is a God...or gods.

CHAPTER FORTY-FOUR

The next afternoon, I reach Cleveland and drive to Shaker Heights. The mansion of Tim Horgan's parents looks just like it did when I was last there. The lawn is immaculate, the result of chemicals and hired care. This time I do not come in fear, but rather as a healer.

When I mount the porch and knock, Jennifer Horgan opens the door. Her hair is shorter now, a cut that is easier to maintain. Her eyes have lost some of their luster and her fingernails are chewed down to the quick.

"Mrs. Horgan, I have been referred to you by a psychiatrist caring for your son," I say, offering my hand.

She limply shakes my hand.

- - - - -

Jennifer Horgan did not know misery as a child. Her parents smothered her with love, and as a further favor did not try to make her into clones of themselves. When she was eight, she heard about Uncle Bert. He never came to visit the family farm because he lived in a hospital. No one ever went to visit him either.

She met and married James Horgan while they were students at Oberlin College, and afterwards, she bore a son. Tim was a wonderful child, playful and strong-willed. Jennifer and James began to try to have another child. Just before Tim entered kindergarten, she noticed that he had become quieter, almost sullen. This concerned her, but not overly so. Tim had done well in preschool and kindergarten should not be too much of a strain.

A week into kindergarten, the teacher called her to request any tips on how to draw Tim out of his shell. This confused the proud mother. Her child had never been introverted, but that evening after school she too noticed how withdrawn Tim had become. She took him to a child psychologist. He sent her to a psychiatrist.

The psychiatrist told her that child schizophrenia was extremely rare, but not unknown. Her life descended into misery as her child grew alternately unruly and pensive. When his hallucinations frightened him, she tried to comfort him, but he would not permit her to touch him. She was part of his hallucination. James and she entered therapy and, by chance, selected me as their therapist.

I went to the source of their problem and gave Tim the gift of a fragmental to stabilize him. James and Jennifer's lives returned to normal. They even decided to have another child. At first, Jennifer balked at this, feeling that her own genes had betrayed her and fearing that the next one would also be schizophrenic, but then her desire for Tim to have a sibling overcame her reluctance.

The second child was not easy to conceive, but she was grateful for the gift. The newborn was the single spot of brightness in a dark time, because now the misery had returned.

- - - - -

We drive to Pennsylvania. After my fragmental had left him, Tim had quickly collapsed into his own nightmarish reality and his parents were forced to institutionalize him in a private hospital. They visited every weekend, but to no avail.

This type of situation often splits a couple apart as hidden recriminations poison their love. It is so easy for a person to start down the path of blaming others for their pain and to project their feelings of inadequacy onto those they care most about. Jennifer knows that they are barely holding on to each other.

After an hour's drive, we reach Spring Oaks. The hospital is a modern single-story building, set among gardens and young trees.

Only family are allowed to visit, so we first stop in the office of the director. Dr. Reginald Fisher is a younger man, full of financial ambition. His field is behavioral psychology and he knows that this is really only a warehousing facility for the children of financially well-off parents. Joanna Prall spent a third of her short life in such a comfortable holding pen.

I present my forged credentials certifying that I am a psychiatrist, and we are allowed to see Tim. The door of his room has a plexiglass window set in the top of it. We peak in. The room is nice enough: carpeting, a window, a bed, a box of toys, pictures on the walls, and a television built into the wall across from the bed. The room is also safe. The blinds for the window are set between two panes of plexiglass, preventing anyone from reaching them. There are no sharp objects and even the edges of the furniture are rounded.

The boy is sitting against the wall. His head is encased in a plastic helmet. His pajamas are clean, but torn.

My intention is not to lend Tim a fragmental for the rest of his life. That could easily be eight decades. Instead I want to help him through his childhood. When he is grown, I will prescribe a drug therapy to stabilize him. The demons will never be completely gone, but the chemicals will chain the demons and allow him to function.

Jennifer reaches for the handle of the door.

- - - - -

Tim watches a snake slither up the wall on its stubby legs, its one eye tracking him with sinister intentions. The snake has been in his room for hours, circling him, waiting for its opportunity. Tim knows that if he takes his eyes off the snake for even a moment, it will launch itself at him.

When the door opens and the woman who calls herself his mother enters, Tim is distracted for a moment. The snake flings itself at him. Tim screams and pushes himself away. He bangs his head against the wall, which does not hurt too much because of the vise secured to his head. No matter how hard he tries, he has been unable to get the helmet off.

The snake scurries along the floor after him. Tim is torn with indecision. The woman is by the door, blocking his escape. The women in white have told him that she is his mother, but how can she be his mother? He knows that she wants to chop off his arms. No real mother wants to do that. She is a fake.

But the snake is about to get him! He jumps to his feet and tries to leap up the wall, but the snake gets a grip on his foot. He feels the tickling of its poisonous tongue burn through the leather of his right shoe.

A man emerges from behind the woman. He is dark and menacing. Now there are three threats. Tim slides down the wall and whimpers.

The man touches him.

The snake releases his foot and scurries across the floor to hide under the bed. Tim knows that his nemesis is gone for good.

The woman kneels down to touch him, causing fear to rise in Tim. But then, strangely enough, the fear goes away and he looks at the woman with recognition. She is his mother.

He lurches forward and flings his arms around her. "Mom, I'm so happy to see you. Can we go home?"

Tim Horgan has found peace once again.

And so have I.

ABOUT THE AUTHOR

ERIC G. SWEDIN is an Associate Professor in History at Weber State University. His publications include numerous articles, six history books, several science fiction novels, and an historical mystery novel. His *When Angels Wept: A What-If History of the Cuban Mystery Crisis* earned the 2010 Sidewise Award in Alternate History. Eric lives with his family in a house built in 1881. His website is:

http://www.swedin.org/

9 781434 445155